The Wedding-Chest Mystery

A Chief Inspector Pointer Mystery

By A. E. Fielding

Originally published in 1932

The Wedding-Chest Mystery

© 2014 Resurrected Press
www.ResurrectedPress.com

Published by Resurrected Press

This classic book was handcrafted by Resurrected Press. Resurrected Press is dedicated to bringing high quality classic books back to the readers who enjoy them. These are not scanned versions of the originals, but, rather, quality checked and edited books meant to be enjoyed!

Please visit ResurrectedPress.com to view our entire catalogue!

ISBN 13: 978-1-937022-83-9

Printed in the United States of America

Other Resurrected Press Books in *The Chief Inspector Pointer Mystery* Series

RESURRECTED PRESS CLASSIC MYSTERY CATALOGUE

Journeys into Mystery
Travel and Mystery in a More Elegant Time

The Edwardian Detectives
Literary Sleuths of the Edwardian Era

Gems of Mystery
Lost Jewels from a More Elegant Age

Anne Austin
One Drop of Blood
The Black Pigeon
Murder at Bridge

E. C. Bentley
Trent's Last Case: The Woman in Black

Ernest Bramah
Max Carrados Resurrected:
The Detective Stories of Max Carrados

Agatha Christie
The Secret Adversary
The Mysterious Affair at Styles

Octavus Roy Cohen
Midnight

Freeman Wills Croft
The Ponson Case
The Pit Prop Syndicate

J. S. Fletcher

The Herapath Property
The Rayner-Slade Amalgamation
The Chestermarke Instinct
The Paradise Mystery
Dead Men's Money
The Middle of Things
Ravensdene Court
Scarhaven Keep
The Orange-Yellow Diamond
The Middle Temple Murder
The Tallyrand Maxim
The Borough Treasurer
In the Mayor's Parlour
The Saftey Pin

R. Austin Freeman

The Mystery of 31 New Inn from the Dr. Thorndyke Series
John Thorndyke's Cases from the Dr. Thorndyke Series
The Red Thumb Mark from The Dr. Thorndyke Series
The Eye of Osiris from The Dr. Thorndyke Series
A Silent Witness from the Dr. John Thorndyke Series
The Cat's Eye from the Dr. John Thorndyke Series
Helen Vardon's Confession: A Dr. John Thorndyke Story
As a Thief in the Night: A Dr. John Thorndyke Story
Mr. Pottermack's Oversight: A Dr. John Thorndyke Story
Dr. Thorndyke Intervenes: A Dr. John Thorndyke Story
The Singing Bone: The Adventures of Dr. Thorndyke
The Stoneware Monkey: A Dr. John Thorndyke Story
The Great Portrait Mystery, and Other Stories: A Collection of Dr. John Thorndyke and Other Stories
The Penrose Mystery: A Dr. John Thorndyke Story

The Uttermost Farthing: A Savant's Vendetta

Arthur Griffiths
The Passenger From Calais
The Rome Express

Fergus Hume
The Mystery of a Hansom Cab
The Green Mummy
The Silent House
The Secret Passage

Edgar Jepson
The Loudwater Mystery

A. E. W. Mason
At the Villa Rose

A. A. Milne
The Red House Mystery

Baroness Emma Orczy
The Old Man in the Corner

Edgar Allan Poe
The Detective Stories of Edgar Allan Poe

Arthur J. Rees
The Hampstead Mystery
The Shrieking Pit
The Hand In The Dark
The Moon Rock
The Mystery of the Downs

Mary Roberts Rinehart
Sight Unseen and The Confession

Dorothy L. Sayers

Whose Body?

Sir William Magnay
The Hunt Ball Mystery

Mabel and Paul Thorne
The Sheridan Road Mystery

Louis Tracy
The Strange Case of Mortimer Fenley
The Albert Gate Mystery
The Bartlett Mystery
The Postmaster's Daughter
The House of Peril
The Sandling Case: What Would You Have Done?

Charles Edmonds Walk
The Paternoster Ruby

John R. Watson
The Mystery of the Downs
The Hampstead Mystery

Edgar Wallace
The Daffodil Mystery
The Crimson Circle

Carolyn Wells
Vicky Van
The Man Who Fell Through the Earth
In the Onyx Lobby
Raspberry Jam
The Clue
The Room with the Tassels
The Vanishing of Betty Varian
The Mystery Girl
The White Alley
The Curved Blades

Foreword

The period between the First and Second World Wars has rightly been called the "Golden Age of British Mysteries." It was during this period that Agatha Christie, Dorothy L. Sayers, and Margery Allingham first turned their pens to crime. On the male side, the era saw such writers as Anthony Berkeley, John Dickson Carr, and Freeman Wills Crofts join the ranks of writers of detective fiction. The genre was immensely popular at the time on both sides of the Atlantic, and by the end of the 1930's one out of every four novels published in Britain was a mystery.

While Agatha Christie and a few of her peers have remained popular and in print to this day, the same cannot be said of all the authors of this period. With so many mysteries published in the period, it is inevitable that many of them would become obscure or worse, forgotten, often with no justification than changing public tastes. The case of Archibald Fielding is one such, an author, who though popular enough to have a career spanning two decades and more than two dozen mysteries has become such a cipher that his, or as seems more likely, her real identity has become as much a mystery as the books themselves.

While the identity of the author may forever remain an unsolved puzzle, there are some facts that may be inferred from the texts. It is likely that the author had an upbringing and education typical of the British upper middle class in the period before the Great War with all that implies; a familiarity with the classics, the arts, and music, a working knowledge of French and Italian, an appreciation of the finer things in life. The author has also traveled abroad, primarily in the south of France, but probably to Belgium, Spain, and Italy as well, as portions of several of the books are set in those locales.

The books attributed to Archibald Fielding, A. E. Fielding, or Archibald E. Fielding, are quintessential Golden Age British mysteries. They include all the attributes, the country houses, the tangled webs of relationships, the somewhat feckless cast of characters who seem to have nothing better to do with themselves than to murder or be murdered. Their focus is on a middle class and upper class struggling to find themselves in the new realities of the post war era while still trying to live the lifestyle of the Edwardian era. Things are never as they seem, red herrings are distributed liberally throughout the pages as are the clues that will ultimately lead to the solution of "the puzzle," for the British mysteries of this period are centered on the puzzle element which both the reader and the detective must solve before the last page.

A majority of the Fielding mysteries involve the character of Chief Inspector Pointer. Unlike the eccentric Belgian Hercule Poirot, the flamboyant Lord Peter Wimsey, or the somewhat mysterious Albert Campion, Pointer is merely a competent, sometimes clever, occasionally intuitive policeman. And unlike, as with Inspector French in the stories of Freeman Wills Croft, the emphasis is on the mystery itself, not the process of detection.

Pointer is nearly as much of a mystery as the author. Very little of his personal life is revealed in the books. He is described as being vaguely of Scottish ancestry. He is well read and educated, though his duties at Scotland Yard prevent him from enjoying those pursuits. In an early book in the series it is revealed that he spends a week or two each year climbing mountains, his only apparent recreation. His success as a detective depends on his willingness to "suspect everyone" and to not being tied to any one theory. He is fluent in French and familiar with that country. He is, at least in the first two books, unmarried, and sharing lodgings with a bookbinder named O'Connor, in much the manner of Holmes and Watson, though this character is absent in later works.

One intriguing feature of the Pointer mysteries is that they all involve an unexpected twist at the end, wherein the mystery finally solved is not the mystery invoked at the beginning of the book. I leave it to the reader to judge whether Fielding is "playing by the rules" in this, but it does keep the books interesting up to the last chapter.

When Fielding wrote *The Wedding-Chest Mystery* the series was already a half-dozen years old, the book being the tenth novel to feature Pointer. The author's style had matured and been refined over that period. Gone are the over reliance on disguises and other dramatic gimmicks that mark some of the earlier books. Despite that, the Pointer mysteries have a certain flair that separates them from the "humdrum" school of mysteries that were starting to appear at the same time. Stylistically, they fall somewhere between the works of Christie and those of Ngaio Marsh or E. C. R. Lorac.

The Wedding-Chest Mystery centers around the chest of the title, or rather on the body that is discovered inside the chest during the reception held for its presentation. Chinese art was very much *en vogue* during this period and figured in any number of mysteries from a variety of authors. Unfortunately, the Chinese themselves were not as well regarded as their art, and the prejudices of the times are evident throughout the book, though in the end, they do not come off that badly in Fielding's treatment.

The Wedding-Chest Mystery is very much in the tradition of locked room mysteries, with much of the story revolving around the question of how and when the body was placed in the chest when it was either under observation or locked in a suite with only one set of doors. In typical Fielding fashion, there are plenty of red-herrings introduced, both as to how the body came to be in the chest and as to who killed the victim and why. Love, greed, revenge, and politics are all proposed as motives, and nearly every one involved comes under suspicion.

Of interest, Chief Inspector Pointer is presented with a foil in the person of a private investigator named Schofild, who remains convinced that he will solve the case before Pointer as the latter is a plodding policeman. Needless to say, he fails. On a technical note, the murder weapons is described variously as an "automatic" and as a "revolver" though it is clearly a small automatic pistol. This confusion in terminology was not limited to Fielding, and is in fact quite common in British mysteries of the period. It should in no way lessen the reader's enjoyment.

Despite their obscurity, the mysteries of Archibald Fielding, whoever he or she might have been, are well written, well crafted examples of the form, worthy of the interest of the fans of the genre. It is with pleasure, then, that Resurrected Press presents this new edition of *The Wedding-Chest Mystery* and others in the series to its readers.

About the Author

The identity of the author is as much a mystery as the plots of the novels. Two dozen novels were published from 1924 to 1944 as by Archibald Fielding, A. E. Fielding, or Archibald E. Fielding, yet the only clue as to the real author is a comment by the American publishers, H.C. Kinsey Co. that A. E. Fielding was in reality a "middle-aged English woman by the name of Dorothy Feilding whose peacetime address is Sheffield Terrace, Kensington, London, and who enjoys gardening." Research on the part of John Herrington has uncovered a person by that name living at 2 Sheffield Terrace from

1932-1936. She appears to have moved to Islington in 1937 after which she disappears. To complicate things, some have attributed the authorship to Lady Dorothy Mary Evelyn Moore nee Feilding (1889-1935), however, a grandson of Lady Dorothy denied any family knowledge of such authorship. The archivist at Collins, the British publisher, reports that any records of A. Fielding were presumably lost during WWII. Birthdates have been given variously as 1884, 1889, and 1900. Unless new information comes to light, it would appear that the real authorship must remain a mystery.

Greg Fowlkes
Editor-In-Chief
Resurrected Press
www.ResurrectedPress.

CHAPTER ONE

MR. Schofild frowned as the door opened. He was busy sorting papers. His confidential clerk murmured apologetically:

"Mr. Farrant to see you, sir, Very urgent. Mr. William Farrant."

The private inquiry agent smoothed his forehead and nodded as he glanced at a calendar of social events which his clerk prepared for him daily. A moment later a young man was shown in. He was of big build, but moved with a step so noiseless that even now, when he came forward and shook Schofild's outstretched hand, no footfall could be heard, and the room had parquet flooring.

Schofild waved his guest to a chair, and pushed forward a box of cigars—his best ones. Mr. Farrant, as one of the private secretaries of Boyd Armstrong, the Australian mining magnate, was to be treated *en prince*. But Farrant declined both the chair and the cigar. He had a plain but very intelligent face, and curiously veiled light eyes.

"I'm late for an engagement with a lady as it is," he explained hurriedly in a low voice, naturally low—that mark of a subtle character—"but I quite forgot to give you a very urgent message yesterday. Mr. Armstrong wants you to meet him without fail at his house in Charles Street at five today. There's a function of some sort on—"

"Chinese tea party," murmured Schofild a little blankly, looking again at the social calendar.

"Tea not to be taken literally," said Farrant, with a fugitive smile, a smile that struck the private investigator as curiously false. "Any amount of men will be there."

"Naturally, hoping for some hint about the expected Westralian Exploration cable," murmured Schofild, who made a point of a certain show of bluntness, and almost of indiscretion, at times.

Farrant nodded.

"Just so. Well, the point is, can Mr. Armstrong count on your being there at five or a little before?"

This time it was at the clock that Schofild looked. The hour was almost precisely three.

"He wants you to go up to the Chinese suite," Farrant went on, "where he will meet you beside the Wedding-Chest, a gift of Major Hardy to the Armstrongs for the occasion. You can't possibly miss it. It's pretty nearly the size of this room. Mr. Armstrong may be delayed, but if so, he asks you to wait for him. You will manage to be there? Good. I can't think how it slipped my mind yesterday. Goodby for the present, then. No, I'm off duty for the afternoon. Going to spend it on the links." And with another flash of his white even teeth, that again suggested no merriment, Farrant was out of the room.

Mr. Schofild stood a moment wondering what had happened to Farrant's tie. It was virtually under one ear, and looked as though it had been tugged or caught in something. Then the investigator turned back to his papers. He had just finished his last case. He was free. Armstrong might have something big to offer him. Mr. Schofild expected big things. In person he was stout and middle-aged, with quite a bald spot, but also with young, alert eyes. Physically he was lazy. The only exercise he took was getting into and out of armchairs. The only walk, one to his car. But mentally, he would wrestle all night long with a knotty problem. He was very intelligent, absolutely reliable, and immensely conceited.

Yes, he decided again, reaching for some pink tape, to be asked to give up everything he might have on hand, and meet Mr. Boyd Armstrong at five o'clock sounded promising—very. He had worked on a case for Armstrong, or rather for the powerful syndicate of which he was the leading spirit, only some months before, and had scored a great triumph. One thing he knew, if it was anything like that problem, an intricate question of embezzlement, he would insist on Scotland Yard being called in. Schofild liked Scotland Yard. They were there to do the spade work, letting him save himself for the mental work, which was, naturally, just a little beyond their powers.

His papers finished, he clasped his hands across a middle whose girth would have pained an enthusiast for physical fitness, but the acquiring of, which had given Mr. Schofild much pleasure, and that, he claimed, was more than could be said for the slim outline. His mind passed from speculations on the coming interview, to running over the one with Farrant just now.

Odd that one of the secretaries of a great financier should have forgotten to arrange for an interview which apparently was so important—or rather since it was an interview with himself, Schofild, which evidently was so important. But then, Farrant was odd, in some way that Schofild felt rather than saw. Schofild did not care for the young man, whose laugh was as quiet as his voice, who talked freely to no one, not even to Armstrong, as far as Schofild had seen when he had stayed with the two at one of Armstrong's country houses while working on his previous case. Schofild thought Farrant deep. And there was a glint occasionally in his light eyes that made the inquiry agent think of a fox. But what Farrant was really like, no one seemed able to say. Unassuming in manner, Schofild had often heard him referred to as shy. The idea amused the astute Schofild. If Farrant talked little to people, it was because they interested him very little. Armstrong believed that Farrant was devoted to him. Perhaps he was. Perhaps he wasn't. Farrant went by the name of confidential secretary, but interpreter would be the better label, for he was a really remarkable linguist. For which reason alone Armstrong said that he considered him invaluable. He had seemed to have a very pleasant position in the household, Schofild recollected.

So Armstrong was going to meet   him, Schofild, apparently in full view of every one, as an ordinary, guest. That, too, was odd, for Mr. Schofild's occupation was well known, though perhaps, not so well known as he fancied.

He had once been an all but starving barrister, when some articles of his on how to size up potential criminals had caught on, and he had found himself listened to for a while with great attention. Then other names eclipsed his, and he turned his attention to the solving of unusual cases.

He was a bachelor—almost a necessity, he maintained, for a crime investigator, as he called himself—and was rather popular in his own quiet way, for he was a genuinely kindly man, and very discreet.

Again his mind turned to the coming interview and its possibilities. Westralian Exploration shares—"Westrex" in the stock market lingo—were much to the fore just now. Seven geological parties were working in the tract leased by Armstrong's group, from any one of which it was rumored that an all-important cable was about to be sent, sent in some code that would protect it while on the way, and after its arrival too.

Armstrong had once told Schofild that the codes he used were based on Australian native dialects which none but Farrant and the man who sent it would have the power to read even when decoded. There was a hint abroad that the cable would be unfavorable, but there were also whispers of a remarkable bed of deposits, so the shares, though quivering, were waiting—like the speculators.

Idly Schofild wondered how much Sir Ellis Herbert, for instance, would give to read it. Herbert, the Great Basemetal Bear, as he was called, would he be at the Armstrongs' Chinese tea party this afternoon? Schofild knew all about the party. It was his business to have such things at his fingers' ends. The Armstrongs had bought the Charles Street house from Lady Nunhead on the death of her husband a few months ago, with its wonderfully fitted-up Chinese suite, and in it Mrs. Armstrong had decided to give her first reception at their new address. As to the "wedding-chest" of which Farrant had spoken, and which had been chosen by Armstrong for the place of meeting, it would evidently be easy to find. As Major Hardy had given it, it would certainly be worth seeing. Like Schofild, the great explorer and Armstrong's closest friend, went in for big things.

Schofild was at the house well before five o'clock and found a crowd. Mrs. Armstrong had been a popular girl before her marriage some ten years ago, and had never lost touch with her old world. She was a very pretty woman. Her mother, Lady Blanche Callard, had taken great care, and consulted the best publicity expert of the day to have her established as a beauty, and Phyllis had been well launched. There had even been an expectation at one time that—however, setting on one side what might have been, Boyd Armstrong was a very wealthy man, and expected to be still wealthier. Most, if not all, of the men who came today were distinctly aggrieved at his absence.

Sir Ellis Herbert was not present, Schofild noted with surprise.

"Boyd was called away unexpectedly this morning. It's a secret, of course, but it really, was a command. Something to do with Westralian Explorations," his wife murmured, with an air of imparting a confidence, "but I expect him every minute."

People looked about for Farrant. He, too, was absent, and most of the guests were trying to bet with themselves as to whether this double absence was a bull, or a bear, point. The trouble was, you could take it either way.

As for the presence of Percy Callard, that was no help. Only natural, said those who knew that Mrs. Armstrong was his sister, and did not know of the strained feelings between him and his brother-in-law.

Only a piece of his infernal cheek, said those who, like Schofild, did. As always, where he was, however, the cocktails were excellent, and Percy himself, sleek, imperturbable and good-looking, though his mouth reminded Schofild of a cat's, sauntered among the guests as though he were the master of the house. Schofild looked at his watch. Close on five o'clock.

At last the move was made for the Chinese suite. The big temple doors that led to it were flung open with a noise like a great muffled gong; tea was served in the first room for those who still cared for that old-fashioned beverage. There were some wonderful blends provided. Such Lapchang Souchong as was not to be easily matched with its true tarry flavor. Such Chang Wong as might have come from a Mandarin's plantation, with piles of almond cakes and great heaps of Gum Lu from a Chinese caterer's. Hidden behind a pair of red lacquer doors inset in the side wall of the farthest room, Chinese musicians played Chinese airs. The rooms, there were three in line, each opening out of the other, were scarlet-lacquered, with dull gold dragons half-revealed, half-dimly glimpsed over walls and ceilings. Schofild found them distinctly frightful.

Suddenly there was a little stir. Every one made way for six coolies supporting, or appearing to support, a scarlet Chinese wedding-chest, huge and handsome and wonderfully carved. Schofild looked about for the giver. Then he recollected that the Travelers was holding a great reception in honor of a returned ambassador, and that Major Hardy was to make the speech of the afternoon.

The coolies chanted as they marched. Six London actors who played their parts well. The Chinese orchestra managed to be only half a bar behind, as they finally left the chest in the center of the end wall in a place that was marked off by cords of gold and crimson stretched from gilded spears.

The head coolie stepped forward and unfastened the huge key tied by more scarlet and gold cord to the dragon handles.

Schofild looked about him. No sign of Armstrong. Mrs. Armstrong was standing just outside the gilded spears enclosure beneath a pagoda-like dovecote of inlay work which topped a jade colored column that rose high above her head. She was dressed in black, and made quite a charming figure against her gaudy surroundings. Not even a Chinese lady could be more painted, Schofild thought, nor more successful.

All around came laughter and guesses as to what was coming.

His eye was caught by a woman across the wide room who, like himself, stood near the chest. It was Lady Grail, supposed to be Mrs. Armstrong's social rival in thinking out new ideas with which to amuse people. At the moment, odd to say for her, she was neither talking nor laughing. Instead, her eyes were fixed on the chest with a look of intense anticipation. True, it was being whispered about the room that the chest contained charming little gifts for all the guests, but Lady Grail's expression was quite unlike any other of the glances around him, Schofild thought. She was a handsome woman, but at this moment she looked very ugly.

Callard was standing beside her, and suddenly Schofild saw that Percy's lips were moving, though his head was turned away from her, and though there was nothing in his lounging attitude to suggest that they were talking together. Schofild could read lips. Callard said, "Now for it!" And Lady Grail, without turning her head either, replied, "Do be more careful!" and moved away.

The Chinese orchestra ended with a last *miaow* as the head coolie—Mr. Buck of the Gaiety in reality—unlocked the chest, hung the key in place again, and signed to the "coolies" to lift the lid and hook it back against the wall.

Half in real curiosity, half to keep the ball rolling, every one craned forward. There came a sort of muffled gasp from the room. Mrs. Armstrong shrieked, and collapsed where she stood in a dead faint. One of the coolies nearly dropped the lid again at the thud of her fail.

Schofild had hold of it before it quite closed. In another second a dozen hands took it from him and fastened it open. Inside the great chest lay a man at full length. He was quite dead. The face was distorted in a half grin, but it was the face of Boyd Armstrong. An ugly, powerful face. The face of a man of strong passions.

Her brother carried Mrs. Armstrong out. The slender figure in its clinging draperies looked like a child in his arms. Way was made for him in a silence of quite unusual quality, then came what was practically a hubbub.

Schofild lowered the lid after touching Armstrong's cheek. "Until the police come," he murmured to Mr. Buck, then he took a step forward and raised his voice. "If there is any doctor here, will he be kind enough—?" No one stirred, so Schofild continued, "There's been an accident to Mr. Armstrong. No one should leave the house for the time being. But any one can leave these rooms, of course. In fact, I think every one should do so except you, Mr. Buck, and your assistants. I'll telephone to Scotland Yard."

"Wait a moment," came in Percy Callard's languid yet metallic voice—he had just re-entered the suite—"not quite so fast, please. It may be a case for a doctor. A fit, you know, or a stroke... or drugged. I don't know who you are," he fixed a supercilious stare on Schofild, "to be talking of bringing in the police."

Schofild mentioned his name and that he was here to keep an appointment with the man who now lay dead inside the great red chest.

"And it's not a fit, nor drugging, I'm sorry to say," Schofild went on. "Mr. Armstrong's dead. Been dead some hours, I fancy. That's why I don't want to lift the lid again."

"I see." Callard spoke more civilly. "Then will you go now and telephone? And you needn't wait, Buck, nor your friends either in this ghastly room. I'll stay here until the police come."

"No thanks—eh—Callard, isn't it?—I'll wait here." Buck had caught Schofild's eye and gave the latter a reassuring nod. The actor as well as the inquiry agent knew Percy Callard by reputation, or the lack of it, and quite patently had no intention of leaving the grim chest in his sole charge, though the rest of the white-faced visitors were glad enough to avail themselves of Schofild's suggestion, and broke back for the stairs in a body. Soft sibilants and hisses came from the Chinese musicians. They could not see into the suite unless they peered through the key-hole, but evidently this was just what they had done, and evidently too they could hear what went on beside them as clearly as their music had reached the visitors. After further quick cluckings and dickings they swept from the room in a body, like a flock of black crows. Passing down the back stairs, they were out of the tradesmen's entrance before the servants had even noticed their passing.

Upstairs in the Chinese suite no one spoke for a few minutes. Then the actors drew together and spoke in low whispers. Callard sat in a ceremonial chair, his eyes unwinkingly fastened on the chest.

Within a remarkably short space of time a young man, tall, erect, and bronzed of face, walked quickly into the suite. Schofild was beside him. Behind them came four other men from the Yard. Schofild introduced his companion to Callard as Chief Inspector Pointer. Percy got up languidly, but there was nothing languid in the glance he gave the officer. Buck came forward at the same time. He knew Pointer, and, in common, with all who were acquainted with that typical specimen of the Yard, liked him. Now together, now in bits, the account of what had just happened was given. The lid of the chest was lifted again, and this time remained open.

"You definitely recognize the dead man as Mr. Boyd Armstrong?" Pointer asked. He himself knew the face by sight, and from photographs.

"Definitely," came from Buck.

"Positively," from Callard.

"Unmistakably," from Schofild.

"And which of you gentlemen last saw Mr. Armstrong alive?"

"I suppose I did," Callard said doubtfully, as Buck murmured something about some days ago. "Last night. My sister and I went to the Bat, after dining with some friends, and Armstrong joined us there. But I heard him about the house this morning at some unearthly hour. He's an early-rising fanatic. They rarely come to a good end, in my experience."

Callard spoke with the air of a virtuous man condemning vice.

"Look here, chief inspector, we've got to get away," Buck said in a pleading tone, "will you take my deposition, or whatever it's called, about the chest now? I know all about it. Or rather—good God, no!—not as much as that! But I know a good deal about it. I'm in a fearful rush."

"Sorry, Mr. Buck, but I must first find out when Mr. Armstrong was last seen in the house."

Pointer had a brief preliminary interview with the dead man's butler and valet. He was told that Mr. Armstrong had left the house this morning around nine, and had said that he would be away until the evening, mentioning eight as the earliest possible hour of his return. What suit was he wearing? What hat? What gloves? The information duly noted, Pointer telephoned a question, a guarded one, to Mr. Armstrong's office. Mr. Armstrong had left around eleven, he was told. No, he would not be back at all today. He had said that he was going out of town for the afternoon. "Did he leave his hat and gloves there?" Pointer went on, "this is Charles Street speaking." A miracle, which seemed to cause no astonishment to the office. No, Mr. Armstrong had only rushed in at eleven for a minute, going into his private room and hurrying out again at once. He had not taken his hat off, and his gloves had been still in his hand when he left.

Pointer gave very strict injunctions to his men to let no one leave the house until it was absolutely certain that the missing articles were not in his possession. For, though the suit in which the corpse was clothed seemed to be the same one that Armstrong, according to all accounts, had worn when, he left the house, there was neither hat nor gloves in the chest upstairs. A woman detective, who had accompanied Pointer to the house on the chance that she might be wanted, would attend to the women guests. This was only routine, the chief inspector had no expectation of finding Armstrong's missing articles of clothing among Armstrong's guests of that afternoon, so that he bore with fortitude the news that the Chinese musicians had gone before he had arrived at the house, though it was a pity. Pointer asked where Armstrong's bedroom and study were, and promptly placed them in Charge of one of his men. After, which he returned to the impatient Mr. Buck, who ran quickly over the facts that accounted for his presence and those of the Other "coolies" today. He had been dining with the Armstrongs three nights ago, and Mrs. Armstrong had told him of a Chinese wedding-chest that Bob Hardy—all London called Major Hardy "Bob"—was giving them. Mrs. Armstrong had spoken of her intention of distributing gifts from it to her guests. These were to be birch trees from Szechuan, stunted to a size not, so far, seen in England.

"I suggested coolies to carry the chest in," Buck went on, "and we discussed it as giving an amusing note. As the weight of the trees and the chest might have been a bit too much, it was finally decided only to seem to drag it, on a little trolley table, from the side of the room to the center. I sent up the trolley yesterday. Bits of teak carving were nailed to it, as you see, to hide the rubber wheels. We ourselves all got here at a quarter to five, had a cocktail or two, and a chat with Mrs. Armstrong, and took up our positions in a little sewing-room that's behind those." He pointed to the carved lacquer doors in the side wall near them. "The Chinese musicians were already in there. At a few minutes past five we marched in through the big doors at the other end of this suite, and picking up the gilt staves of the chest which was waiting behind a curtain there, trundled it along to the middle of the wall. As for the rest, well, we've just told you it."

"Where was Mrs. Armstrong standing when the chest was opened?" was Pointer's next question. That, too, was promptly settled. She had stood at the foot of the pagoda dovecote, and the pillar was fastened to the floor.

"Did she seem as usual before the chest was opened?" Pointer asked Buck confidentially.

"Just as usual."

"And how was the key tied on? With elaborate loops, or simply?"

"Very simply. Like this." Buck illustrated how the key had hung in place, and the other "coolies" agreed with him. After showing him where the chest had stood in a little alcove behind a scarlet curtain, the actors were asked if they minded having their fingerprints taken, and were delighted at the idea. That done, they hurried out, promising to come and "depose" later on at Scotland Yard.

"Do you, know when this chest came to the house?" the chief inspector asked Callard.

"Today. Around two, I think. I know it had just arrived when I got in at that hour. Major Hardy could tell you more about it. He was here when it came, helping the men get it into place."

Pointer knew that the major was at the Travelers, but one of his men was sent to telephone him, asking him to come to the house as soon as possible, as an accident had happened to Mr. Armstrong.

Only the police were allowed to use the telephone for the present. Downstairs, the guests were leaving in droves, after submitting to the very mild form of searching requested by the police, and giving their names and addresses.

Their accounts of what each had seen, when compared with those furnished by the "coolies," added nothing to the known facts surrounding the discovery of the body. None of them seemed able to suggest any possible motive for a murder, least of all a possible murderer.

The private inquiry agent had told Pointer how he came to be at the house, and had ended up with the statement that, being there at the dead man's wish, by his especial request, he considered himself doubly bound to help find his murderer.

"My specialty is explaining things," Schofild had continued, "probing into motives, reading people. Yours is, of course, the noting of facts and the gathering of information. I always work well with Scotland Yard. Together we ought to solve the problem, thought it may be a difficult one."

Pointer replied that he would be very glad of his help.

"Where is this Mr. Farrant?" he then asked.

"Playing golf, unfortunately. As he lives in the house, he might have been of the greatest use just now. While I waited for you to come, I telephoned Armstrong's offices in Queen Victoria Street, and asked them if they knew where he could be found. They don't. Incidentally, of course, I made no mention of what has happened. I left that to you. Theories and combinations are province."

Apart from the people in the house, the thing that interested both Pointer and Schofild most for the moment was the room and the chest. The latter was photographed from every angle, fingerprints were taken, collected, and numbered. Unfortunately they were few in number and very blurred, as the chest was elaborately carved.

The stretcher was now placed on the floor beside it, and Armstrong's body was lifted out, after its position against, the walls of the chest had been outlined with chalk. Schofild noticed the great care that Pointer took to ensure that this should be done with accuracy and detail. He had milk brushed over the chalk marks to keep from from smudging. The cause of death was was quite clear. Armstrong had been shot through the head from a little behind one ear, the bullet was still in the head. The weapon had, almost touched him, for it had singed his thick, curly hair.

'In my opinion," Schofild said to Pointer, with quite unconscious stress on the "*my*" that he always gave to that phrase, "the wound in itself does not absolutely preclude the idea of suicide. But he couldn't have shot himself lying down in that wooden chest, nor could he have been accidentally, or intentionally, shot by any one else while in it. Suicide, and spite that tries to stage a crime? Quite possible in my opinion. Quite possible."

There were definitely no marks of a struggle. Each garment as it was removed was examined. Any articles that could possibly retain a fingerprint were tested. Over the letter-case Pointer for the first time paused a long moment. Then he glanced up at Schofild, who was scrutinizing it too.

"Been what the Americans call 'frisked' in my opinion," said the crime-expert promptly. "Wonder what they were searching for?" He asked the question of himself. Quite definitely of himself.

Pointer thought that the search had not been for anything definite. He based his idea on the fact that the contents of all compartments, even the one with a few of. Armstrong's cards in it, had—to his keen eyes—been taken out, flipped over, and hurriedly replaced, which would not have been necessary had a definite paper of known size been wanted. He thought that the search had been merely to make sure that nothing incriminating was in the case, or had been left in the case. There were many fingerprints on the various papers inside, but nothing else that promised any help. Pointer motioned to his men to cover up the body, and began his search of the Chinese suite itself. As has been said, the three rooms of which it consisted, opened each out of the other in a straight line. There was no way into or out of the suite except through the one main doorway, since the small lacquer double doors inset in the side of the end room were, Buck had told them, purely ornamental.

Investigation with Pointer's tiny surgeon's mirror showed the dust of many years thick in the keyhole. On the other side was the room, almost empty of furniture, which Buck had called "the sewing-room," where he and the other "coolies" had waited before their entrance, and where the small Chinese orchestra had been stationed. Here, too, as in the suite, the most careful scrutiny showed no spot of blood, no smear, or stain. Everything went to show that the body had been placed in the chest before the latter had been set in the alcove. Schofild said as much.

A question put to Callard, who was drinking cocktails below, confirmed the statement that there was no key in existence to the lacquer side doors. Lord Nunhead had brought them and the large entrance doors from a nobleman's house in China, and even at that time the smaller pair had been without a key, but as Nunhead intended to use them for the place they occupied as part of the wall decoration, this was immaterial.

"Rufus will give you all the details about them," Callard said indifferently; "he got my sister to keep the suite unaltered and go in for Chinese things. Rufus Armstrong, Boyd's cousin."

"And where is Mr. Rufus Armstrong?" Pointer asked.

"God knows. Not here. That's all I can say."

"Who is this cousin?" Pointer asked Schofild as they left the young man, "do you know anything about him?"

"Only that he's in existence," Schofild replied, and that he's a well-known collector, especially of Eastern things. Wealthy man. I seem to remember that he has a beautiful old house off Fitzroy Square—" Schofild was groping in his recollection of chance remarks and idle gossip. A glance in the telephone directory gave his number, but apparently the household of Mr. Rufus Armstrong, as well as the master, were out, for they got no reply.

Too much, however, depended on whether the small side doors could have been opened, for there to be any mistake made, and Pointer promptly telephoned for one of the Yard's best locksmiths to come at once to Charles Street.

As for the windows in the suite, they were covered with wrought iron ornamental gratings cemented into the walls, which permitted the windows to be raised or lowered in the usual way, but absolutely precluded the idea of any entrance through them.

By this time the police surgeon had arrived. All he could say was that, to the best of his belief, death had occurred over six hours ago—though he could not be positive. But of two things he was sure. The first was that the body had been placed in the wedding-chest very shortly indeed after death had taken place—within half an hour. And he gave as another thirty minutes the probable time between the shot and the moment that Armstrong had actually died.

CHAPTER TWO

ARMSTRONG'S valet had meanwhile been asked to go through the dead man's clothing. He could only be sure that one thing was missing, beyond the hat and gloves, and that was Armstrong's gold fountain pen, a Swan, with his initials on it. Mr. Armstrong always carried it on him by day.

Pointer now asked the man for further details of when he had last seen his master.

"This morning, sir. Around nine, or a few minutes before." He went on to say that Mr. and Mrs. Armstrong were dining out with Major Hardy, and that his master had stopped him on the stairs to tell him that he might be very late, but would do his best to get home by eight, but could not possibly be in before that hour at the earliest.

The other question was a general one. Had he any idea, however fantastic, that might throw light on his master's end.

The man said that he had none whatever, except that, as every one knew, tremendous financial issues hung on Mr. Armstrong's various Australian enterprises.

As to any domestic trouble, or any personal reason for Armstrong having taken his life, his manservant scoffed at the idea. He considered Mr. and Mrs. Armstrong to have been an unusually devoted couple.

Pointer touched the doctor on the arm. The body was being carried down to the ambulance waiting below.

"I think Mrs. Armstrong needs you. I'll go up with you and wait outside the door. If it's in any way possible—without danger to her, I must see her. I don't want to speak to her, if she's at all overcome, but I do want to see her."

Dr. Birckbeck nodded. He was a man of few words. They hurried up the stairs. The doctor was a bare minute in the bedroom when he came out.

"She can't possibly be questioned. She needs a hypodermic at once."

"I'll be your assistant," Pointer said promptly. 'I've often seen them given."

Again Birekbeck nodded, and they entered together.

The room was very modern. The walls seemed entirely made of mirrors except for inset cupboards of aluminum. The ceiling was of the same metal. The chairs were mere puffs of satin held together by what looked like wires. On the bed with its black silk pillows and sheets lay Mrs. Armsong fully dressed. Her eyes were closed at the moment. Yes, Pointer thought, she looked as though she had had a very complete, and very recent, shock. He did not need to ask the doctor if this were acting. While the latter opened a bag that he had brought upstairs with him, Pointer swiftly took out a flexible steel rule from his waistcoat pocket, one that coiled up at a touch into a neat metal case. One stretch of his long arms and he knew that Mrs. Armstrong's height from the top of her neatly parted hair to the tips of her high heels was five foot eight.

Birckbeck was used to strange doings on Pointer's part, but he shot him a questioning look which the chief inspector did not choose to see. The doctor on that, motioned to a small bottle marked *ether* in his bag, a packet of wool, and finally to a place on Mrs. Armstrong's arm.

Pointer swabbed obediently. A woman standing by the window turned and watched him as though she hardly saw him. Mrs. Armstrong's maid brought in a quilt. Pointer told her to come out onto the landing for a word with him as soon as the doctor could spare her.

She did not keep him waiting long. He opened the first door beside him and they stepped into a plainly furnished, comfortable bedroom, Armstrong's room. A constable stood by the window.

"When did you last see Mr. Armstrong?" Pointer asked. Her eyes had told him that she knew who he was.

"He looked in at Mrs. Armstrong this morning before she got up. I was just turning on the bath. About nine, that would be. She's an awfully early riser, too. Though not as bad as he is. He only stood in the doorway for a moment to say that he was off for the day on something very important, and couldn't possibly be back to lunch and very possibly might be late for dinner, too."

"Was his manner as usual?" he asked next.

"Oh, no! Not at all as usual. He had a paper—a letter—in his hand, just drawn out of its envelope, and he kept looking at it as though half-reading it while he talked. Seemed to have given him a rare shock I thought even then. Spoke hastily, too, as though only half thinking of what he was saying. And in a hurry, too. As though impatient to be off. Just opened the door and stood there as though longing to be away."

"What did Mrs. Armstrong say?"

"She said, 'But what about this afternoon, Boyd?' He said impatiently, 'I can't help that. Make some excuse for me. I've got to leave at once and can't possibly be back till this evening.'"

"And what did she say then?"

"Nothing, except 'Very well, Boyd,' or something like that. Anyway, he didn't wait to hear what she said before he shut the door and ran down the stairs."

"Did he speak as though there had been any quarrel between himself and Mrs. Armstrong?"

"Oh, no!" The maid's tone was honestly amused. "Oh, dear no! Simply preoccupied and in a tearing hurry."

"Did Mrs. Armstrong make any comment to you on his leaving like that?"

"Yes, several times. She said, 'I wonder what is calling Mr. Armstrong away so unexpectedly,' and 'I can't think what he's in such a rush about.' And once she laughed a

little and said, 'I do believe he's running away from the
tea party this afternoon, Meade.' Meade is my name.
'How cowardly of him!' But that was only her fun. Mr.
Armstrong was terribly rushed by something. Looked as
if he hadn't a moment to catch the train, you know what I
mean."

Pointer did. There came a tap on the door of the room
and a man put his head in. He was one of Pointer's plain
clothes men, and said nothing, only showed himself and
then vanished, very much as a ghost might do at a
séance. But Pointer, unlike sitters at a séance, was in no
doubt as to the meaning of the apparition. Major Hardy
had arrived.

"Who is that lady in Mrs. Armstrong's room?" he
asked, as he thanked the maid and prepared to go
downstairs.

"That's Lady Grail. A great friend of Mrs. Armstrong.
She was in the Chinese rooms and saw it all. She nearly
fainted herself. I had to get her a lot of brandy before she
could help with Mrs. Armstrong at all."

"And did Mr. Callard need brandy too?" Pointer
asked, a little dryly.

"Didn't he take it coolly! I was in the room when he
brought Mrs. Armstrong in, and he said—all he said was,
'Here's your mistress. Mr. Armstrong's just been found
dead in Major Hardy's chest.' And laid her on her bed
and walked out again. I didn't believe it. Not until Lady
Grail came tottering in a moment later."

Pointer had heard from Schofild about Lady Grail's
expression before the lid of the chest had been raised, and
about Callard's remark to her, and her reply to him. He
now asked for a word with her. She came out after some
minutes.

"I know nothing whatever about it. Well, then, if I
must go into all the horrible details, I'll come downstairs.
I need a couple of cocktails first."

Downstairs Schofild joined them. She led the way into
one of the roams and pressed a button in the automatic

cocktail mixer that stood in a corner behind a so-called bar. Only when she had a glass in her hand did she turn again to the chief inspector. She had large brown eyes that looked either frank or bold, according to her mood, or possibly according to one's point of view. Pointer was amazed at the speed with which that cocktail vanished. She pressed the button again. He decided that if they wanted a clear account from her, the sooner they got it the better.

"Will you be kind enough to tell us just what happened in the Chinese suite," he said in his pleasant, grave way. "This gentleman"—she evidently did not know Schofild, nor recognize him as having been present at the afternoon's 'horrible happening—expected to meet Mr. Armstrong here this afternoon. He is helping us to investigate the case."

The glass in her hand shook violently.

"Horrible!" said she, half under her breath. "Quite too shattering for words." She bit her lip, and, tossing down the liquid left in the tumbler, turned once more to the metal friend behind the bar.

"Sorry, but as an eyewitness?" Pointer murmured.

"Well, when she opened the chest she fainted," Lady Grail rapped out sharply, "fainted dead away. I didn't know women ever did that any more."

"But before the chest was opened?" Schofild asked. She looked vaguely at him.

"I don't know what happened before the chest was opened," she spoke impatiently. "I was too far back in the room to see well—until just at the last, when I happened to be near the end of the rooms. I can only tell you that when the lid was lifted, she pitched forward as though some one had struck her down from behind. It really was ghastly."

"What time was this?" Pointer now asked.

"I don't know. Long past five. They were fearfully late in bringing out the chest. I thought they would never come along with it."

Now Schofild knew that the chest had made its appearance from behind the curtain that covered the niche where it had stood—at just a quarter past five.

He suggested this time to her. "Much more like a quarter to six!" she maintained.

Schofild decided that impatience had made the minutes drag; but why the impatience? Further questions brought no new facts to light. Had Mr. Callard been there before the chest was brought in, Pointer inquired. She said that she did not know. He might have been. Probably was, but she had not noticed him.

She was thanked, and allowed to continue her cocktails alone. Before meeting Major Hardy, Pointer telephoned to the family solicitors. They knew the contents of Mr. Armstrong's only will, they said. Told, in confidence, that Mr. Armstrong had been found dead at his house in Charles Street, the head of the firm assured the chief inspector that there was nothing in the will left with them long ago that could have any bearing on either suicide or crime. The will had been signed after his marriage. Everything was left to Mrs. Armstrong absolutely with the exception of a few unimportant legacies. The solicitors in question and Mr. Rufus Armstrong were the trustees.

"Anything left to Mr. Rufus Armstrong?" Pointer asked.

"Nothing except any four objects of art which he cares to select from Mr. Armstrong's house, the term to cover furniture as well."

Pointer thanked them, and arranged with them to let him know as soon as they got into touch with the dead man's cousin. Had he any other relatives, the chief inspector asked next. Not close ones, no. The firm in question had poked after the family affairs since the days of Armstrong's grandfather.

Pointer turned away from the instrument not quite so sure as the telephoning solicitor seemed to be that Armstrong's will could have no bearing on the crime—if

Armstrong's death proved to be, what it seemed, a crime. Percy Callard, for instance, might have a much better chance of dipping his hands in Armstrong's money bags with only a sister in charge of them. And she, as here was no clause about her re-marriage, became a very wealthy prize, and was still considered by many to be a lovely woman.

"Now for the major—do you know him?" Schofild asked, when Pointer, rejoined him and assed on what he had learned of the will.

"Only by sight."

The chief inspector opened the door of the library now, and a figure as tall, well set-up, and soldierly as his own, turned at the sound. Major Hardy was a well-known explorer and collector of trophies. His lean, hard face was bronzed to a point that made the chief inspector's tan look like pallor. The features were strongly molded. The dark eyes, with their thick lids, were set rather close together beneath powerful brows, but that only gave his glance a strongly-concentrated look like an eagle's rather than any hint of slyness. There was daring in the jaw, resolution and perhaps cruelty in the mouth. The small, trim ears were placed unusually high on the well-shaped head.

"I understand that there's been an accident to Armstrong," Hardy began, as Schofild shook hands and introduced the Scotland Yard man. It was to the latter that the major spoke.

"Yes, I'm sorry to say he's dead," Pointer replied. "He was found shot."

Major Hardy's brows drew still closer together as he listened.

"Do you mean suicide, or accident?" he asked.

"Murder probably." Pointer, too, could be as direct as any man.

"Murder!" Hardy stared from one to the other.

"In my opinion suicide is by no means excluded," Schofild said in a comforting voice.

"Where was he found? When?" Hardy demanded next.

"Did you send in a Chinese wedding-chest as a present to Mrs. Armstrong today?" Pointer asked, instead of replying.

"To her husband and to her, yes. What's that got to do with it?"

"Was it sent in today, sir?" Pointer persisted.

"At noon, yes. Why?"

Pointer told him of the events' of the afternoon.

It was said of "Bob Hardy" that he did not blink once when a wounded rhino charged him, but his dark, weather-beaten face grew crimson as he heard just what it was that, enclosed in his gift, had been presented to Mrs. Armstrong and her guests. Even his eyes shone red. Hardy was shortly to take up an important position in the colonies. That helped him to keep back some of the words the two with him could almost see struggling to get past his locked lips. For a second he stood rigid. Then, suddenly, without intending to say the words, both Pointer and Schofild thought, he asked sharply, "Where's Farrant?"

"He's not here at the moment. Why, sir?"

"He should be here—to take charge. However"—he pulled himself up, breathing hard. "And Mrs. Armstrong?" he asked thickly—"this must have nearly killed her. They were devoted to each other, she and Boyd."

"Mrs. Armstrong's in the doctor's hands. He's given her an opiate," Schofild replied while Pointer asked:

"The name of the firm from whom you bought the chest?"

"Lee and Son, 19 Limehouse Street. But where are the trees that were inside?" Evidently the major was unable to believe that no trees had been found on the place. "I saw them put in myself," he added in explanation.

"Will you come up a moment, sir, and see if the chest upstairs really is the one you bought? After that, of course, we want to hear how you came to buy it, and all about it."

Once in the Chinese suite Hardy examined the outside of the chest very closely.

"It looks to me like the one I chose. But it might not be—I'm no authority on things Chinese any more than Armstrong was. But that one was filled to the brim with three hundred dwarf birch trees that Armstrong was buying to be distributed as presents to his guests.

"Those"—he gulped—"Chinese must be at the bottom of this, in some way. Armstrong had told me he might come on to Limehouse to have a look at the trees. But I thought that he had changed his mind."

"When did you buy the chest?" Pointer asked.

"This morning at eleven. The order had been placed a fortnight ago, but the two Lees wanted me to wait the arrival of a better example that had been shipped to them. They told me this morning that it had got damaged on the way, so I decided to be content with the one in stock, and arranged for the trees to be packed inside and for it to be sent up at once."

A look crossed Hardy's face, as of a man who suddenly remembers something which he considered trifling before but now sees as being of importance.

"It was to be here at noon. I dropped in around twelve to learn what Mrs. Armstrong thought of the trees. As nothing had come by one, I telephoned to the Lees, who told me that there had been a breakdown, but that we should have the thing without fail as soon as possible. It came around two, as a matter of fact. I stayed to see it delivered, helped to have it placed in that alcove over there, locked the door of the suite, hung up the key, it weighs half a ton, and rushed off. It must have been well past the half hour by then."

"Was the chest empty when you bought it?" Schofild asked.

"It was. I had the trees packed in my presence. They just went in."

"Was there any other similar chest on the premises, do you know?" Pointer asked.

"They told me there wasn't. But Chinese assurances!" Hardy finished savagely.

"And about Mr. Armstrong intending to be there?"

"Yesterday afternoon he and I were chatting at Boodle's about a bronze that he had bought. Without being a collector, like his cousin, he had a fancy for bronze, and Rufus Armstrong had told him he ought to see a Han leopard that had just arrived at the Lees' establishment. It had already been decided that he would buy for Mrs. Armstrong a consignment of dwarf birch trees which the Lees had offered me at a great bargain, and Armstrong said he might look in himself this morning and have a glance at the bronze. I told him I should be there at eleven, as I intended to wait till the last moment for something better to turn up—though Rufus Armstrong had already vetted the chest for me and told me it was a wonder in its own line and that we could look at the bronze together. But he evidently forgot all about it, as I did."

"What makes you think that, Major Hardy?"

"Because he didn't refer to it when he called me up this morning on the telephone around nine, or a thought before, and said that he had to go out of town for the day on a very important matter that he couldn't put off."

"He didn't say what it was that called him away?"

"No. All Armstrong said—he was evidently in a tearing hurry—was that he was called out of town for the day and might be late for the dinner Mrs. Armstrong, he, and I had planned to have together before going on to a friend's dance."

"Have you yourself any idea of what called him away in such a hurry?"

"Probably something connected with Westrex, his Westralian Exploration Company. That's a safe bet. For a cable's due any day now. The fact that he was willing to leave town today makes me think it must have been connected with it. But Farrant will know. Farrant is sure to know. That's why I asked for him just now."

"Now, going back to the chest, sir, did you look inside it when it came?"

"Most unfortunately, no! Mrs. Armstrong wanted to, but I was in a hurry. Where can those damned trees have got to?" The major stared around the room, as though they must be in sight.

"Was anything put in the chest to hold them? I mean, could they be lifted out all together, or would they have to be taken out one by one?"

"A piece of embroidered Chinese linen was laid in first. A kumshaw from the Lees. The trees were packed in, and the ends folded down over them and pinned firmly, in place."

"So that they could have been lifted out as one bundle?" Pointer persisted.

"Very possible, I should think."

"Were they damp at all? Would they drip?"

Hardy explained that the trees were planted in small mandarin oranges which had been treated until they were as firm as balls of copper. The aperture for the trees was exceedingly small, and the earth had been covered with some sort of plaster that would break up when watered, but until then would keep the mold from spilling.

"They were as clean to handle as wiped apples," he finished. "Mrs. Armstrong made a point of that. They were Armstrong's, you know. I only bought them for him."

"Can you come with us now to where you bought the chest, or at least one like it?" Pointer asked, leading the way out of the suite and motioning to one of his men to draw his chair against the door inside.

"You don't suppose I'm not going to take a part, however humble, in clearing this up, do you?" the major almost roared. "It was my gift, you know, that chest. Armstrong was a friend in a thousand. And he, was found dead—murdered—in my present to him and his wife. Well, if you think I won't do my best to have this cleared up so as to wring the neck of the man who did it with my own hands—" Again the major found a glare safer than words.

This was not exactly the consummation for which Scotland Yard allowed its officers to work, but Pointer only asked:

"When did you see Mr. Armstrong last, sir?"

"Yesterday afternoon at Boodle's, around six."

A constable murmured something to Pointer. The Yard's locksmith was waiting to speak to him.

"Well, Dewar, has a key been turned in the lock of that side door recently?"

"Not for years and years, sir," came the unhesitating reply. Without taking a lock to pieces, Dewar had a way of inserting thin wires with absorbent pads on the ends that told him all that could be known as to the condition of any lock's interior. "Say five years since a key was even put in, and you'll be on the safe side. And as for the wards—it's not merely dust on them, sir, it's more like the muck of centuries."

"And the hinges?" Pointer asked, though he was sure they had not been tampered with.

Dewar shook his head. "That double door's only a piece of the wall, sir. Except for the fact that you can see through the keyhole, it might as well be bricks. Just put there like a handsome panel might be." And with that the locksmith slung his bag over his shoulder and hurried away.

Pointer told one of his men to telephone to Lee and Son, and ask them to send up a responsible person at once to identify—or not—the chest in the house as the one which Major Hardy had bought of them this morning, telling them in explanation that the trees which were to have been delivered inside it were missing.

The reply of Lee and Son was a sentence in good English that their foreman should start off at once and would be at Charles Street as soon as humanly possible.

Meanwhile the chief inspector had a word with the servants.

Mr. Armstrong was always an early riser. He breakfasted generally at half-past eight. This morning he had done so, and seemed as usual when he came down. While he was still at table, the telephone rang. There were four in the house. It was the library bell that rang. Mr. Armstrong had gone to answer it himself, as he preferred to do when near by.

A little later the butler had seen him going up the stairs and heard him speaking as though to Mrs. Armstrong from the door of her room. He had not heard the words. The voice had sounded as though Mr. Armstrong were hurried and impatient to be off.

The butler had noticed his face as he went upstairs, it had looked so pale that he had wondered if his master were ill, but he had not ventured to ask him if he were feeling ill. A footman in the hall had noticed nothing. Both agreed that he had an opened letter in his hands.

What letters had come this morning for Mr. Armstrong? The butler made a motion with his hands. A pile like that. But Mr. Armstrong hadn't opened any of them when the telephone bell rang, and had told him to put them all on his writing-table in the library, where they were at this moment. He could not say if one of the letters had been opened by Mr. Armstrong while in the room to answer the telephone, but he could say that at lunch he had noticed without meaning to notice, that the letter which he had laid on top of the pile was still on top unopened. It was a New Zealand letter.

Continuing with the events of this morning, Mr. Armstrong had told him to telephone to the garage and have his Sunbeam Sports sent around at once. That always meant, the chauffeur told Pointer, that Mr. Armstrong was going alone, and going far.

All three servants had seen him open out a map and jot down some names and directions on a piece of paper. He had left the map open on a table. The butler now produced it. Pointer only gave it a glance to see that it was unmarked, and a small scale map of the counties lying between London and the Bristol Channel. Such a map as a man would look at who was going some distance west to a familiar place, and wanted to have an idea of main-traveled roads only.

When the car came around, Mr. Armstrong told the butler, as he had his valet, that he would not be in before, at the earliest, eight o'clock in the evening, possibly not till later. Then he drove off, and that was the last that the house servants had seen of him—alive.

"How about having come back earlier than he intended? Could Mr. Armstrong have done that?" Pointer asked.

Humanly speaking, he could have, but the butler seemed to think that human speech counted for very little in this affair. True, the house was upset with preparations for the afternoon's reception, and with a burst pipe in a bathroom over the Chinese suite. There was a door opening into a side street, one Mr. Armstrong often used, but it only led to the library, and Mrs. Armstrong had had lunch served in the library today, as she often did when Mr. Armstrong was not there.

"Mr. Armstrong never came back into this house walking on his own feet, sir," the man finished gravely.

"Who else was in the house? The secretary, Mr. Farrant?"

"Mr. Farrant had left us yesterday, sir. Mr. Armstrong wished him to undertake some very important mission, it seems, that may take months."

Pointer was now told that Mr. Farrant had moved his personal effects out of his two upper rooms yesterday afternoon.

"Who told you about the important commission?"

Mr. Farrant had told one of the footmen. "What about Mr. Callard; he's staying here, isn't he?"

Yes, Mr. Callard had arrived for a visit the day before yesterday, and had spoken this morning as though intending to stay some time. But Mr. Armstrong had mentioned three days. Well, no, one could not say that

Mr. Armstrong was pleased to see his brother-in-law. He had very patently ignored Mr. Callard whenever the two were alone together, and had tried, the butler thought, to have such occasions be as few as possible. Mr. Callard, on the other hand, had seemed not to mind Mr. Armstrong's manner. He was just back from Cannes, and had let his own rooms at Knightsbridge for a week. There was an idea among the servants that Percy Callard was in low financial water, but as that impression was due to his saying on every possible occasion that he hadn't "a bean," things might not be so dark as they seemed.

Mr. Callard had breakfasted around nine this morning, very unusually early for him, and had then left the house. He had got back about two this afternoon.

"Just when we were all busy getting that huge chest up the stairs, sir. I never thought we could do it."

"What about Major Hardy? Does he often come to the house?"

Very often indeed, he was told. He and Mr. Armstrong were good friends. The major had come around twelve today and seemed surprised when he heard that a Chinese chest, which he had ordered as a present for the Armstrongs, hadn't arrived. He had been heard telephoning for it, and then telling Mrs. Armstrong that the van carrying it had had engine trouble, but that another would bring it on. He had lunched at the house and the van had finally arrived around two. Major Hardy had superintended the carrying of the chest up to the niche. He had barely glanced at it, the butler thought, and had not opened it. Mrs. Armstrong had suggested doing this, but he had said, "Oh, everything's all right inside. They're packed as tight as peas in a pod, three hundred of the little beggars tied up in a princely napkin. I kept tally myself."

Had the chest seemed heavy when it was taken upstairs?—Very heavy. Pointer went over every detail of the carrying in of the chest and of its placing in the Chinese suite. He made quite sure that it had not been

out of sight until the major had locked the great double
doors and hung up the key, except for one short interval,
when Mrs. Armstrong had stepped back to take a last
glance at the suite. The men had all stood panting about
the doors until she reappeared. It had seemed long to the
butler, but he had had his eyes on his watch, and it had
not been three minutes all told. The doors were in full
sight of the stairs and front hail. Pointer had already
found that it was impossible to open or shut them without
a sound like the beating of gongs, and that the key,
though it turned easily, made a noise that could not
possibly be missed anywhere in the house.

The men sent with the chest by Lee and Son were
Irish, said the servants. They had asked if it contained
stones or cement when drinking their beer afterwards in
the servants' hall.

Major Hardy had left as soon as the doors were locked
again. The butler had heard him tell Mrs. Armstrong as
he hurried off that he would like to stay and support her
through the afternoon's 'fuss' "his word, sir," the butler
interpolated primly—"but that he had another of his own
to worry through, and that there was no need to give up
their little dinner party—it could, and would, wait until
whatever time Mr. Armstrong got back in the evening."

As for the preparations for the tea which was to be
served in the first of the three rooms, the butler had
superintended its arrangement. At no time was he, or any
one else, alone in the suite, as the tables had been
prepared downstairs and set up quickly in the one corner
of the big room. A service lift beside the entrance doors
made all this part of the work exceedingly expeditious.

Pointer had already given orders to his men to search
the house for any trace of the missing dwarf birch trees.
Not that he expected them to be found at Charles Street,
but the improbable as well as the probable must be
investigated.

"And when was Mr. Rufus Armstrong last in the
house?" Pointer asked the butler.

"He came this morning, sir, around eleven, just after Mrs. Armstrong had gone out, but when he heard that the chest wasn't expected until twelve, he said he wouldn't wait, and shouldn't be able to see it in place until next week."

"When did he leave?"

"I suppose at once, sir," the man suggested vaguely.

"Did you show him out?"

"No, sir. I was trying to find the main cock below stairs and turn off the water."

"Then who did show Mr. Rufus out?"

The butler left Pointer to make some inquiries. He returned to say that all the servants had been too busy trying to help mop up the overflow, or get to the plumber, to remember.

"In other words, you don't know that he left the house at all," the chief inspector said quietly.

The butler looked tolerant. "well, sir, as he isn't here now, and hasn't been seen since Mrs. Armstrong spoke to him, I should say he left the house there and then. He said he couldn't wait, you remember."

Pointer thanked the butler, and collected Major Hardy and Schofild on his way to the car.

CHAPTER THREE

PERCY Callard strolled up as the three were about to shut the door of the car

"Nothing private in your visit to Chinatown, is there? I should like to come along. I really should. Let me drive. I can drive quite nicely," and without waiting for a reply, Percy insinuated himself into the seat with practiced ease. The Yard chauffeur, standing on the pavement, looked at Pointer, who, in his turn, looked at the major.

"Can he be trusted with government property and our valuable lives?'" he asked.

"He drives like a racing pro," was the reply, then, as they were off with a smooth ease that bore out his words, he added, "The trouble with Callard is in himself. He's such a shiftless beggar. He can do anything he sets his hand to. That's what makes us—his friends—a bit wild at times with him. He won't try. However, about that chest... " The major went into greater detail about the purchase.

"How was it that Buck of the Gaiety knew that your present was going to be a chest, if you only bought it this morning?" Pointer asked.

"Oh, I had told Mrs. Armstrong a month ago, when the question of fitting up the Chinese suite first came up, that I'd dash them the biggest thing in wedding-chests I could find in town. Mrs. Armstrong wanted something in which to keep the robes and shawls she collects. As I told you, Lee didn't think much of this chest, he hoped to get hold of a really fine one for me, but, as I also told you, Rufus Armstrong thought it a splendid piece of work."

"Is he considered a good judge?"

"It isn't a case of what he's considered, but of what he considers himself," Percy threw in over his shoulder, the glass partition was down between him and the others. "And judged by that, no one can pull the wool over the eyes of R. A. He was, out in the legation for a while at Peking, and since then poses as a heaven-inspired critic on all things celestial."

"He's a quite good enough judge for Armstrong or me," the major said easily.

"Do you know who engaged the Chinese orchestra?" Pointer asker next.

"That was Rufus's own contrib," Percy murmured.

"Do you know what agent he went to?"

"Same firm. The Lees. As he recommends every one to them, he could hardly go elsewhere."

"Do you know when he arranged for them, Mr. Callard?"

"Must have been this morning. As he only proposed it to my sister last night at the Bat. She thought it a capital idea. Hoped it would send every one into roars of laughter."

"I bought the chest at eleven," Hardy put in. "Rufus Armstrong hadn't been down by then, or I think they certainly would have mentioned it to me."

"When he recommended you to go to these Lees, sir, did Mr. Rufus Armstrong say why he liked them?"

"Yes. Said they were the old, almost extinct, type of China merchant. If they said a thing was genuine, genuine it was."

There was a short silence on that.

"I hear from the chief inspector that Farrant has left Charles Street and is away on some sort of a private mission," Schofild now put in, "do you know anything about it, major?"

"I don't. You mean that he wasn't at the house at all today?" Hardy asked.

"He seems to 've left it yesterday," Pointer said, as Schofild had no answer to give. "What is this Mr. Farrant like, in character, I mean?" He had had a terse, accurate description of his outward appearance from the private inquiry agent.

"Silly, superior ass!" came from Callard.

"Genius at languages," Hardy said; "that's why he's got the post with Armstrong."

"Not a bit of it," contradicted Callard, "William Farrant got the post because he was Phyllis's old friend. He kept it because he's good at languages—That's the right of it, chief inspector. It was Mrs. Armstrong who got him the post."

"I wonder you don't say it was you!" scoffed Hardy.

"But that wouldn't be strictly true," minced Percy. "It was my sister's liking for dear Willie that impelled her husband to offer him the job of confidential secretary. And it was his liking for her that impelled him to accept it."

Something in the young man's tone made Pointer wonder if he himself had tried for the post.

He asked him the question in a roundabout way, and learned very plainly that Callard had been tried for a week and been found wanting.

"Everything once, was his motto," Callard said, with apparent frankness, spinning the wheel with one finger and passing through a narrow opening between two cars.

"Make it yours!" begged Hardy, "and don't try that again. One more coat of varnish and we'd have stuck fast there. You're a careless devil, Callard. It's not that you're plucky. You don't see the risks you run."

"Everything once," Pointer repeated thoughtfully. "Was that Mr. Armstrong's character as well as his motto?"

"Not a bad summary of him, in my opinion," Schofild said, with a faint smile.

"Only there was a great deal more in Armstrong than that," Hardy spoke in a tone of deep affection. "Splendid fellow!"

"But he certainly was fond of testing things," Schofild maintained.

"He was! Fond of testing anything, old or new." Callard spoke in a by no means affectionate tone. "Tell Armstrong anything, and his first thought was how to test it if he didn't believe it, or prove it if he did. Fatiguing trait in a brother-in-law, I assure you!"

"You mustn't take our dear Percy's idea of light and airy persiflage at the foot of the letter," Major Hardy said to the chief inspector. "Coming back to Farrant, Armstrong doesn't employ people merely because they were acquaintances of his wife."

"Has he ever sent Mr. Farrant off on a mission before?" Pointer asked. No one seemed to know. Again there was a short silence, which Pointer broke.

"By the way, I might as well ask you now where you were today, Mr. Callard. As you know, I shall have to put that question to every one connected with Mr. Armstrong, merely as part of the routine work."

"I spent the hours from ten until my lunch at two at the National Gallery," Callard said promptly.

"Did you see anybody there whom you knew?" Pointer asked, looking hard at him.

"At the National Gallery?" Callard's tone was one of such deep amazement at the idea that Hardy gave a short laugh; though he said a trifle gruffly, "Don't try our patience too far by saying that you spent the afternoon in Westminster Abbey."

"But I didn't. I lunched at Simpson's, saw nobody there either that I knew bar the waiters, and sat on in the lounge until I finally wended my way on foot to Charles Street, arriving there just as you, major, were bursting your coat seams over the Chinese chest. Next time, you'll give something smaller, I fancy." And Percy Callard, with his constant half-smile, turned his face towards the traffic again. His face really had something cat-like about its retreating chin, mouth with upcurving lips, and long nose.

Hardy looked at him for a lingering minute. Both Pointer and Schofild thought that a longing to have Percy alone with him in some distant corner of the globe, just for a little while, surged through the explorer. But if so, he only turned to Pointer without putting his thoughts into words.

"My own movements today have been..." He detailed them as closely as was possible. And as he had been on an important colonial committee practically all morning, the police would have no trouble in verifying his whereabouts.

Percy began to slow up.

"Do you mind waiting here for a minute, sir?" Pointer said to the major, as they drew up at the address in Limehouse Street, "with Mr. Callard? I have some routine questions to put first."

"Oh, certainly," Major Hardy said stiffly, but again he looked as though he would like to add something not at all stiff. However, he pressed his firm lips together instead, and stared out of the window, while Pointer and Schofild quickly got out.

The ground floor of Messrs. Lee and Son suggested a lawyer's office rather than an importer's. Two big, bare rooms beyond the small room where a clerk sat typing. In the one room sat Lee father, in the other Lee son. Both looked at a glance about the same age, grave, round-faced, small-eyed men, whose lids drooped as they talked, thin lids that showed the darkness of the pupil through them like moving shadows. No opium den keepers these, the word of Lee and Son was a bond in the eyes of the East-End police, or the Chinese around them.

As Pointer had expected, both bore out, only in fuller detail, the account given by Major Hardy of his two purchases this morning. As to Mr. Rufus Armstrong, they knew him very well indeed, they said, from Peking days. He had been their patron ever since they first opened up business here some ten years ago. Mr. Rufus had only telephoned them to send Mrs. Armstrong a small but very good Chinese orchestra—five men—to play at her house from five to six. He had telephoned them this around ten. As a rule it was not the sort of thing they concerned themselves with, but Mr. Rufus could ask nothing of them which it would not be an honor to do.

While Pointer was talking, a message came through from their foreman who had reached the house in Charles Street. The wedding-chest was most certainly the one purchased by Major Hardy, which, filled with dwarf trees, had left Limehouse this morning.

"And Mr. Armstrong called here this morning about the trees, I understand?" Pointer threw in, "after Major Hardy was here, I suppose?"

The two Lees looked at him and asked him just what he meant, they had not had the honor of Mr. Armstrong's presence at any time.

Pointer explained that Mr. Armstrong had spoken of coming in this morning to have a look at the trees and also at a bronze of the Han period that Mr. Lee had on his premises, which his cousin had praised.

The older Lee bowed and waved a hand at a safe behind them.

"No one has seen the Han bronze these last four days, not since Mr. Rufus Armstrong saw it last. Mr. Armstrong has not come. Either today or at any time."

"He couldn't have come and seen one of your clerks?"

"Either my son or I am always here. If my son is out, I stay. If I am out, he stays. Perhaps you would like to question the man who showed you in here? You are, of course, trying to trace the trees?" Both the Lees looked at him very intently as the elder asked this.

"I am," Pointer agreed.

The clerk who had shown him in, the only clerk to be seen, was summoned. The two Lees left him alone with the chief inspector. The man was half-English, half-Chinese, and answered in a very concise, apparently straightforward manner. There had been no visitors this morning except Major Hardy. As to Mr. Armstrong, except for Mr. Rufus Armstrong, no gentleman of that name had ever come to the place. Pointer set some quite neat and very well-concealed traps, but the man seemed to have nothing to hide, and, after a few minutes, was allowed to go.

Pointer went out to the car. He asked if Major Hardy and Mr. Callard would like to ask the Lees any questions without waiting for Mr. Schofild and himself to finish. He mentioned that the chest had been identified as the one bought by the major.

"Any questions?" The major gave a mirthless laugh. "A thousand! Look here," he turned to the elder Chinese, who shot his dark eyes to and among his callers like little shuttles, "have you heard exactly what was in your chest when as opened in Charles Street?"

Mr. Lee murmured that he had not, but that foreman had seemed almost inarticulate with surprise and agitation over the telephone, and as man knew before he started out that the trees were missing, he, Mr. Lee, wondered what had caused it.

"When that chest was opened the dead body of Mr. Armstrong was found inside," the major it on, staring at the man. "Mr. Armstrong, gentleman to whose house the chest and the trees inside were sent. The buyer of the trees, in fact."

Both the Lees drew in their breath sharply. Turning, they began to talk to each other rapidly. The Chinese are said to be an impassive race, but when the veneer of impassivity cracks, they can seethe like any Sicilian. What struck both Pointer and Schofild was that they seethed so long. Backward and forward went the swift interchange of sentences, before they turned to their visitors and in English asked for enlightenment. Pointer told them the outlines of the case as so far known.

"Now," he went on, "when, exactly, was that chest sent away from here?"

A Chinese was sent for—Mr. Sing, their "number one clerk." He brought in a ledger to show that the chest had been sent off exactly five minutes after the major left the premises.

"And it stood meanwhile?" Pointer asked.

Sing took them all out to see where it had stood. In a shed at the bottom of the yard close to the double doors through which the vans passed in and out. There was a man, an Englishman, on duty at the gates as they were called. Pointer took Mr. Sing on one side and talked to him for a minute. It would have been possible for any one to slip in unnoticed, and slip out again, just as in Charles Street. Mr. Armstrong could have come back and gone out and come back, but here, too, it seemed most unlikely. Mr. Sing explained that he was always in and around. The firm employed ten men in all, and had three vans. A combination of circumstances might have let some one slip in and exchange the heavy bundle of tied-up trees for the equally heavy if not heavier body of a dead man, but to chance it, the murderer would have had to have a faith in his lucky star outrivalling Napoleon's.

"No van of any other firm drove into this yard this morning, between the time Major Hardy bought the chest, and the time it was sent off?" Pointer asked.

The man at the gate, Randall was his name, said no. But when it was ready to leave, a laundry van had driven up, and the driver had got down for a word with Ogle, the driver of the van that carried the chest. He explained that he was a pal of Ogle's and in passing had caught sight of the latter, and wanted to know when he was coming along to Canning Town to see him and his missis. Nothing else. What laundry was it? Somewhere out in Ealing—Sunshine—or Sunlight. No, it wasn't Sunlight— but something of that kind. He had wondered why they didn't launder their own canvas covers. Dirty old turn-out, and no mistake.

How many men were in it?

"Only one. The driver."

"Van fully laden?" Pointer asked.

"Good few baskets in it," the gatekeeper conceded, "say a dozen or so, of the usual kind."

In answer to further questions, he said that one very big one, yes, by that he meant very long one, was the last in the cart, riding on the tailboard.

"Was the laundry man bearded?"

"No, sir. But Ole Bill mustache, and hair like a Jew's wig. And kept on grinning fit to split his face. Terrible amused he was at everything. I thought he'd taken his tea just a bit too strong for breakfast."

"And his hands, rough and browned?"

"Gloves, sir. Thick driving gloves."

"Drive well?" Pointer asked, passing him a couple of very good cigars.

"Never saw a van turn in that length before," the man said warmly. "Turned her as on a swivel, he did. And, judging by the look of her, that took some doing, I'll lay."

Pointer and Schofild returned to where, some distance off, Callard and Major Hardy were deep in discussions about the route the van had taken.

Pointer learned that the chest had not been put into a packing case as they thought there might be difficulty in getting it out. It had merely been laid down on a mattress in the small padded van.

"And now, what about the breakdown?" He had purposely given them time to get it all straightened out.

Mr. Lee explained that the driver of the van with the chest—they had made a special delivery of it—-had kept to the quieter streets, and it was off Fleet Street that the accident had occurred. Something wrong with the magneto. They had managed to back the car into a little cul-de-sac, and had then reported the mishap to Mr. Lee by telephone. Another—an empty—van, which was by chance on its way home, had been sent to the place at once. The men on it handing over their van to the men with the chest and going off duty. The second van took the first in tow, and the chest was duly delivered, though later than at the hour set.

"Where are the men who seem to have been in charge of the chest throughout?" Pointer asked.

"I have sent around to their homes. As today is Saturday, they may be out. They had but that one job to do this morning."

The four visitors next inspected the van. Percy Callard with his perpetual half-smile more marked than usual. Major Hardy with a black frown. Pointer and Schofild with non-committal expressions.

The chief inspector had already arranged from Charles Street with the Yard that one of their most expert men was to be sent to the Lees' place to investigate the car and the cause of the breakdown. He now asked Mr. Callard meanwhile to inquire about the make of the laundry van's tires from the gatekeeper. The reply Percy passed on to him was that they were Dunlops, very much patched. Pointer slipped away and had a word with the gatekeeper himself. Randall stared at his first query. "Tires? Nobody hasn't asked me about no tires, sir," he said, puzzled, arriving at a negative again in his circle. "Nobody hasn't."

"Didn't the fair-haired young man with us ask you about them?"

"No, sir. Hasn't opened his mouth in this direction," was the reply. Pointer thought how exactly the man's phrase hit off what he had noticed Percy Callard had not at any time opened his mouth in Mr. Randall's direction—which was precisely why the chief inspector had given him the commission about the tires.

He now was told by the man that the latter had not paid any attention to the tires of the laundry van. Why should he? Mr. Randall asked in an injured and bewildered tone.

"There's some mistake," Pointer said, as though vexed, and asked Mr. Callard to be kind enough to come to them for a moment.

Percy came, munching something sweet and sticky. The Lees had pressed some Chinese delicacies on their guests.

He looked interrogatively at Pointer, and went on eating with a faint wave of the hand that said, "Excuse me. I'm stuck."

"There's some mistake here which I want to clear up," Pointer said crisply. "You told me, Mr. Callard, that the gatekeeper here said that the laundry van I'm interested in had much-mended Dunlop tires?"

Callard nodded affably. But Pointer's eyes were on his notes.

"Didn't you?" he asked, still writing.

Percy mumbled, "My mistake. Sticky stuff, this. Better to make your own inquiries. I'm apt to forget messages". His voice hardly reached the others through the glutinous mass, and his words were all but impossible to understand. But Callard turned away with a bearing as nonchalant as ever, and as unhurried, as he went back to the others. The next move was to examine the place where the breakdown had occurred, and the two detectives hurried to the car.

"It's all rubbish about that breakdown having anything to do with Boyd's murder. The body was put in the chest in the house. Take my word for that," Callard said. Major Hardy and he had come out on to the pavement with the other two.

"I'm afraid we want better security." Hardy spoke contemptuously.

"You're keen on having it connected with the breakdown?" Percy asked, his smile more like a cat's than usual.

"It was connected with it." Hardy spoke sternly. "Unfortunately, I didn't open the chest when it arrived. It's no use harping on that great mistake, for the body couldn't have been put in at the house. The servants were all over the place, and those doors into the Chinese suite make a sound like a gong when they're opened. Besides, what of the trees that filled it level with the top?" The major stood a moment with his arms resting on the top of the window.

"I've got a chap who's very good at finding things out. I'll put him on to this," he muttered. "At first I thought whatever had happened had taken place down here, in Limehouse Street, but it must have been where the van broke down."

"Of course, if so, the idea of suicide is impossible, or very improbable," Schofild said.

"Idea of suicide!" Hardy's dark brows drew together. "What on earth should Armstrong commit suicide for? Of course it's not suicide!" Major Hardy spoke as though the suggestion were a personal affront.

"Well, I'm off," Callard replied indolently, "perhaps you'll put me down at the nearest tube, chief inspector, there's bound to be one somewhere—anywhere." Without waiting for an assent, he installed himself on the cushions.

Pointer only nodded and pulled up within a few minutes. Percy languidly collected his legs and arms together, and slouched off with a patronizing wave of the hand to the two in front.

"I wonder he didn't offer to tip me," was Pointer's amused comment, as he made off at a swift pace towards the river. But his mind was still on the young man as he drove.

The good driving of the man with the laundry van, his alibi so carefully prepared, so triumphantly given, that Pointer felt sure it would be difficult to break down in its entirety. Not that Callard was a formidable antagonist to any one's brains. It was bantam against heavyweight. The trouble was, that with young men of Callard's type it took so little to send them crooked. They were pretty well born crooked. He very much expected to find that little Percy Callard had been a liar, if not worse, at school. And a liar, if not worse, at the university, supposing he had been able to pass an entrance exam. He was, unless Pointer was all wrong about him, absolutely unmoral.

Percy Callard... that laundry van... three hundred very special dwarf trees. Pointer would be quite prepared to find that Percy had stolen the trees to sell them. Lee had told Schofild that, sold singly, they could easily fetch two guineas apiece, instead of the ten shillings for which he had let a friend of the purchaser of the chest have them. Major Hardy was a new customer, and a famous man; Mr. Armstrong was still newer, and, in his own way, as famous. Hence the price of the trees, and the embroidered linen sheet in which to wrap the tiny things.

Turning, he told Schofild about the gate-keeper and Callard.

"The major's right in saying that he's foolhardy," was Schofild's comment. "It looks as if he hadn't quite realized that the same gatekeeper would be on duty at the Lees', and that a walrus mustache is not, after all, a mask and domino. Of, course, he may be cleverer than he looks."

"That shouldn't be difficult," Pointer murmured.

"But, in my opinion," Schofild went on, "he was in all probability the driver of that laundry van. I know it sounds a bold jump—"

Pointer did not say that he had already taken it, unaided.

"But he's done some close sailing to the wind before now. Very close." The private investigator nodded portentously. "Introducing wealthy visitors to disreputable places, and moneylenders, that sort of thing, not in your line at the Yard, but in mine. Yes, in my opinion, Percy and the disappearance of those dwarf trees are linked. The trouble is, is that the extent of his guilt?"

Lady Grail's look of intense anticipation came back to Schofild now. Gossip had linked her name with Hardy's some year or so ago. But since his return from his last hunting expedition Schofild had heard no more whispers. The chest was Hardy's gift... if it could be linked with a public social fiasco... Yes, Lady Grail might have joined forces with Percy Callard... He had felt sure that there was spite in this crime. Pointer was stopping the car. They were in the cul-de-sac off Fleet Street. They found nothing on the spot itself except oil where the van had stood so long.

The constable on duty near by had been duly notified of the breakdown, and had noticed that a laundry van at one time was pulled up end to end with the other. It had driven off after five or ten minutes' stop. In other words, it had only been there long enough for the driver to have a glass of beer, he had thought. Had he noticed any name on the laundry van? Yes. Something to do with Sunshine or Sunbeam or Sungleam. He thought the last. The district had been Ealing.

And the time when he noticed it?

"Noon. Just struck twelve."

Pointer and Schofild looked the street over. There was a publichouse on the corner. The place of breakdown was exactly at one of the lampposts.

Pointer strolled on to the publichouse, and saw one of his men having a cup of bovril and a chat with barmaid, noticed that from the window of the public bar, the engine of the van would certainly have been in sight, but probably not the rear. Yet the vanmen had telephoned to Mr. Lee that they were keeping their eyes on the chest all the time.

There were no empty houses around. None where one could easily fancy that a murder might have been committed. Every house and every room would be investigated, quietly but thoroughly, but there was nothing to suggest crime here.

They had another talk with the constable, who knew Pointer by sight. The policeman was told briefly what was suspected of having happened at the spot when the two vans had met and remained end-on for a few minutes. Would it have been possible?

"I saw," P. C. Fisher said, going carefully back, "I saw a chap leaning against the lamppost there when the laundry van drew up. I thought he had come with the breakdown van, but I can't be sure. I saw him talking to the driver of the laundry van. But as to what happened?" With a sigh the man in blue had to confess that he had no idea. But he was sure of one thing, no vans other than the van that broke down, the laundry van, and the van that finally took the breakdown in tow had been in the cul-de-sac this morning.

"Did you see the van that took the breakdown in tow?" Pointer asked. Here the man knew all there was to be known by an onlooker. He had insisted on a fluttering paper being tied to the connecting cable. Had done this himself. "You are quite sure that the relieving van was empty?"

"Certain, sir. I clambered through her to tie on the paper."

"How about the top?"

"Canvas top. Nothing on top, sir. Nor slung from the top."

"How about the bottom of the van? Could it have carried a false bottom? Think carefully, constable."

Constable Fisher shook a neat head with desicion. "Impossible, sir. It was a Leyland chassis. Ordinary commercial make. Van was light wood as thin and as cheap as they can be made. Nothing thick or double-bottomed about her, sir. You see, I walked over the boards while the engine was running to tie on that paper. You could fairly feel the cam shaft turning."

He gave more details of the men and the car.

Pointer now asked over the telephone for the best Chinese interpreter whom the Yard could get to be sent to Limehouse. He wanted a white man. That proviso meant Mr. Wilkins, he was told. Mr. Wilkins, the Limehouse police-court missionary, who had been a China Inland missionary until his health broke down. But it was most unlikely that Mr. Wilkins could be got at an instant's notice. However, the Yard would do its best.

Back to the Chinese merchants' house went the two men. Schofild made but one remark on the drive there.

"Murder," he said, out of a brown study, "not suicide. No mere spite would account for Armstrong's dead body being transferred into that chest in the open street. Only necessity."

Back in Limehouse the mechanic from the Yard had given the car a look over. No more was needed. The accident was most certainly not an accident at all, but an intention. "A speck of paper between the make-and-break; Regular chauffeur's dodge, sir."

Pointer passed this on to Mr. Lee the elder, who murmured that he would be delighted to see again the three men of that particular van, but that there was a fear clouding his mind that the meeting would not be at once. Both Pointer and Schofild agreed with him. Mr. Lee's man had drawn blank so far in trying to find the trio. They were all unmarried men, and each had left his room, or his share of a room, that morning with his belongings packed up or tied up, and rent settled. All three had seemed in very high spirits.

"And that, as your proverb says, is very much indeed that," murmured Mr. Lee "This affair is a great disgrace. I can arrange for another consignment of little trees, but the occasion for their presenting will have passed. My customers have been, as you would say, 'let down' by me and my son."

"How was the key tied on, Mr. Lee? A simple loop?" Pointer asked, after a moment.

"No. A ceremonial knot. Like this." Mr. Lee showed him a carved casket with a key fastened to one side.

"Would it take long to untie it?"

Mr. Lee said that they were quite easy to undo.

His son joined him, and for a moment the two of them went off the deep end again in their own tongue. Then the younger turned to Pointer.

"As you asked, I have sent for the musicians who performed at the house of Mr. Armstrong. They are refugees from noble houses now destitute. They are here. As most of them speak no English whatever, I thought you might like to have some one not connected with this terrible tragedy to speak to them for you, and to you for them. I have obtained Mr. Tong, the scholar."

Mr. Tong proved to be a melancholy elderly Chinese, who now entered the room followed by four others of his race, the little orchestra that had played in Charles Street. They looked distinctly frightened. All of them had their instruments with them, and, one of them had brought his pet lark in a cage as well, apparently for moral support.

"We will take oath according to the custom of our country," Mr. Tong explained to the Englishmen. Advancing, he spoke swiftly and solemnly in Chinese, then turning, he translated, his words in a sing-song voice.

"I declare, as in the presence of Buddha, that I am unprejudiced, and if what I speak shall prove false, or if, by coloring the truth others-shall be led astray, then may the three Holy Existences, Buddha, Dhanuna, and Pro Sangha, in whose sight I now stand, together with the Devotees of the Twenty-two Firmaments, punish me and also my migrating soul."

Each of the musicians in turn knelt on the floor and repeated a Chinese formula while blowing out a candle. The formula Mr. Tong translated into, "I tell the truth and the whole truth. If not, as this candle is blown out, may my soul be blown out."

This much was interesting, but there followed a very tedious quarter of an hour, which only firmness kept from extending to an hour.

Nothing was learned from any of the men. Mr. Tong had all the virtues, except brevity, and the musicians seemed to think that only a ceaseless flow of protestations could save their lives. The tallest of the little group, the one with the lark, kept his gaze fixed on the chief inspector, and seemed greatly relieved when Mr.

Tong finally told them, translating Pointer's words, that, though they might be wanted for the inquest, and were not to change their addresses without letting the police know, they could go. He himself set the example by hurrying off. The tall young Chinese swept Pointer's face with a final glance as he passed out with a quaint, ungainly bob. His eyes remained in Pointer's memory. There was a quite unconscious, and therefore important, expression in them. Pointer searched for the right name for it. Malice?—Too strong. Amusement tinged with malice?—Better, but not quite it. Yet there was a hint of derision.

Why was Mr. Wong—Pointer learned that the young man's name was Wong and that he came of a very high family—why was Mr. Wong amused? At what? And why the faint tinge of mockery? Unfortunately he professed to speak almost no English at all.

Mr. Wilkins was now announced. At the name, the younger Lee murmured something to his father, who met it blandly, but said a quick word under his breath before replying to the clerk. "We are honored by a visit from so well-known a friend of our race."

And both Lees certainly showed every sign of respect as they advanced to meet the pale-faced, shabby little man, who now entered hurriedly. Pointer, introducing himself and his companion, thanked him for having come, but explained that the need for his talents was over for the moment. Mr. Wilkins made for the door promptly. Pointer walked a few steps into the street with him. He told him that he believed Mr. Wong knew something that might help the police. Would Mr. Wilkins try to prevail on him to tell it them? Pointer did not make the mistake of asking the little man before him, with the blunt features, scrubby cheeks, but honest eyes, to try and get it out of Mr. Wong. He knew that he would have been met with a decided refusal. But the Yard had just told him that Mr. Wilkins was popular with the Chinese exiles who had managed to find a home in Limehouse with friends or relatives.

Mr. Wilkins told him at once that young Wong could understand no English whatever—only French or German. He had but very recently arrived in this country, and, like many others of his countrymen, was really living on the charity of Lee and Son.

CHAPTER FOUR

THE telephone bell rang. The chief inspector was called to the telephone. He learned, in code, that the bullet had been extricated from Armstrong's head. It was one to fit a small automatic of the .38 caliber so commonly sold in gun shops. As the doctor had thought, death could not have occurred for some little interval after he was shot, but he must have become at once unconscious, with—perhaps—a lucid moment at the very last.

The next step was to hurry to Armstrong's offices in the city. A word from Scotland Yard had ensured that however late Pointer might be, there would be some responsible person waiting there for him.

The Lees took a most elaborate farewell of Major Hardy, and a polite one of both the Yard man and the private investigator, and repeated their assurances that nothing could ease their burning sense of humiliation, but the complete exoneration of their house from any share in the accident and the loss of the trees, let alone in the terrible end of the most honorable Mr. Armstrong.

"Yet they were none too pleased to see Mr. Wilkins," Hardy said, as the three drove off. Pointer and Schofild agreed with him.

There was a short silence.

"I don't know what to say!"—the Major spoke in a tone of a man in genuine difficulty—"nor what to think. What possible link can there be between these Chinese and Armstrong? Yet, they're in it. Somehow. The only idea I have at the moment is the well-known fact that Armstrong was on the side of an all-white Australia, and so against yellow immigration. But that seems a wild notion to account for his murder."

"What about Mr. Rufus Armstrong, he might be able to suggest something?"

"He might." The major did not sound hopeful. "He's not much of a hand at solving problems of this kind, I fancy. Rufus is the true collector. Likes to keep the world shut out, while he dusts his jades and polishes his ivories in a museum of his own. Still, it's most unfortunate that he's not at hand at the moment."

"Were they on good terms, he and Mr. Armstrong?" Pointer asked casually.

"Excellent. Boyd hadn't an enemy in his own world, I assure you. At least, not one that any of us can guess as such. Will you drop me here, chief inspector? I'm going back to Armstrong's house. It's still that to me. I'll stay till Rufus, or Farrant, take over. Can't leave the place with no one but a dazed woman to look after it. And you'll want to be by yourselves at the office."

The two watched him stride away towards a taxi.

"There goes a sorely puzzled man," said Pointer, as he moved off.

"In my opinion," Schofild said, "his idea of Armstrong's objection to Chinese immigration into Australia as the cause for his murder is quite possible. It would all depend on whether he had, as they thought, harmed any relations of the Lees or disgraced them in any way. I have rather an idea that as there was an idea of making a fool of both Hardy and the Armstrongs, mixed in with blacker motives in this murder, it's quite possible that that, too, is in revenge for some slight, or disgrace, inflicted by Armstrong, or suffered because of him. You never know with the Eastern mind. However, I happen to know a son of the Mr. Wilkins we met today. He and one of my boys are scoutmasters, working in the same part of the East End. I shall cultivate the father a bit, and get him to take an interest in those two Chinese merchants for me."

"I've already asked him to take an interest in Mr. Wong the flautist for me," Pointer said.

"Oh?" Schofild was all interest. "He may know more English than he claims to, and have overheard something." They had learned that the musicians, afraid of being late, and not sure of how much time to allow from Limehouse, had arrived in a body, with the exception of Mr. Wong, well before five. But Mr. Wong had come first. Alone. The servants had said that the first of the "Chinks" had got there somewhere around half-past four. The housekeeper had found the room empty when she had looked in at four. "Yes," Schofild murmured, "he may have heard something.

"Or seen something," Pointer thought that the more likely. "The keyhole, dusty as it is, gives a view of one end of the chest, and of the pagoda dovecote."

"Now I come to think of it," Schofild put in, "Percy Callard and Lady Grail were standing just against those doors—those inset decorative panels one could really call them—when the lid of the chest was raised. Yes, right against it, and also when they rushed forward, both must have been well in the range of that big keyhole. Yes, it's possible."

"And it's also possible that it was something connected with Mrs. Armstrong, who would be full in the range of vision while standing against the pole of the dovecote," Pointer put in. "That's the question, rather, those are the questions. Anyway, I fancy that Mr. Wilkins can be of the greatest help to us if we could get the young man to talk."

"Supposing Wong knows something," temporized Schofild

"Oh, he knows something all right," Pointer spoke with confidence as he stopped at the big building where Armstrong's offices occupied two of the floors.

A few questions put to the horrified head clerk told nothing that threw any light, on Armstrong's murder. The dead man had been at the office in the morning from half-past nine to ten. Then at eleven he had hurried in again just for a minute, dashing into and out of his room, evidently to fetch something, and had left, saying that he would be away all day. Considering that a very interesting cable was, hourly expected from Perth in Australia, the head clerk had been slightly surprised.

"Has the cable come?" Pointer asked.

It had not.

"I thought Mr. Farrant would be expected to decode it," Schofild put in.

"One would have thought that," the head clerk agreed, "but evidently some other code is being used, for Mr. Farrant is off on some private mission. He left yesterday afternoon."

"Will Mr. Armstrong's death send the shares of any particular companies down?" Pointer asked.

The clerk thought not. Not for any length of time. The companies in which the dead financier was interested depended on facts, not on his personal life, to send them up or down. "Mr. Armstrong wasn't at all one of your one-man rulers. In all his companies there were two or three men who could carry on just as well as he had."

"Was there any one man who would step into his shoes as head of all?"

"No particular man, no."

Pointer was watching the head clerk without seeming to do so. This man had no hand in his employer's death, he felt certain of that. He was the kind of man who kept straight from cast-iron principles.

"Had Mr. Armstrong any enemies?"

"Any enemies? Well—the Herbert group were enemies all right, but not murderers."

Asked by Pointer to explain who the Herbert group were, the head clerk looked surprized and disappointed. What did Scotland Yard know, if it didn't know all about the Herbert group, his expression said. Almost pityingly he explained that by that name the City meant Sir Ellis Herbert, Mr. Isidore Macpherson, and Mr. Julius Parkinson, the three biggest men in the Southern Cross Base-Metal Trust. And the greatest of the three was Ellis

Herbert. But these gentlemen were commercial enemies only. Dangerous financially—very! But not physically.

And as failing these three magnates, no one else in the City had any pecuniary interest in Mr. Armstrong's death, the head clerk seemed to think that in the end Mr. Armstrong's death must turn out to have been an accident.

The door opened at that point and Percy Callard came in.

"I was sure the shop would be open. Just occurred to me that I want a word with Mr. Castle about Farrant. Howd'ye do, Castle? What's this about Farrant being off on an important mission?" Percy sank languidly to a chair and lighted a cigarette. He conveyed the impression that he and the chief clerk were alone in the room.

"Quite true, Mr. Callard, he is." Something in Castle's glance over his glasses suggested that he was not one of Percy's admirers. Pointer did not interfere. He wanted to see what that young man was up to.

"How do you know that he is?" Callard asked. "Because he told you so, or because my brother-in-law told you so?"

Castle made no immediate reply.

"Come, now, which was it? World of difference, you know," Percy said, with his head on one side.

"Mr. Farrant told me," Castle said at that.

"In front of my brother-in-law?" Percy continued. He seemed to be harping a good deal on his relationship to the dead man.

"When we were alone together. Why?" Castle asked bruskly.

"Because it's important, Castle, that's why." There was rather a nasty undertone to Callard's voice. "That's very much why!" He strolled on into the empty room which Farrant had used as an office.

"Pretty thorough cleaning up," he said aloud,"looks as if Farrant never expected to return."

Which was the impression the room made on the chief inspector and on Schofild.

Percy opened all drawers, lifted out a book or two, before he finally let the outer door swing shut behind him.

The two detectives did not stay much longer. A chartered accountant was on his way, who would be joined by an expert in big business, a man who knew the little, tight world of high finance as another man might know the fingers on his hands. In due course they would pass on any information to Pointer that might have any bearing on Armstrong's death.

Back at the house in Charles Street, they found Major Hardy waiting for them. He promised to help with the investigation of the dead man's papers and letters until Farrant or Rufus Armstrong could relieve him of the task.

Pointer was leading the way into the library, a room which was Armstrong's special study and almost his den, when Callard came down the stairs.

"She's still asleep," he answered the major's look. "And I'll bet that Farrant's still not returned. Look here, can I be of any help with Armstrong's correspondence? There's a terrifying constable in there who as good as told me he would arrest me if I crossed the threshold, but as poor Phyl is helpless, and probably half the drawers are chock-a-block with her letters to Armstrong, I thought I might come along."

Hardy evidently did not think so. Neither did Pointer or Schofild.

"We can manage," Pointer said, closing the door. A word to the man in plain clothes, and they had the room to themselves, without fear of eavesdroppers,.

"I wonder why Callard is so interested in Farrant," Schofild asked Hardy.

"Trouble with Percy is, he's such a spiteful little devil," was the rather vague reply. It was one that peculiarly interested Schofild.

"But why the spite against Farrant in particular?"

"Probably because of Mrs. Armstrong's secretary, Miss Dickins. Nice little girl. Pretty as paint. Last kind to give our Percy a second look, but he doesn't quite see himself as others see him. At any rate he's making himself very ridiculous just now."

"In what way?" Pointer seemed puzzled. Not too much so. Major Hardy looked a clever chap.

"He'd like to think that Farrant had something to do with Armstrong's murder."

"You don't think Farrant had?"

"I'm certain he hadn't!"

"Yet you don't know all the facts, nor even the half of them, major," Schofild warned him.

"Yes, but I know Farrant! He's a quiet chap, not given to protestations, but he's devoted, body and soul, to Armstrong."

"Was he particularly friendly with Mrs. Armstrong."

"Farrant? The other way, I should have said."

"I thought she got him his position?" Pointer, asked.

"So she did. But perhaps she found a daily dose of Farrant a bit wearing. And she's not his style for long, either. He's well—staid is the best word I can think of, and very dependable."

"Yet you were surprized when you heard that he had gone off so suddenly on this mission." Pointer seated himself in front of the knee-hole table.

The major hesitated.

"Yes," he said finally, "but simply because I wondered what lay behind it. Important missions just now might mean almost anything. And there's that cable. The cable that hasn't arrived yet. Thinking reasonably, something connected with Westrex seems the most likely reason for Armstrong's terrible end; if it weren't for that damned chest, and the odd feeling those Chinese gave one."

"Gave all of us," Schofild murmured. "But they may easily be tools only. But about Farrant—"

"I would like to hear Farrant's own account of what he's going for," Hardy said promptly. "Besides, he should be in the house. It's his post. Don't like to see a post vacant at a moment like this."

"Westrex may be at the bottom of the murder," Pointer agreed, "or some financial reason, but it would hardly account for Mr. Armstrong's body having been put into that wedding-chest."

"In my opinion, that was an act of spite against you, major," Schofild added.

Hardy raised his head sharply.

"Eh?" was his only reply, but in a tone of great interest, "Eh?"

"Have you any enemies of your own?" Schofild went on.

"I hope so," was his prompt rejoinder. "I've stopped any amount of little games in my time, and hope to do plenty more of it. I'm not at all a popular man."

Schofild remembered hearing, as Pointer had already reflected, that it was just because he was not a popular man that a certain government post was to be offered to him, a post where nerve and unyielding carrying out of unpopular orders would be expected of the holder.

"Yes, I have lots of enemies," Hardy went on cheerfully, "but I don't think even hate would murder a friend merely in order to annoy me by putting his body into my present to him."

"Though it has an oriental sound about it," Schofild said quietly, "in my opinion a decidedly oriental sound about it."

And a silence fell on the three of them. Put like that, something sinister and Eastern, something veiled and threatening, something that suggested it might only be a prelude to worse, seemed to be evoked.

They were just about to tackle the desk when one of the chief inspector's men reported that Miss Dickins had arrived.

She seemed to know nothing of the tragedy. As instructed, he had told her that an accident had happened, and that a detective officer from New Scotland Yard would like a word with her.

The major slipped out, and Miss Dickins was shown in. She was a pretty girl, with pleasant but timid eyes, and a skin that suggested love of the open air. Indeed, except for her shoes, she might have just stepped off a putting green in her soft, blue-gray woolen coat and skirt, with her bag of clubs still in her hand.

"What has happened?" she asked breathlessly. "I'm told there is something wrong, and that the police are in charge. Are you the police? Is it anything to Mrs. Armstrong?"

"No, it's Mr. Armstrong. He's had an accident. He's been killed." Pointer spoke with a pause between each sentence. His eyes were on her, not apparently watching her, but as one does look at the person to whom one speaks.

Her bag fell to the floor with a clatter, and he picked it up awkwardly, so that the clubs were scattered over the floor. She did not notice them.

"Oh, I must go at once to Mrs. Armstrong!" she said in a tone of horror. "I must go to her at once." She rose and would have made for the door.

Now, as a rule, in accident cases, it is the investigator who has to call time, not the innocent member of the household where something terrible has happened. Miss Dickins had asked no detail, had made no inquiry as to place or time or manner of Armstrong's death.

"The doctor has given her a sedative. Please sit down again."

"Where was he killed? How was he found? By whom?" She now asked, and with a suggestion of genuine tenseness.

"Mrs. Armstrong found his dead body in a Chinese wedding-chest, that Major Hardy had sent in, when it was opened this afternoon at five o'clock," Pointer replied.

"How terrible!" she muttered faintly. Then, "I can't seem to grasp it. She opened the chest herself?"

Schofild now told her of what he had seen. She kept her blue eyes fastened on his with almost painful fixity.

"Now, do you know anything, however trifling, that can help us to find out any one who may have had a grudge against Mr. Armstrong or may have thought that he had? Or against Mrs. Armstrong?" he asked, when he had finished.

Breathlessly she said that she had no faintest notion.

"Do you know if he had anything on his mind?" he asked again.

She hesitated. Whether to collect her thoughts or to decide what to say, even Pointer could not be sure.

"He always had plenty of business things worrying him," she replied. It sounded evasive. She seemed to think that it did, for she straightened up, and said more firmly, "But, of course, I should not know anything about that."

"Were he and his wife on affectionate terms?" Pointer asked.

"I think so." She did not sound certain. "Yes, I suppose so. I hardly ever was with them when they were together."

Pressed, she could not apparently amplify her statements.

"Do you know where Mr. Farrant is?" was the next question.

"I left him at the club house. Roehampton club. He and I have been having a round there together. How horrible it sounds with this dreadful tragedy." She spoke jerkily.

"And when did you leave him?"

"About an hour ago. Around six, or a little past. He stayed on trying some new steel-shafted clubs."

"And you, neither of you, had heard anything about what had happened here at the house?"

"If we had, is it likely that we would have stayed on!" she replied in a shocked voice.

"You, neither of you, knew anything about Mr. Armstrong being in danger, or dead?" Pointer persisted calmly.

"Of course we didn't," she said, looking very indignant.

Pointer had arranged with Schofild to keep any one talking if the chief inspector passed a hand over his hair and then went on out of the room.

Pointer did so now, and heard Schofild saying, "By the way, Miss Dickins, could you tell me—" as he closed the door behind him. He went to the telephone and got on to the Roehampton club head steward.

"Mr. Farrant?" came the reply to Pointer's question, "he has just left. About half an hour ago. Left on foot. He set out as if for the station. Is Miss Dickins there? Who is it speaking, please?"

Pointer told him, in confidence, adding that there had been an accident at the house and that he had to check off Miss Dickins's hours and those of Mr. Farrant merely by way, of routine.

The steward became precise, but he could give no hours of arrival. The two had not lunched at the club. Nor had they had tea there. But he had seen them on the course together around half-past four. They had come in about six, and Miss Dickins had gone when he brought Mr. Farrant a cocktail into the lounge a little later.

Pointer asked to be put through to the caddy-master. To him he gave the same explanation as to the steward. Had he seen Miss Dickins this afternoon? The man said that he had—seen her playing with Mr. Farrant. No, he had not actually seen either of them playing; it had been a case of lost ball at the moment.

Who had caddied for them?

"No one. Mr. Farrant never took a caddy."

"Miss Dickins?"

"Yes, she usually did. But she had not done so on this occasion."

"Did either of them leave their clubs to be cleaned?"

"Now, that's an odd question, sir," the man said. "I've just been asking the caddies about that. Miss Dickins always has her clubs cleaned. I've never known that to fail. Yet she hasn't done so today."

"You're sure of that?"

The man said he was. Quite sure.

Pointer next asked for the secretary, again explained himself, and asked him for a more precise time-table of the young people. Here again he got little information. The secretary had been playing himself all day. He, too, had seen Miss Dickins and Farrant once. Time? The secretary did some calculations, necessarily vague, and thought it must have been around five or a little before.

"What's the handicap of each of them?" The figures were good.

"Are they keen on the game?"

"As mustard."

"Play often together?"

"Every Saturday afternoon."

Pointer thanked him and rang off. He had learned quite a good deal. For when he had picked up Miss Dickins's clubs, as her bag dropped just now, he had noticed that, though none of her irons had chromium-plated heads, all of them were as clean and polished as only a well-tipped caddy leaves them. It had rained steadily yesterday, and any inland links would have left uncleaned clubs in a very, different condition to this perfection.

As for having cleaned them herself, Miss Dickins had very much over-manicured hands, each nail was rosy pink and polished to a mirror. Those hands had not plied sandpaper, polishing paste, and oiling rag just now, and the clubs in question had had all three applied to them. Nor did Pointer believe that Farrant had done this as a labor of love. There was a professional touch about the cleaning of those clubs.

In other words, Miss Dickins had gone to the links, but he did not think that she had played on them. But even lovers do not usually take the trouble to go to a golf course for the whole of an afternoon, and never play one hole. They could have gone for a run in a car or on a bus. But car and bus would not have created an atmosphere of a care-free, unconscious-of-evil Saturday afternoon which was to be like all other Saturday afternoons. Love-making? Golf links are too public for that, nor did Pointer think that it would have kept two keen players off their game from at least four until six.

He returned to the room where Schofild and Miss Dickins were talking.

"I wonder if you would tell us how you spent yesterday and today," he began again, seating himself once more where he could see her face in a mirror.

Yesterday had been spent in hard work preparing for today's function. Miss Dickins gave him place and hour for each statement. This morning a little after' nine o'clock Mrs. Armstrong had told her over the house telephone that she could have the day to herself. So Miss Dickins had spent the morning having a look round the shops, preparatory to some re-fitting. She had met Mr. Farrant by chance outside Harrod's around one, they had lunched there together at two, and he had told her that Mr. Armstrong intended sending him away on a very private commission, but that it would only begin with the late evening, so they could have their usual Saturday couple of hours on the links together. He had had some sort of a message to take first, however, which he had forgotten to deliver. So she waited for him at Harrod's. He came back for her, and they must have got to the club a little past four, or nearly four, she thought. They had played until six. And, there, as she had said at the beginning of the interview, she had left him.

"Did he tell you where he was putting up?" Pointer asked. "We ought, of course, to get into touch with him at once. It's not fair to him to let him know nothing of what has happened here in his absence."

"He spoke of having gone to an hotel in town, waiting for some instructions of Mr. Armstrong's to reach him tonight—but of course, when he doesn't hear from Mr. Armstrong, he's bound to telephone here." Apparently she could not give the secretary's present address.

"Are you and Mr. Farrant engaged, by any chance?" Pointer asked. "The question is merely put to get things clear."

Miss Dickins said they were not engaged. They were merely good friends engaged in similar work.

"You say you spent from about four to six on the links. Could you give us the names of any one whom you met, or who saw you there?"

Pointer again explained that these questions were merely part of the regular routine.

Miss Dickins promptly mentioned the pro., and a Mr. Norfolk, with whom she and Farrant had exchanged a word or two.

"How many holes did you play?" he asked, as though anxious to fill as many pages of his notebook as possible.

"Eight," she replied promptly. "And then we played about practicing with Mr. Farrant's new clubs."

It all sounded quite easy, and natural, but, as is so often the case, Miss Dickins had talked too much. Eight holes of soft grassland this afternoon, those shining club heads, those immaculate finger tips! The combination was simply impossible.

"How long have you been with Mrs. Armstrong, Miss Dickins?"

"Not very long. Barely six months."

"And before?"

"I was assistant almoner to the Haverstock Hill Hospital for a time, and then assistant secretary to a laundry."

"I must have all the dates," Pointer said, looking as though this were all part of a very dull day's work and of no interest to him beyond seeing that everything was correctly entered.

She gave the dates with what seemed careful precision. "Mrs. Armstrong looked me up very thoroughly," she added, with a confident smile.

"The address of the laundry?" Pointer was writing as though lost to anything else.

"It was the Ealing Sungleam Laundry, but they sold out to the United Northern Laundries."

"The exact address, please?"

She gave it, and added that when the laundry was taken over she applied to Lady Grail, who was one of the principal shareholders and a member of the Roehampton golf club. Lady Grail very kindly spoke to Mrs. Armstrong of her.

And to Mrs. Armstrong, after the usual preliminaries, Miss Dickins had gone.

Pointer chased Miss Dickins's career back to her school days, with apparently her willing help, and then thanked her and let her go.

When the door was shut behind her, he and Schofild looked at each other.

"So she has been a secretary to the laundry whose van certainly has some connection with the van that brought her employer's dead body here," Schofild murmured. "Evidently she's involved, whether innocently or not. In my opinion, innocently. I thought she was not nervous of talking about it. But Farrant—and the game of golf this afternoon—that's quite another matter. Were they playing, as she said?"

Pointer repeated what he had learned from the club in question. One of his own men, a man who had been a caddy in his time, was dispatched to Roehampton at once with orders to find out all he could about the two on the spot.

CHAPTER FIVE

POINTER now really did make a note or two of Miss Dickins's statements and of the condition of her golf clubs. As he blotted it, he noticed a bulge in one of the leather corners of the blotter which he was using. From force of habit he touched the bulge. It yielded to pressure. The top sheet of paper had got folded under in some way. Pointer examined it. Yes, the top sheet had been inserted by hand, not by a machine, and one of its corners had buckled. Had the sheet in question been merely turned, he wondered, instead of having been thrown away when used? Taking it out, he saw that the other side was fresh. Saw, too, that it was a fraction larger than the other sheets of the pad, and a shade lighter in color. He held it to the mirror. It showed several scraps of what he was soon to learn was Mrs. Armstrong's writing. Nothing that seemed of any importance. Nevertheless, he put it away in an envelope in his pocket. In detection, the stone that the builder rejects, so frequently turns out to be the head of the corner, that Pointer rejected none.

He and Schofild looked about them to find from where the piece might have come. The library ran below the Chinese suite, and was, like it, divided into three rooms. Here, too, each opened out of the other, and there was only one door leading into the rest of the house.

Only here the order was reversed. The largest room came first, book lined, sparsely furnished, then came a gay little writing room much used by Mrs. Armstrong, and finally the end room, little larger than a cupboard where rarely wanted books were stacked on double shelves. In the second room they found two blotting pads

with unused surfaces, but whose paper exactly matched
the sheet which Pointer now held in his hand.

Obviously a used top sheet had been taken from one of
these pads, and inserted in the one in Armstrong's
writing-table. Pointer rang the bell, and had a casual
word with the butler. The blotters were not tidied up
daily, but from time to time. Yes, Mr. Armstrong used the
first room a great deal. Just as Mrs. Armstrong was very
fond of the second room.

Major Hardy now came back. Pointer asked him
whether, when he had lunched here today, he had noticed
the blotter on Mr. Armstrong's desk. He must have used
the telephone that stood on it. Was the desk changed in
any way, had anything on it been altered? Or was there
anything missing?

Major Hardy looked about him very searchingly.
Finally he said, that, as far as he could see, or could
remember, everything was now as it had been then.

"I can't be sure, of course," he wound up with.
"Fortunately, it's not important, I suppose," and with
that, the inspection of the desk began in earnest.

The letters that had arrived by the posts of the day
were neatly stacked on various small salvers side by side
at one end of the mighty table. The first of these piles
showed, as the butler had said, a New Zealand letter on
top. None of the correspondence seemed capable of having
any bearing on the murder of the man to whom it was
addressed, though this would be gone through in detail
later on. That out of the way, Pointer and Schofild each
took a drawer at a time, the major merely represented
the family, and looked on.

Schofild was working the left-hand drawers. The top
one, locked, contained nothing of importance. As he drew
out the second, he gave a low whistle. On top of
everything lay a large fountain pen. Such a pen as the
dead man's valet had missed from his master's
belongings. A gold Swan. Hardy gave a slight twist of his
thick, powerful brows, and a muttered "Damn funny!"

more to himself than to his companions. "That's Armstrong's pen," he said with certainty, "the one Johnson missed from his things. Besides his monogram, there's the mark of Armstrong's teeth. He used to bite the end in moments of great impatience." The major drew a deep breath. There were no fingerprints on the pen. There hardly could be, with its heavy chasing.

Schofild sat back while Pointer tested for them. Then he said suddenly, "That pen! In my opinion Armstrong was writing something, signing something, when he was murdered, and the pen was forgotten along with his hat and gloves until the body was put into the chest. The hat and gloves are burnt, and the thing that can't be burnt is brought here and put in Armstrong's desk, the safest of all places—the dead man's own writing-table!"

"Then the murderer came on here to this house, into this very room, this afternoon? One of the guests?" Hardy's face looked very terrible.

"He or she," Schoflld said.

"No woman could have lifted Armstrong into that chest," Hardy protested.

"A woman could have shot him first," Schofild pointed out. "Not that I see any reason to think that, but neither, in my opinion, is there any reason to exclude a woman from a share in the crime. *Cherchez la femme* is still as true as when first stated."

"But a bit more hackneyed," Hardy said, with a twisted smile.

"So's murder!" Schofild retorted.

They went on with the examination of the desk, but nothing more of direct interest came to light. Though letters from Mrs. Armstrong in two locked drawers, written to Armstrong on his many trips away from home, bore out, in the one swift glance given each page, the idea of a very great affection between the two. Then why, Pointer wondered, had Miss Dickins seemed unaware of its warmth.

They were just finishing when a plain clothes man reported that Mr. Farrant had arrived and wanted to see Mr. Schofild. It had been arranged between the two detectives that, if possible, the private investigator was to have a preliminary talk with the secretary, who might be more communicative to him than to a stranger, let alone a stranger who was a Scotland Yard officer. Schofild found Farrant looking very pale, standing by the window, twisting and untwisting his gloves between nervous hands.

Schofild was struck afresh with the breadth of his shoulders, the long reach of his arms. Not so big as Major Hardy, broader built than Callard, though the latter suggested to Schofild's eye unsuspected strength if Percy should ever care to use it. Farrant had a certain spring in his carriage which went with the extreme silence of all his movements.

"I hoped I should find you here!" Farrant spoke with apparent warmth. "I've just seen the evening papers with an account of the finding of Armstrong's body. For heaven's sake tell me what it all means! You were here? Is it true? Was his body found in that chest sent in by Major Hardy?"

Schofild told him what he himself had seen. "And you're going to find his murderer now you *are* here," Farrant said urgently.

"I've no real standing in the case," Schofild pointed out. "I was sent for by Armstrong to have an interview with him at five. He was dead by then, so that, strictly speaking—"

"I ask you to undertake the clearing up of this crime." Farrant interrupted. "There's no one I should entrust with such a task but you. You work independently, I know. Not with the police."

Schofild stiffened.

"I'm working with Scotland Yard in this case. A civil offense is another matter. But murder—I'm most certainly working with Chief Inspector Pointer."

Schofild had an idea that door might be shut by his saying those words. But he had to say them. One of the reasons that made him generally trusted was that he was trustworthy.

"And where do you think Armstrong was murdered?" Farrant went on, after a moment's pause, raising rather impenetrable light eyes for a second, and then dropping them again.

"It looks as though his body had been substituted for some plants that were in the chest before it reached here." Schofild explained the situation.

"A breakdown! And you think the body was placed in the chest outside—in the open?" Farrant looked incredulous. "Murder is hardly an outdoor job."

Schofild did not explain just what he thought. There were plenty of houses—rooms—places—where Armstrong could have been lured and killed within four walls, and then his body placed in a hamper in the laundry van, to be transferred at the right moment into the chest.

"That interview Armstrong wanted me to have with him today," he said instead, "have you any idea as to what it would have been about?"

"Connected with what was the cause of his murder probably," was the reply, given in Farrant's low voice, that yet carried as clearly as a loud one.

"What makes you think that?" Schofild asked with interest, fixing his keen eyes on him.

"Because it wasn't financial—the reason on which he wanted to see you," Farrant said slowly, "or he'd have chosen another man—a commercial expert. The choice of you makes me think, or rather feel sure, he wanted you to investigate something definitely not connected with business. And as, in my belief, his murder had nothing whatever to do with business either—why, I think it and the interview with you, that Armstrong didn't live to have, are linked."

Schofild had a feeling that Farrant was concealing something. He rose. "I'd like you to see the man in charge

of the case—Chief Inspector Pointer. He may have some
questions to put to you." And without waiting for Farrant
to excuse himself, Schofild went in search of the detective
officer. Major Hardy moved the papers which had been
handed to him into another room, the library was locked,
and Pointer accompanied Schofild to where Farrant
turned to him with what some people called his shy
glance. Pointer did not care for light eyes, as a rule, but
here, at any rate, he felt that they were no sign of lack of
feeling. Farrant, in his opinion, was capable of great
depths when stirred.

"I understand that you are both hunting for the
murderer together," Farrant began, after a few
commonplace sentences had been exchanged.

"Unless it was suicide," Pointer put in, to see what he
would say.

The secretary's eyes flashed round at him. "Out of the
question!" he said, in very much the same tone as that
which Major Hardy had used, "absolutely out of the
question! How did he get into that chest? Where's his
weapon? Why should he kill himself?"

"Lifted. Taken. To be found out," Pointer replied
succinctly.

The secretary eyed him for a moment, then dropped
his lids and eyed the floor; then looked at Pointer.

"I'd like immensely to help you. You see, apart from
being Armstrong's secretary, apart from personal
feelings, I'm naturally keen on being of use. Anybody
wants to catch a murderer. There may be lots of ways in
which I can be useful—"

"Certainly there will be," Pointer agreed. Not quite so
many as there might have been, had not something about
Farrant's voice or manner suggested—perhaps only the
young man's natural caution. But it struck Pointer as
more than that, as something secretive—just as it had
struck Schofild.

"This commission you were to be sent on, for
instance?" he began promptly.

Farrant shook his head. He had thick, glossy and rather long chestnut hair. "Unfortunately I was to receive my orders at my hotel—the Audley—in the course of this evening, or tomorrow morning from Armstrong himself. Too bad, isn't it!"

"Do you mind going into it in detail? It may be very important."

"As helping to catch his murderer" Farrant spoke swiftly for once. "Oh, no, chief inspector. As I say, the motive for Armstrong's murder had nothing to do with any business he was interested in, or about to be interested in. Whatever the reason of his death, it was private, not —not—well, professional. Not financial." Again both Pointer and Schofield had that curious impression of something concealed, something hidden.

"I would like the fullest possible account of how the commission was given you, please," he said quietly.

Apparently he got it. Apparently... but Pointer felt again equivocation in every sentence. What Farrant said was this:

"Yesterday morning about eleven Armstrong told me that there was a very important, very private commission for him which he wanted me to undertake. It might last a couple of months, and I should probably have to leave England. I was to take rooms at some convenient hotel, and wait for a telephone message which would reach me either this evening or tomorrow, telling me when and where to meet him and receive my, definite instructions. As the commission would take so long, I cleared out my room both at the office and at Charles Street too, telephoning him my new address."

"Have you had any message from him today?"

Farrant hesitated. "Yes," he said finally, and he paled noticeably. Pointer had an idea that he found it hard to speak that affirmative.

"And when was that?"

Again there came an infinitesimal pause, again something in his voice suggested a resolute forcing of himself to say what he had decided to say. It did not convey an impression of truth, though he might be speaking the truth for all that.

"Around two. I can't be sure of ten minutes before or after." And on the instant both his listeners knew that he had been leading up to this, and in some way nerving himself to make just this statement.

"Are you sure of the time? It's very important," Pointer asked.

Farrant hesitated. "I told you I can't, be sure of the exact minute," he said finally. "I lunched with Miss Dickins at one. Towards the end, at half-past or a little more, I telephoned Charles Street. I do know for certain that it wasn't two when I telephoned, but that's all I can say with certainty. Armstrong wasn't alone." Farrant did not meet either Schofild's intent gaze or Pointer's equable one. His gaze fastened itself on the opposite wall. "He wasn't alone," he repeated, and waited.

"What makes you say that?" Schofild asked.

Pointer doubted if he would get an exact answer to that query. What made Farrant say any of this would have been most interesting to know, and most enlightening.

"I heard some one speaking as Armstrong took down the receiver."

"You didn't recognize the voice?" Schofild pressed.

"No. I didn't recognize it." The reply was toneless and heavy.

"Man or woman? Could you tell that much?"

"A man."

"Threatening in tone?"

"On the contrary. Very conciliatory." Farrant spoke carefully. "Rather as though I had broken into the midst of some explanation that he was giving Armstrong. I rang Armstrong up to say that I had forgotten to give his message to Schofild, but that I would do so at once without fail, but I didn't finish my sentence. Armstrong gave some exclamation of impatience and hung up with a slam."

"Then how were you certain that it was he?" Schofild let some scepticism show.

"He was speaking as he took the receiver down."

"Did his voice sound just as usual?"

"No." Farrant spoke in an even lower tone than was usual to him. "No. It sounded tremendously agitated. As though he were in a perfect storm of very fierce anger."

Again his light eyes swept both Pointer's and Schofild's faces and seemed to quiver a little as he met their gaze. Both his listeners were certain that the man was lying. They questioned him nevertheless, but he added no further details.

He was asked whether Mr. Armstrong carried any letters of importance on him. For a second Pointer thought that he was about to reply in a negative, but, after a second of indecision, Farrant said that he could not tell. Mr. Armstrong might easily have had some very important letter, or memoranda, on him of which he alone knew.

Pointer asked him next about his time on the links. Farrant's time-table fitted in exactly with the hours mentioned by Miss Dickins.

"And where were you this morning?"

As he expected, he only received vague replies. The fact that Farrant, for some reason, found it impossible to arrange an alibi for the danger hour of noon, seemed the most likely explanation of his claim that he had heard Armstrong speaking on the telephone around two o'clock.

"Do you mind telling us what you had for lunch?" Pointer asked next, and on the instant he knew that this simple question had not been expected and provided against.

"Oh-h, I think a cut off a roast of some kind. I never do know what's set before me. I choose quite at random."

"And for drink?"

"Beer," Farrant said promptly, "a bottle of Bass."

Pointer passed his hand over his hair. "Will you excuse me a moment, one of my men wants me," and as though in answer to an unheard signal he stepped into the hall. He asked for Miss Dickins. She came down at once. Pointer met her in the little sewing-room.

"Just a word," he said pleasantly. "I think you said that you lunched at Harrod's?"

"Yes." She looked uneasy. "Yes?" she repeated inquiringly.

"Oh!" His voice sounded patently doubtful. "Indeed. *Harrod's*? You're quite sure?"

"Of course I am."

His face still showed doubt.

"What did you order, may I ask?"

"Chicken, lettuce salad, new potatoes. Banana Royal for a sweet, and black coffee." The reply came instantly.

"And to drink?"

"A stone ginger."

"I see." He looked as though he quite accepted her statement now. "And Mr. Farrant?" he asked as he was turning away, "the same, I suppose?"

"The same," she agreed, after a slight fraction of a pause.

"He tells us that he telephoned to Mr. Armstrong towards the end, do you recall his doing so?"

"Yes. To Mr. Armstrong, I know, that's a fact."

"How do you know?" Pointer seemed puzzled.

"Because he told me so," she replied, with a lightness that seemed to smack of the lamp. He looked at her very gravely.

"But a fact isn't something you're told, Miss Dickins. You may get into very serious trouble indeed if you act on that belief."

She did the equivalent of tossing her head.

"In this case it was a fact," she insisted. "Mr. Farrant hurried away to telephone Mr. Armstrong about some message or other that he had forgotten, and rushed away to give it, and then came back for me, and we went on out to the links."

Pointer asked her again some of the questions which he had already put to her, then he left her, and returned to Schofild and Farrant on the ground floor. In passing, he asked the butler if any telephone calls had come to the house a little before two for Mr. Armstrong.

None whatever. By Mrs. Armstrong's orders the butler had this morning unhooked all the receivers except the one in-his own pantry, so that messages would come to him. There had been none, barring Major Hardy's inquiries for the chest.

Pointer had barely seated himself again when a buzzing sounded in the corner.

"That's the house telephone," Farrant said, rising and going to it. "I hope Mrs. Armstrong isn't any worse."

They heard his voice: "Speaking. Yes, speaking myself." Then, "The chief inspector and Mr. Schofild are with me if you want them." A straight tip that talk at his end might not be free. "Oh!" came next, and his voice had an instantly suppressed, startled note. "Oh! No, it doesn't matter." And with that the receiver was hung up. His eyes met Pointer's as he came back again. Pointer felt quite sure that Miss Dickins had passed on to the young man their luncheon menu.

And he also felt sure that Farrant was desperately uneasy—if nothing more.

"By the way," he said easily, can you tell us how to get into touch with Mr. Rufus Armstrong?"

"I'm afraid he's off for one of his usual weekend sailing trips. He has a little yacht which he keeps down at Burnham-on-Crouch, and blow high, blow low, he spends every Saturday to Monday or Tuesday at the least in her. She's *The Winkle*. No, he has no wireless aboard. Rufus Armstrong has no use for wireless. I've sent telegrams to all the possible places where he may put in, but unfortunately, as a rule he often doesn't put in at all, until he comes back when his trip is over. I have known him to spend a week in her. Fortunately there's a big sale on on Wednesday at Messrs. Yamanaka's. He never misses their sales. At least he once told me he never did. Mr. Rufus Armstrong is a collector, you know. It's his passion. He has no other interest in life."

"Except yachting? What kind of a boat is *The Winkle?*"

"Tabloid cruiser. Outboard engine. Only room for himself and his man, and his catalogs. I sometimes think he goes off in her for no other reason than to get plenty of time to look them over."

"Great friend of his cousin, Mr. Armstrong, I understand?"

"Very great, indeed," Farrant said warmly.

"A wealthy man?"

"I doubt that." Farrant spoke carelessly. "I fancy he spends all his money on his collections, from the size of his boat and his address."

"Chinese collection chiefly, I am told," Pointer went on.

Farrant nodded.

"Which are his clubs?"

"As far as I know he has only one, the Connoisseur."

"And now to turn to a very important question," Pointer said briskly. "Did you know that Mr. Armstrong had any enemies?"

"Half the people who pretend to be a rich man's friends are secret enemies," Farrant said soberly and very sweepingly. He would not, or could not, be more particular. They learned nothing more from him of any importance. Both men felt that the whole interview, as far as he was concerned, had been for the purpose of maintaining that Armstrong had been alive around two o'clock.

For a moment after he left there was silence. Then Schofild asked:

"What about his lunch? Did you compare notes with Miss Dickins?" Pointer told him the result.

"Clear enough," the other replied. "As we thought, she's standing in with him. Funny that he didn't arrange for her to give him an alibi over the noon hour. In my opinion he was seen at that hour or very close around it, and daren't try a fake on us therefore. He may be the driver of the laundry van, a part I had assigned to 'our Percy.' Yes, in my opinion he knows that we can find out where he was around twelve. And I shall set about getting at that first of all."

Pointer was wanted on the telephone. His man was reporting from the Roehampton golf links.

Mr. Farrant's clubs were in Mr. Farrant's locker. They could, it was true, hardly be dirtier than they were, but it was dried earth and grass on them all. Not one showed traces of use today except a new steel-shafted iron which might have brushed over the surface of the grass, say in a swing or two on the approach of a real golfer, or in brushing the surface of the land in an ostensible hunt for a lost ball. But not a ball had any of the clubs, wooden or iron, driven today. That much the detective was prepared to swear. As to the time of Mr. Farrant's arrival and departure from the club, they tallied with the information given by Miss Dickins.

Pointer hung up the receiver and turned away. It was hardly likely that Farrant, who neglected his own clubs, would, or could, have given that look to Miss Dickins's set. He was just passing on the information to Schofild when Major Hardy came in.

"I was told Farrant was here. I want him very badly."

"I'm sorry to say he's gone. I wish I knew, Major Hardy, why you are so certain that he has nothing to do with Mr. Armstrong's murder," Pointer said.

"And I wish I could get it across to you two why I feel so damned sure," Hardy said on that. "I know men. Have to, of course, in the kind of picnics I go on. Besides, I always could sum up a man fairly well. Farrant is utterly incapable of murdering any one, least of all Armstrong. On that I stake everything I have in the world."

"And Callard?" Schofild asked.

Hardy looked at him hard. "Do you call this cricket?" he asked finally. "I hope Callard has nothing to do with this crime because of his sister, poor woman. And I feel fairly certain he hasn't, because he's such a coward."

"And do you think Mr. Farrant physically brave?" Pointer asked.

Hardy gave one of his twisted smiles. "No. Anything but. Sensitive as a woman, I fancy. But he's not on the same plane as Callard. I hope young Percy is all right, but I know Farrant is. Nothing can shake me on that. Don't think I'm blinded by liking. I don't care for the fellow, but I'm, absolutely certain he's not in this crime, just the same."

"Thank you, so much," came in Farrant's quiet voice. The door had opened behind the major. "I left my stick behind me, and I couldn't help hearing your kind words."

Hardy turned and looked at Farrant, who looked back at him. Neither spoke. Time has no reality, say the philosophers, and we know it for a fact in moments of emotion. The glance that passed these two was as swift as a glance could be, swifter than most, yet it had all the effect of a long, hard stare. Pointer and Schofild both felt it, more than watched it. There was a non-committal absence of meaning in each eye that spoke for enmity, yet to Pointer at least, there was something that linked them. It might be mutual dislike, Pointer rather thought it was of that order, but there was a link.

"Not at all," Hardy said shortly. "I happen not to be a fool. Some men are, when murder's been done."

"Yes," Farrant's voice shook a little, "some men are."

"You're staying, of course." The major's tone did not suggest a question.

"Yes. At my hotel." And Farrant left as noiselessly as he had drifted in.

The major stood a moment, then with rather a whimsical look at the two detectives, a look that said, "Well, what do you make of that?" he, too, left the room.

Schofild drew a deep breath. He actually asked a question not of himself:

"How do you sum up the position, so far, chief inspector?"

"Percy Callard is deceiving us, or thinks he is. Major Hardy is keeping back some belief, or suspicion, or even knowledge of the criminal's identity. Mr. Farrant is both actively deceiving us and passively withholding information which he thinks might be too useful to us, or too dangerous to himself." Pointer spoke dryly. "Yet he's extraordinarily difficult to understand. He gives himself no alibi for the danger hours, and yet he spoke to you this afternoon of that wedding-chest, where, according to him, you were to meet Mr. Armstrong, as though he had seen it. At least your account of the interview with him suggested that, but the chest didn't get to the house until two."

"You're right," Schofild's eyes were dancing with excitement; this was a problem such as he had long hoped to get hold of. "You're right! He certainly referred to it as a man does to something he's seen. And his tie! His tie! By jove, his tie!" Schofild was almost lyrical.

"Seems a very neat affair. What was wrong with it?" Pointer asked.

"It was under one ear when I saw him. Yet Miss Dickins had been lunching with him, according to their made-up little tale. I said *cherchez la femme* just now. I wonder if Mrs. Armstrong is in this... Callard's her brother... he might be in with her. Hardy—there was a hint of their having been very much together at Biskra last winter—he might want to shield her. Farrant—there was a boy and girl attachment between them, so she told me one evening when I was at their Yorkshire place. It only amused Armstrong at the time. Farrant—do you think Major Hardy really is as convinced of his innocence as he makes out?"

This was a tremendous compliment to Pointer had he known it, that Schofild actually consulted him on things not connected with the handling of clues.

"I do think so. I think he really *is* sure—certain of his innocence."

"Mistake," Schofild said soberly, "to be sure of any one in a murder case. With an uncommonly pretty woman in the circle."

"And an uncommonly wealthy one since her husband's death," Pointer added.

"That message Farrant gave me, purporting to be from Armstrong—to meet him this afternoon beside that chest... I wonder... "

So did Pointer. He had, from the first.

"Supposing Farrant wanted an eye-witness of all that happened when the chest was opened. And wanted to start a current of good opinion of himself, in my mind as it were... In my opinion that message may mean absolutely nothing whatever, except an effort on Farrant's part to get me into this case as a reporter—to him—of all that I learn while investigating it. If so, he's tripped up on his man. Mrs. Armstrong—yes, in my opinion, Mrs. Armstrong might explain all this feeling of being up against blank wails of deception at every turn. Where are you going?"

"To the Chinese suite. It's a little experiment I have been waiting to make. Care to come? As you are talking of Mrs. Armstrong, it may interest you."

Pointer, once in the suite, locked the great doors. He wanted no interruptions. Next he marked on the jade pole the height of Mrs. Armstrong. Holding a camera at the place where her eyes would have been, he had Schofild slowly lift the lid of the chest inch by inch, and took a careful exposure of what each inch showed.

"What's the idea?" Schofild was puzzled. Then, as Pointer did not reply at once, "Found anything?"

"Found another bit of the problem, yes." Pointer, his camera swinging from his hand, looked at his shoes, deep in thought. "Even allowing for a slight error in position, from where she stood, how did Mrs. Armstrong know that it was her husband who lay inside that chest? And, above all, how was she sure that he was dead? Her faint at the time, and her present condition, mean that she did know."

Schofild looked his intense interest. His very nose was quivering.

"It is possible, barely possible, that she could see that a body lay inside it. But it was not possible," Pointer still thought as he had when the place was first shown him, "for her to have seen the face of the dead man, nor anything of him beyond, perhaps, a bit of a farther shoulder, and, possibly, the farther hand." Careful tests on this point would be made, but, if established, it suggested some very terrible ideas. Schofild now tried it for himself, having the lid carefully lifted while he stooped until he was at the height of the woman lying upstairs, the wife who had collapsed when the lid was but barely ajar.

"Yet, that's where she stood," he muttered, intrigued, "not a foot farther forward."

"Granted that, and the actors agree with you and Lady Grail, and they are, of course, like yourself, accustomed to notice position very carefully, then it is a riddle how she knew so instantly, and above all so certainly, what lay inside the chest."

"She was alone in here for just a moment," Schofild said slowly, "alone after the chest came. The lock of the chest turns soundlessly. She might have had time to look inside. But—"

"But she didn't faint then," Pointer reminded him.

"She seemed just as usual at the reception," Schofild muttered... "Still, it fits my theory, that she's in the murder in some way, and that the others know it, or guess it."

"As Major Hardy says, Schofild, no woman lifted Armstrong into that chest."

Schofild nodded gloomily, and they parted. Pointer to walk to his rooms in Bayswater. Yes, Pointer acknowledged to himself, as he lit a cigarette, a pipe was unfortunately out of the question in the festal garb in which he had had to array himself to pass muster at an afternoon reception in Charles Street, yes, it was a puzzling case. But out of all the whole struggle, what remained most in his mind was the enigmatic smile in the eyes of the young Chinese musician. Wong really knew no English whatever, Mr. Wilkins maintained. Nor did the look that he had turned, as he left the room, on the chief inspector quite fit the supposition that he had overheard something, for, Pointer thought, if ever intelligence mocked at what it considered lack of intelligence, it was when the black, almond eyes of the flute player had met the clear, gray ones of the chief inspector. Now, Pointer could not possibly be expected to have known anything that was said on the other side of the closed and locked door before he got to the house... then why that look? Pointer felt certain that in Wong's eyes he had not been as clever as he—Wong—was. Pointer had missed something that the Chinese had not missed.

Or was the reason for that curious haunting gleam connected with the Lees. Did Wong know that they had more of a share in the crime than seemed possible without any knowledge of a motive. Did Wong know that a very good motive existed? Armstrong—Western Australia—Chinese immigration—Chinese labor—Major Hardy had tentatively suggested that as a possible line of search. The two Lees were already down for close inspection on the part of some competent man of Pointer's. Their present and their pastas far as the latter could be ascertained. One thing was certain, or at least seemed probable, and that was that the motive, if it existed, would not be money. The firm was wealthy. But Rufus Armstrong—Rufus Armstrong, the Lees' patron, was he behind them? Were they more or less his employees, or at least bound to him by ties they could not, or would not, break? Rufus Armstrong, who could select any four articles from his cousin's houses now that the latter was dead... a collector... any four... the wedding-chest...

Pointer reached his rooms deep in thought.

CHAPTER SIX

THE chief inspector did not stop long at his comfortable quiet rooms that night. But he had a talk over the telephone with the Burnham-on-Crouch harbor-master. Pointer himself knew only the West Coast, the matchless coast to his mind of England and Scotland. But he learned that *The Winkle* was well known at Burnham. She stayed there from year's end to year's end. Mr. Armstrong had bought her from a doctor who had left the place. He paid sixty pounds for what had originally cost a hundred. *The Winkle's* expenses would come to a pound a week, all told so that Mr. Farrant had rightly spoken as though Rufus Armstrong spent his money on other things. *The Winkle* had set off this afternoon around three for a couple of days' floating. The harbor-master did not call what *The Winkle* could do sailing, least of all yachting.

Was Mr. Armstrong well known in the place? Not known at all. He never came on land. His servant, silent and elderly, did the shopping. Apparently master and man were content with the simple life, which, in a boat, means the tinned life. "No," wound up the speaker, "I don't think any one in Burnham has ever had two words with Mr. Armstrong. Nice quiet gentleman, and generous when there's any collection going, but comes down for rest and quiet, his man once said, and by gum, he gets it."

"Any companions? Any friends join him?" The reply was that, like the engine, they would have to be out-board; *The Winkle* was a tight fit for two. Measurements followed which bore this out. Pointer thanked him, and made a note. After a little wait, as soon as it was dark enough, the house off Fitzroy Square was broken into, if one can call as careful an entry as Pointer's breaking. He left no traces behind him, and the collection behind steel-shuttered cases cemented to the walls, did not interest him. He was looking for signs and portents. But he finally slipped out, quite certain that no tragedy had taken place in these rooms. The master and his one servant had evidently, Pointer thought, left them unhurriedly before noon, and whether Rufus Armstrong was linked with his cousin's murder or not, he had not killed him here. That was something learned. For the rest, it was midnight when Pointer switched on the small electric searchlight fitted to a head band which he wore. He had found, or, strictly speaking, others had found for him, that back of the former offices of the Ealing Sungleam Laundry were the laundry's garages Both office and garages were empty. They were locked as well. But Pointer had no difficulty in letting himself into them.

Two very ancient motor vans, and two old horse vans stood there. Emergency surplus, he thought, not scrapped yet, but evidently not used since the larger company had taken this over. He was to learn next day that the Ealing office and garages were for sale, and that the vans were to be included in the sale—if possible.

One of the vans was standing much nearer to the door than the rest. its canvas sides were less dusty, its engine more so than those of the others; also, the latter seemed to him to be faintly warm. There was petrol in its tank. Its tires were still inflated. And in it, among smaller ones, were a couple of large, long hampers such as that of which Lees' gatekeeper had spoken. One of the large baskets was close against the backboard. Opening it, he found it full of something hard and knobby completely folded up in a very big white embroidered sheet fastened here and there with safety pins which had torn the linen.

When he opened it out, he found, inside, crowded close together, tiny dwarf birch trees planted in what looked like old gold lacquered bowls, the mandarin orange rinds of which he had been told.

This, then, was the van and the hamper into which the plants had been lifted from the wedding-chest. What had it carried to the place? Armstrong's dead body? Going over the sheet inch by inch, he found a long but faint smear of blood at one corner. Very lightly marked, showing that the smear had been on something else, and that the cause of it had not actually touched the sheet itself.

He stood the hamper up on end. It was over six feet long, and Armstrong was under that height. Working his torch over it slowly, and very carefully, he found several more faint blood smears on the wicker rim at one end. They might have been caused by many things. But among these possible causes was the dead body of Armstrong, supposing, as it was natural to suppose, that it had been tightly wrapped in some stout cloth, which would allow of its being lifted into the chest in place of the plants.

Pointer imagined that around the stout, more or less waterproof, cloth would be something white, to carry out the idea of laundry work, should the man have been detected carrying it from one van to the other. But wrapped in white or not, it was a very risky thing to do in broad daylight... Yet it seemed to have served its purpose of preventing any search of the place where the murder itself had been committed. He continued his examination of the hamper. There was another unmistakable smear of blood inside one of the end handles, as though the hand that had grasped it had had blood on it. But there was nothing further.

Just as he had finished, a faint sound outside made him turn out his electric lamp and stand in the darkness, his finger on a torch in his pocket.

Very gently some one could be heard crossing the cobble stones of the yard. So faint was the sound that it was clear that rubber-soled shoes were being worn. Peering through the keyhole, he saw a torch advancing very slowly. Evidently the holder was in unfamiliar ground. It went round in circles, until it focused on the garage, and finally on the keyhole. Pointer hurriedly withdrew his eye. The light continued to stream through the hole. Pointer heard the soft click of keys being turned over in some one's palm. A little later the lock was carefully tried. The choice had been good, for it opened, and Pointer, who was behind it, flattened himself against the wall.

It was a man who entered—a small man. Then the door was cautiously closed and locked. To do this the intruder trained the light of the torch that he carried on to the lock. It lit up also the hand that turned the key. It was the hand of an Easterner. Small, very long-fingered, yellow and withered. The door locked, Pointer stepped forward and switched on, not his pocket torch, but his head lamp. It shone full in the face of old Mr. Lee. Mr. Lee blinked, then he called shrilly:

"Who there? I am the manager of this place, who there?"

"I'm the assistant manager," Pointer said blandly. Twisting his lamp down so that it shone on himself as well. "Suppose we have a committee meeting."

Mr. Lee gave a funny little chuckle, higher pitched than a European's.

"This must be looked at the right way," he said, bowing. "I hope that your piercing orb will see through the seeming falseness to the abysmal truth. In a way, I rejoice to meet you, for it shows I am on right, hot trail. But I naturally regret appearance of false position."

"What brought you here, Mr. Lee?"

"Who, not what, Mr. Chief Inspector. And the answer is—yourself." Mr. Lee was evidently enjoying himself.

Pointer had no bias against the Chinese race. He thought that every town should have a monument to the great mandarin who brewed the first cup of tea, and sent its blessing afloat in a world of brain-workers. Also there was *Go*, the great Chinese war game. The finest game in the world, in his opinion. The emperor of all intellectual games, if chess be the king.

"Just how did I bring you here?" he asked now.

"Quite simply," Mr. Lee bobbed affably. "By leading the way. For finding out criminals is a thing that needs practice. You have the practice, so I keep watchful eye on you. I gathered from quietness of attire and footwork and look of old car that you were on some important work. I followed with equal caution. In equally old car of mine."

This might be true. If so, it was the first time that Pointer had been followed when he thought himself alone.

"I wonder your son didn't come."

"He is too young," Mr. Lee replied promptly. "The young should be cautious. They have so many years in which to pay for mistakes. At my age one can afford to take risks."

Pointer opened the hamper again, asked him not to touch it, and showed him the white cloth inside.

"Is that what the plants were wrapped in?" Mr. Lee nodded. Then he pointed to the faint smear of blood.

"That was not on it when it left our house. Ah, as I thought, this must be looked at the right way..."

"The blood may have come from a cut on a hand, a shallow cut," Pointer hedged.

"True, it might have," Mr. Lee agreed, "but is it too imaginative to think it probably blood from murdered body?"

Pointer could not honestly say that such an idea would call for an excessive exercise of fancy.

"We pinned the cloth with these safety pins," Mr. Lee went on, "neatly folding it so that, when opened, the white cloth, filled with the green of the little trees, and their brown trunks with the orange of the containers, would be pleasing against the vermilion lacquer of the chest."

Pointer opened the cloth out a little. The Chinese nodded.

"Those are the dwarf trees Major Hardy bought on behalf of Mr. Armstrong. You would not think to see those tiny things that in my home, Western Szechuan, they rise a hundred feet up, magnificent trees, with leaves as long as a hand and broader. And"—he pulled himself up and blinked like an elderly owl for a minute — "the mind of the old reverts easily to the place where it was young," he murmured apologetically. "Yet there is enough in this affair to keep it from wandering... what a strange story... to make the wife a present of her husband's murdered body... " Mr. Lee lit a cigarette of a peculiarly sickly smell. "Yes," he repeated, "this must indeed be looked at in the right way. There is subtlety in this plot. More like a man of my race than yours. Being of your race, I should say a woman was the criminal. Not the changing of the plants for the body, but the planning for the body to be found by the man's wife. But I am presumptuous, to instruct the instructor!"

"I should be very glad to know your real opinion of it all," Pointer said truthfully. He would have been. "Have you been able to find out more about the men who drove the van?"

"My detectives—we are employing two of the best Chinese detectives in town—are sure that they have left London, and separated. There has been money spent on this job. I should venture to opine, much money."

Pointer privately agreed with this. Mr. Lee seemed able to give no other help, so Pointer, to keep an eye on him, got his assistance in carrying the hamper out to his shabby little car and place it beside the driver's seat. It was the sort of car that could carry a laundry hamper without attracting any attention whatever. The driver, one of Pointer's men, was also the kind to attract no attention in driving such a car.

"Hold hard! What's all this?" came the time-honored query, as a young constable ran up, his whistle between his teeth.

Pointer took off his tweed cap and let the light of the car shine full on his face for an instant instead of replying. The constable took one look at the—to him—well-known features, and then apparently decided that the chief inspector, the Chinese with him, the car and its driver were all hallucination, for, without another word, he passed on, and continued his task of testing gates and doors. Even when the motor began to wake to life, it did not attract P. C. Leather's attention as he rattled a bolt with his back to the street.

Mr. Lee now took an ornate farewell of Pointer, and hurried down a turning to his own incredibly dilapidated Ford, to which he had tied a silk rope ladder, one end of which he had swung over the low wall. The Chinese with him had hauled it in again, and was holding it ready to throw over once more at a hand-clap from his master.

Pointer returned to the garage. Others might be interested in the plants too. That other, or the others, who had put back the van with the plants in it, for instance. Mr. Lee had just pointed out that there was an Oriental touch in this crime. Was his pointing out of it another Eastern touch? It was not impossible for any member of the Chinese orchestra, say Mr. Wong, to have dropped Mr. Armstrong's gold pen into Mr. Armstrong's writing-table drawer, supposing it to have been handed to one of them by Messrs. Lee and Son. And in that case, the odd little Farrant-Dickins combination was outside the crime. Pointer could not trust to that. He was the sheep dog ceaselessly rounding up all the flock—accounting for every straying lambkin even. Farrant's manner... Miss Dickins's manner... their unused clubs... their lunch... Farrant's alibi, which she provided, for a time, that was of no importance if Armstrong had been murdered before noon, but which covered the vital part of the day if, according to his own statement, Armstrong had spoken to him over the phone around two.

Pointer took another hamper from the van and made himself comfortable on it. He dared not smoke. Head down, he thought, instead. Then he heard something plop with a thud into the courtyard with a louder sound than Lee had made. A click reached his listening ear. Peering through the keyhole, Pointer saw an electric torch, apparently walking about the courtyard and finally coming to rest on his eye, as it seemed, come nearer and nearer. Pointer stood behind the door. Some one tried it, and then began to try a number of keys. At the eighth, the door opened and a man stepped quickly in, set his torch down on the floor and turned to close the door behind him. Pointer leaned forward, picked up the torch and flashed it full on Major Hardy.

In an instant the major had side-stepped, and shot out a fist full and square in the direction of the holder of the light.

Pointer ducked, and called out the other's name, and then his own.

A second later he let the torch pass over his own face. Hardy burst out laughing. "'Pon my word, here I nearly break my neck and do break the law, I suppose, and find you in possession."

"How did you know where to come, major?" Pointer asked.

"By putting an innocent two, and a not so innocent two, together," was the reply. "Laundry van, said the man at the Lees. Ealing. Sun-something or other. Now, I happened to have heard Lady Grail saying only a week ago that Miss Dickins had been secretary to an Ealing laundry called Sungleam."

"Saying it to whom, major?"

"Saying it to Callard. Oh, Callard, mopped up those trees all right, but as to murder—that's a very different question... So I brought all the outhouse and cellar keys I could find with me—" He stopped.

Something clinked, rattled, and chinked. Metal on stone—then came silence. Then the same sound, repeated, came clearer, and this time it was followed by the unmistakable rattle of chains being dropped full length.

"Chain ladder?" murmured the major. Pointer had already guessed as much.

A few minutes later and again a torch seemed to waver its way toward the door of the shed where the two men now waited. But this torch knew the way better than Hardy's. It kept a fairly straight path. There came the sound of a key inserted in the lock, and a sound of its turning to and fro. Then the door was pushed open and, the torch still on, Some one entered. Instantly Pointer pulled him in, flung the door shut behind, and drew out the key which he put in his own pocket, while the major flashed his torch over, the newcomer. And again he burst into a laugh.

"This is pure vaudeville," he gasped. "Percy! Our well-beloved Percy!" It was Callard who stood there, quite unruffled, his little half-grin still curving his mouth up like a cat's.

"You, major! And the chief inspector! And how about the van that I came to hunt for? Is it here?"

Percy Callard certainly had plenty of nerve.

"What brings you here?" Pointer asked him.

"This." Callard solemnly touched his forehead. "These." He laid a finger on each ear in turn. "A laundry van suggests Miss Dickins somehow. That may not be prettily put, but you know what I mean. Miss Dickins leads me to the Sungleam Laundry, and meditation on it led me here tonight. Even as it led you two, I fancy. But the point is, has it led us all three aright?"

"Suppose you help us look," Pointer said briskly, and Callard certainly betrayed by no look or gesture that he was other, than the greatest stranger to the place or all in it. He looked into every van, opened every likely hamper. Then he turned to the others who were doing likewise.

"I might have known it was too easy. There's no sign of the little what-you-may-call-ums. Well, that's that! I shall go home and try to have another brain wave."

"How did you get in?" Hardy asked curiously. "We heard you—it sounded like a cross between the family ghost and the faithful hound who had got loose from his kennel and was dragging his chain with him."

"Our wine-cellar key happened to fit the lock, I found. As to the rest—collapsible fire-escape ladder." Percy smiled. "There's one on every landing in Charles Street. You hook it on to something and let go, and it falls down as steps hung on to two chains. It did rattle a bit, but fortunately there's a wind, and it's blowing away from the bobby down the other end of four streets. Coming back with me?" he asked affably.

The major said rather shortly that he supposed he might as well. Pointer motioned them to precede him, and said he would also let himself out through the building. As they passed on out into the yard he flipped back the lid of the other large hamper which he had left in place of the one he had taken, the one with a small smear of blood on it.

While Percy was talking to Hardy, he had dropped a tiny spray of dwarf birch tree into it. The spray was gone now. It had been there before the major had looked in. But Percy, the apparently inefficient Percy, had seen it. It was gone since he had looked over the hampers. And he had not spoken of it. True, the amateur sleuth on the trail can cause a lot of trouble to the real detective, but Pointer doubted very much if that were the cause of the silence in Percy's case. Just as he doubted very much if it was his brains and his listening to the talk of others that had brought him hunting for the van this evening.

Pointer now finally got into a bus and made for his rooms. Before he let himself in, however, he dropped a note in a letter-box of a house where young Rickitt's mother was caretaker. Young Rickitt was Armstrong's office boy, and Pointer had noted the nearness of his home to his own rooms.

He found a telephone message was waiting for him. It seemed to come from his tailor, but to Pointer it meant that the Yard had some information for him. It was, he speedily learned, to the effect that the telephone message which Armstrong had received that morning at breakfast came from Willesden. From a public phone booth at the station there. There had been no other call at that hour.

That much learned, Pointer went to bed and to sleep. Next morning at eight he was at the door of Master Rickitt's house in his comfortable two-seater. The lad, a bright looking boy, was flattered at the idea of a drive with a detective officer in charge of the case. So flattered, that Pointer did not have to draw anything out of him. It flowed out. Among other things came the news that there had been a scene at the office between Mr. Armstrong and Mr. Farrant day before yesterday morning. The boy had heard the "row", as he called it. In other words, he had heard the voice of Mr. Armstrong rising to a final forte. Mr. Farrant had begun moving his things from his room as soon as it was over, and had spoken to the head clerk, before the boy, of leaving on a long Commission which would keep him away for at least a couple of months, and which would probably take him out of England. The boy had heard nothing of what had actually passed in the interview between Mr. Armstrong and his private secretary. The former's room was sound-proof, not so sound-proof, however, but that the engineer's voice, pitched in what appeared to be ungovernable fury, had clearly reached the outer room.

"Was any one in the outer room, except the staff?" Pointer asked.

"Yes, sir. Mr. Larkin—from Sir Ellis Herbert—was in one of the waiting rooms, and heard everything. I was afilling up the ink, and he stood there listening with all his ears, and making no bones about it, either—gave me a wiggle of the hand to step more quietly so that he could hear better."

"What, exactly, was the end of the interview?" Pointer asked.

"Mr. Farrant came out in a hurry, sir, and went on out, and Mr. Armstrong started telephoning, and I went in to say that Mr. Larkin was waiting."

"Do you know to whom Mr. Armstrong was telephoning?"

"Yes, sir. Mr. Armstrong said, 'Of course it's a dreadful blow, Hardy, but I've had my suspicions of Farrant for some time. This is between ourselves, mind.' Then he saw Mr. Larkin, and called into the phone 'So long. See you tomorrow.' And hung up."

"Was Mr. Armstrong given to losing his temper?"

The boy said that he had never overheard such a scene as that of the day before yesterday.

"And Mr. Farrant? Does he lose his temper?"

The boy said that, on the contrary, Mr. Farrant was the quietest speaking gentleman one could imagine. And always kind, though he was not very popular at the office. Too quiet; never talked to anybody. As for the chief—Mr. Armstrong was a prime favorite. He evidently was a hero to his office boy if not to his valet, and that spoke well for the dead man.

"Now about any cable that came the day before yesterday," Pointer said after a pause. The boy hesitated. He flushed painfully.

"Mr. Armstrong was murdered, Edgar," Pointer said quietly. And Rickitt nodded.

"That doesn't make it like sneaking to tell things, does it, sir. Well, in Mr. Farrant's room after he left, I had to empty the paper basket. And I just dumped it into the chute and carried it back, and there sticking to the side was a tiny fragment of a cable—I know the color of cables well enough—on it was a word, a whole word by the little space in front of it and behind it. The word wasn't English, sir. It was MEZ. That was all. I don't know if that means anything to you, sir?"

"Everything means something, Edgar," was the copybook maxim that he received and which he stored up for future quotation.

And MEZ did mean something to Pointer.

He had applied yesterday, Wednesday, for a copy of all cables received that day or during the last fortnight by

Armstrong. He had received by this morning's post copies of all that had arrived this week. The others would be sent to him later. Among those in his possession was a copy of a cable sent from Perth in Western Australia the day before yesterday. It must have arrived not long before the quarrel of which the boy had just told him. It contained just that word or combination of letters, MEZ. Yet the head clerk had told Schofild and himself that no cable from Perth had been received the day before Armstrong's murder. When he now went on into the office where the chartered accountant and the Yard's financial expert were starting work, he found Schofild waiting for him. The experts told them that they had come on no record of any cable from Westrex, but they had found ample proof of a growing divergence of interests between Armstrong and the Herbert group of interests.

Pointer had another word with the head clerk, and learned that in the ordinary way Mr. Farrant opened all cables intended for Mr. Armstrong. If Mr. Farrant were out, he, the head clerk, saw to them. He, too, had heard the loud voice of Mr. Armstrong day before yesterday. Yes, Mr. Larkin was waiting for an interview. Who had given him the appointment? The head clerk had made it on instructions from Mr. Armstrong himself.

Pointer went on to Charles Street.

"By the way," he asked the butler, "do you keep the key of the wine-cellar?"

"Certainly, sir."

Pointer asked to see it. It bore no slightest resemblance to the key of the Sungleam garage which had been, as Major Hardy found, of the old-fashioned, large, out-house type. The Charles Street wine-cellar had a key of the Yale kind.

In one of the lower rooms the chief inspector found Major Hardy busy answering letters. "She's better!" Hardy said, as Pointer was shown in. "I mean Mrs. Armstrong, of course. She ought to be able to leave after the funeral, and that means I can leave too. Lady Grail proved a broken reed as usual, but Farrant's sister, also as usual, turned up trumps. She's going to look after Mrs. Armstrong for a bit. Can I offer you a cocktail, chief inspector, or a spot of anything simple and pure?"

Pointer declined, and indeed the major's offer had only been made in the tone of a man trying to simulate a lightness that he does not feel.

"It's a damnable business," he now said, turning his chair towards Pointer, "utterly damnable."

"Major Hardy," Pointer said bluntly, "why didn't you tell me that Mr. Armstrong practically dismissed Mr. Farrant the day before yesterday? And told you at the time that he had had his suspicions of him for some time?"

Hardy clipped off a cigar and lit it carefully, four square, before he replied. Even then he first looked at Pointer with a lift of his thick brows.

"I did know of it, yes. I plead guilty to that much. But you see"—he paused—"to be frank, I was afraid of your making a mistake. Of your thinking that such a quarrel had any connection with Armstrong's death."

Pointer said nothing.

"One does hear of the police making mistakes occasionally," the major said a little dryly.

"Keeping back the truth won't help to prevent them," was the cold reply. "you, of all men, sir, know, that. Then there was a quarrel?"

"There was," conceded the other.

"Caused by Mr. Armstrong's suspicions of Mr. Farrant proving themselves to be well founded?"

Hardy did not reply at once. Instead, he rose and leaned an arm on the mantel. Then he said rather curtly, "I wish this could have been kept from you. Quite frankly, I wish it. However, since it has come out, there's no use my keeping back anything. Armstrong phoned me the day before yesterday somewhere before noon, that he had just found out that Farrant had not told him of a most important cable that had come from the Westralian

Exploration Company's head office. They're hunting for telluride, you know, of which there's supposed to be chances of a deposit of considerable richness. The cable was sent in Wodi-wodi, a native language, which only the man who sent it and Farrant could understand, and in code at that. Wodi-wodi code. Well, Armstrong had arranged for another—a one-word cable—to be sent to him privately when the all-important informative cable was dispatched to a secret address, where Farrant was to collect it.

"Armstrong got his one-word notification-of-dispatch cable, but when he got to the office Farrant insisted that no cable had come. Armstrong grabbed him, and pulled the very cable itself out of his pocket. That's what he told me when I met him at Boodle's later in the afternoon. He was done with Farrant, and, but for his having served him splendidly in the past, would have hoofed him half across Europe, he said But, for value received, Farrant was to be allowed to claim that he was sent on a commission. The understanding with him was, that Armstrong would maintain this for six months. By the end of that time, Farrant was to have found other work. He could easily, of course, with Armstrong speaking of him as Armstrong would—and as Farrant deserved—in all except this cable business."

"Rather a big exception, it seems to me," Pointer murmured tentatively.

"He was tempted a bit too much for himself, unfortunately. But that has nothing to do with Armstrong's murder. And I felt sure you would think it had, and so perhaps lose the real criminal."

"If not with the murder, then with what did the suppression have to do?" was the chief inspector's not unnatural query.

"Speculation, probably, if not, of course. We, Armstrong, and I, all the City, are speculating on what the drills will show. In point of fact, Armstrong had the cable repeated in another code, and this time he had it read for him by a British Museum man who knows the Australian dialects. The result of the assay is very disappointing, but there's reason to think that another bore-hole, a little beyond this, will give a very different story. My belief, and in his heart I think Armstrong's belief too, was that Farrant was certain—he has been certain all along—that the results of the second bore-hole would reverse the finding of the first, and for that reason very stupidly decided to keep silent about the first message. He also has many friends out there. I don't doubt he's had private news that made him sure that a later cable would tell a very different tale. Neat way Armstrong caught him out, though. Armstrong was fond of setting traps."

"Was he a quarrelsome man?"

"Calmest chap in the world. Up to a certain point. That point past, he had a way of bursting out with extraordinary violence. Extraordinary, that is to say, to those who had only judged him by his quiet exterior up to the moment that the lid blew off. And from what he said to me I imagine that the lid blew off in his office, that morning of the cable. If so, as he had a voice like a bosun's when roused, it was evidently heard by some one who has passed the information on to you."

Pointer asked a few more questions, but, about this incident, he felt that the major had told him the full story.

CHAPTER SEVEN

ON leaving the major, Pointer had a brief interval with Sir Ellis Herbert. Not that he expected to get much out of him. Big financiers, like big poker players, do not, as a rule, betray themselves. He found Sir Ellis to be a man with a body almost as big as his reputation. He looked a formidable personage in every way. Yes, he and his friends had had an interview with Mr. Armstrong yesterday morning at their offices in Threadneedle Street from ten to around ten-thirty. The meeting? Just a discussion between friends. Mr. Armstrong had seemed quite his usual self? "Oh, quite!" This last assurance came with a sudden effect of deep disgust.

Pointer asked if Mr. Armstrong had written anything or made any notes, if so, had he used his own fountain pen or one from the office? Mr. Armstrong had made an entry or two, and used his own pen. Sir Ellis was certain? Sir Ellis was, and as he described briefly the pen found in the writing-table drawer there seemed no doubt on the matter.

"Have you got any clue to the murderer, chief inspector?" the financier asked, looking at the clock.

"You don't think it's suicide?" Pointer asked dubiously, a way he had.

"I do not! Absolutely out of the question. Wealthy man with millions in sight. Beautiful wife who adores him. Why should he kill himself? And who put him into that box? Obviously it's murder. Can't think why people want to have dealings with Chinks. Mr. Armstrong was very strong on an all-white Australia, you know. He's paid now for some of his sinophobia." Sir Ellis looked almost defiantly at Pointer.

"Can I see your Mr. Larkin for a few moments?" the latter asked, rising.

Herbert's eyes flashed oddly. "Mr. Larkin is not with us any longer. Blundering fool! I dismissed him yesterday. He—he made a mistake over Mr. Armstrong's appointment. My clerks are too well paid to make mistakes." Sir Ellis was actually quivering with suppressed rage. "As to where he is, I have no idea. He spoke of going for a cure somewhere. He certainly needs one."

"Mr. Larkin's home address?" Pointer asked.

"Willesden Terrace, Willesden."

Pointer left Sir Ellis with a good many things to think over. So Armstrong had had the pen on him at ten-thirty yesterday morning. And Mr. Larkin lived at Willesden, whence the telephone message had come that had reached Armstrong at breakfast. And Sir Ellis considered Mr. Larkin to have been a blundering fool... and had dismissed him yesterday... and would not hear of Armstrong's death having been suicide.

This was the first case that Pointer had ever had where so many people seemed roused to fury at the mere suggestion that there was no foul play in the matter. Major Hardy, Farrant, and now Sir Ellis Herbert, all underscored the fact that it was murder.

He decided that he would see Mrs. Armstrong, since she was now able to be questioned. He found an absolutely prostrate woman still. White, haggard, she did not open her eyes, and replied in the faintest of whispers While he questioned her, Pointer had the doctor with him. For his sake as much as hers. But he had to give up any attempt at an examination, for he found that no question, however guarded, could include any reference to her dead husband without Mrs. Armstrong bursting into sobs that shook the couch on which she lay. Pointer finally beat a retreat, leaving word with her doctor that if Mrs. Armstrong could think of anything, at any time, however trifling, that might help the police, he would be glad to come instantly and hear it.

Lady Grail passed him on the stairs and stopped for a word with him in one of the rooms.

"I'm leaving Mrs. Armstrong to Daisy Farrant," she began. "As she's Willie Farrant's sister, of course, she's just the person to look after Mrs. Armstrong in this damnable affair. I've told her that Willie must come back at once. The house needs him. Men are so selfish, and Miss Dickins is no good whatever and too much given to listening at doors. Yes, I caught her at it this morning. But now about the case, haven't you got any clues? I always understood that criminals left clues!" She looked at him very intently.

"Have you found any?" she repeated, as he did not at once reply.

"Heaps!" Pointer said on impulse. "Simply heaps, Lady Grail." And at that he saw her eyes waver for a second.

"Oh! indeed! Such as?" she asked invitingly.

She had a charming way with her when she chose, had Lady Grail. A way that had, been of great help to her in the past and in the present.

He shook his head, looking very official. "You'll learn before long," he could not resist saying meaningly, and on that there was no mistaking it, she paled to a real and rather dreadful pallor that made her weirdly-colored make-up look like a chromograph, purple lids, white forehead, bluish markings around her eyes, orange cheekbones, blush rose ears, and all the rest of the tinting.

"I must see how Mrs. Armstrong is," she said suddenly, and hurried from the room.

Pointer went to the telephone and had a talk with one of his men who had been sent to the office of the Ealing Sungleam Laundry. He had learned that there was practically no guard kept on the garages, that if one knew of their existence and of the old vans still in them, and could either obtain a duplicate of the key, or pick a lock, there was nothing to prevent taking one of them out early in the morning and returning in the afternoon, provided the borrower had a fair idea of the hours of the only caretaker, who concerned himself with the offices and not with the garages at all.

All this information was of the kind that one could find out by a little observation, it was also of the kind that a former secretary could easily supply. If she had done as much, had Miss Dickins done more? Had she had a hand in the actual murder? She had been away from Charles Street at the all-important noon hour. She had no alibi for the hours preceding it. Could it be that the two secretaries, the husband's and the wife's, were in this murder together? If so, what could the motive be? Granted that Farrant had been speculating, he was supposed to have kept back an unfavorable cable... that would mean that he was a bull of Westrex... Armstrong's death was certainly not a bull point for the shares of his companies, even though, according to the head clerk, it would do them no lasting harm. There were no irregularities in Farrant's accounts or in the accounts with which he had in any way to do. That much was already ascertained.

At this stage Schofild joined him. He had been able to find out nothing as yet that would link Farrant's morning hours with the wedding-chest in which Armstrong's dead body, had been found. But he had set his own two very capable men at work, and hoped for some result shortly. He was very keenly interested in the account of Pointer's talk to Sir Ellis Herbert.

"In my opinion," he said finally, "it looks as though Farrant were their tool. Promised some enormous prize by them, and they have big enough ones to offer in all conscience."

Pointer said nothing. Of all the wily foxes in London, his chief had told him that none were held to be keener-witted than Sir Ellis. The chief inspector thought it difficult to believe that he would find it necessary to use force rather than finesse, or be willing to do so. On the whole, with many provisos, the assistant-commissioner at Scotland Yard rather agreed with the head clerk, that the men in question, though ruthless and keen, were not of the kind to commit murder. Nor was, as far as could be learned, Armstrong's death a necessity to them, though doubtless a convenience.

Pointer gave instructions over the telephone for Mr. Larkin to be looked up, if it were possible to reach him in England. If he had gone abroad already, then the foreign police were to be notified.

"Armstrong learned something from Wikesden over the telephone yesterday morning that put, or would have put, the extinguisher on Farrant, in my opinion," Schofild said, deep in thought as Pointer hung up the receiver and turned to him.

Then he hurried off, still intent on picking up Farrant's trail near the place of the accident, while Pointer went on to see the Lees again. He wanted to see if he could link up Lady Grail with them in any way.

Questioning old Mr. Lee, he was told that three days ago, a lady had come to Limehouse Street and ordered some lily bulbs, and had also bought a couple of old Nanking vases. Mr. Lee said he remembered an old lady with white hair and a veil of black lace falling from her hat brim. He remembered her chiefly by her hands, which, when she took her glove off to examine the vases more closely, were white and smooth and beautifully cared for. The hands of a smart young woman, he would have said.

Had he noticed any rings? A wedding ring, for instance? Pointer held out the finger in question.

"The lady wore three very narrow rings on that finger. Gold, platinum, and gold again." This was the wedding ring of Lady Grail, and Pointer had hoped for much from it, for a woman often remembers to take off all betraying rings set with stones, and yet often forgets that a wedding ring may be as peculiar. In this case hers had caught the eye of the chief inspector at once among a mass of flashing stones, just as it had that of old Mr. Lee when it was the only one worn.

The purchases, Mr. Lee went on, were delivered at a certain address near Sloane Square that same afternoon—three days ago—to a Mrs. Warnett.

At the address Pointer found that a Mrs. Warnett of Guildford had taken a furnished suite for a day or two, she was up for some shopping, she had said. As a matter of fact, the old lady had met some friends and had only used the rooms one afternoon. That was three days ago. Some packages had been delivered, a basket of bulbs among them. Mrs. Warnett had been in at the time, and had left orders that the vanmen were to be shown into her sitting-room as she wanted to ask some question about the bulbs. Three men had come with the order, and had all been shown in as Mrs. Warnett had requested. A few minutes later still another had arrived, a big hulking young fellow, with a thick mop of hair and a long drooping mustache. Apparently they had had a good deal to show the old lady, for it was some twenty minutes later before they left. All but the tall young chap. He had remained on another few minutes, and left later by himself.

Mrs. Warnett had not stayed in the Sloane Square house over night, but she had been in again yesterday, and the men in question had come back about three in the afternoon. They were gardeners really, Mrs. Warnett had told the woman of the house, and were giving her important directions. She had thought it a little odd, and had kept near the sitting-room, and what she heard had sounded still odder to her. Yes, she had heard the old lady apparently scolding, or at least she had heard one of the men replying, half-humorously, half-impatiently.

"It's not at all what I wanted," the old lady had said in a sharp voice. "The van was not to drive up till just before five."

"Yes, but lady, it wasn't our fault—another van was sent along, see, that we'd never dreamed would come... but it was all done as you said. And neatly done, too."

"I certainly paid you enough," the woman had said shortly, and then had apparently paid them still more, for the landlady had heard her add: "However, here's another something for each of you to keep your mouths shut. Remember, you know nothing whatever!"

"We shan't be there to know," the man replied, laughing and coming out.

No, she had not seen the tall one with the mop of hair yesterday. Mrs. Warnett had given up the rooms immediately and walked away. She had only had a small handbag with her throughout. "And what it all means I'd like to know," the landlady finished. Pointer had told her that he was a detective officer. He now asked her to describe Mrs. Warnett, and heard again the description given by Mr. Lee. Could the landlady remember any rings that Mrs. Warnett had worn?

She wore three wedding rings, thin as wires: gold, platinum and gold. The woman of the house, too, had been struck by Mrs. Warnett's beautiful hands. She had never seen her lodger without her hat and veil. Pointer thanked her, and decided that he had now enough interesting material for a heart to heart talk with Lady Grail.

She was in her comfortable flat in Cadogan Gardens, and saw him at once. Coming in fully dressed for outdoors, and buttoning her gloves as she came, with an air of sparing a minute to a not too deserving case.

"Lady Grail," he began in his most awe-inspiring manner, and Pointer could be very daunting, "I want the names of the vanmen whom you paid to leave their employment with Messrs. Lee and Son, and who let Mr. Armstrong's murdered body be placed in the wedding-chest that they were taking to Charles Street, instead of the dwarf trees which Mr. Armstrong had ordered."

Lady Grail looked as though her spine had suddenly given way.

"We know that you disguised yourself as an old lady, a Mrs. Warnett, and went to the Chinese importers for some bulbs and a couple of Nanking vases, also taking rooms in Sloane Square under that name, where the purchases were delivered to you, and where you arranged the plan with the men who brought you the bulbs, once you heard that they would be on duty next morning and would be the ones who would take on to its destination any purchase made at that time."

For a full second she only stared at him, then she ripped her gloves off with what looked like the energy of despair, and sinking into a chair pointed to one near her.

"I've been expecting this. It's true. But my plan was only to prevent the trees being delivered on time. A horrid plan, I admit. I'm frightfully ashamed of it. But it was really only a practical joke. As to the substitution of Boyd Armstrong's body—I swear I know nothing about that. Nor of his death. Nothing whatever. Nothing! Nothing!" Something in her eye suggested hysteria not far off. "Oh, chief inspector, it's too awful. I'm thankful in a way that the truth is out now—provided you keep it to yourself, of course. You see, I only meant it as a joke. I knew from Bob Hardy that he was giving the Armstrongs a chest of some kind. And Miss Dickins let slip to me— she coaches me in golf—that Mrs. Armstrong had arranged with him to buy the dinkiest little dwarf birch trees yet seen in Europe. She was getting them at a wonderful bargain. They were to be sent along in the chest, and there was to be a sort of state opening. And—it was quite disgusting of me, I admit—but I decided to arrange for the chest to be delivered empty. That was all I did! All! All!" she gulped.

"How did you intend to get the plants out of the chest?" Pointer asked.

"You know I'm president of the Laundry Girls' Holiday Camps? We're giving a garden fête for them next week. The idea is to use laundry vans and baskets as part of the fête, decorated with flowers, of course, as platforms for singing and dancing turns. Some very good stage people are giving their services. I spoke of it to Miss Dickins when I was practicing approach shots with her, and she told me of some laundry vans I could probably get the use of for the afternoon for next to nothing. She had been secretary to a laundry, you know."

Pointer nodded. Yes, he had been quite aware of that, he said.

"I wrote to the laundry in question, and they said I was welcome to the use of the vans on the day of the fête for nothing, supposing they were still unsold. Would I care to have a look at them? I saw them, and noticed how no one was looking after them. Well, all this was about a week ago. Only when I wondered whether I could"—she hesitated—"borrow those plants in the chest for a while, I remembered these vans. And Percy Callard was just having a cocktail or two with me. He drives magnificently. That made me think of him... And Percy— he'll undertake anything that strikes him as being amusing. And above all he loves to do people in the eye."

"Even his sister?"

"Except that she supplies him with money, Percy doesn't care that for Phyllis!" She flipped a finger in the air.

"What was his part to be?"

"Oh, don't you know? He thinks you've guessed all about it. He got the van out on the quiet that met the breakdown van, and took out the plants into a hamper. Then he put the van, plants, hamper and all, back in the garage, also without being seen. I think he had tipped the man not to be on the lookout. My idea was that the plants would be delivered late that evening. Or sent on somehow..." She looked a trifle awkward. Pointer did not believe that she had the least interest in what happened to the plants, provided they were not there when the chest was opened, so that the little ceremony would be a

complete fiasco. "But, as you see, chief inspector," Lady
Grail went on, "all this has nothing to do with Boyd
Armstrong's murder. Nothing at all!"

We speak of whistling to keep up one's courage. There
is talking that serves no other purpose. Lady Grail was
trying to make herself believe what she said.

"Percy's a bit off color, we all know that. Born that
way, poor lamb, like all his branch of the Callards. But as
to killing Boyd—oh, preposterous!"

"He's rather by way of being great friends with Mr.
Rufus Armstrong, isn't he?" he asked casually.

"Just lately. He talks of setting up a secondhand
clothes shop."

Pointer stared. This really was unexpected. "I mean
furniture shop, and thinks that Rufus Armstrong could
give him points as to what to go in for, and afterwards
buy it off him."

"And is Mr. Rufus Armstrong falling in with Mr.
Callard's simple plans?"

"Oh—it's just talk! Percy couldn't keep a shop. He
can't add to save his life. His manager, or, salesman, or
whoever he would put in, would simply skin him alive.
Besides, now that poor Boyd is dead, of course Percy will
have an easier time. Not a condition attached to all that
money! Really Phyl is—" Lady. Grail bit back something.

Pointer asked her further questions about the taking
of the plants. She seemed to answer truthfully, "I'd give
anything not to have done it," was her cry.

So, on the day of the reception, she knew that the
chest would not contain the dwarf trees. Did she know
more? Pointer thought not. Her horror at its contents
seemed real and deep—for one of her shallow nature. But
some one else seemed to have utilized the chest that she
had had emptied. Who?

He asked her if she had discussed this plot of hers
with Percy Callard in any place where they could have
been overheard. She was sure that they both had been
most discreet. Pointer doubted it. And apart from

indiscretion, there was the possibility of Callard having served two masters.

Pointer decided to see Callard at once. Percy began the interview very brightly. He was at his own rooms near Knightsbridge, whose letting seemed to have been more or less a fictional excuse for staying at Charles Street.

"Mr. Callard, I want a clear account from you as to your share in the murder of Mr. Armstrong. Unless satisfied, I shall have to take a very unpleasant step," Pointer said, after, some minutes of Callard's chaff.

"Indeed?" Callard snuggled his shoulders still more comfortably into his armchair, "my share in Armstrong's murder... rather a hectic way of talking, isn't it, chief inspector?"

"We know that you purloined a laundry van and took out the dwarf birch trees Mr. Armstrong had bought to be distributed yesterday afternoon. This isn't guessing, Mr. Callard. We can prove this. In place of the trees, the dead body of Mr. Armstrong was found, when the chest was opened. Who else had the means of putting it there but yourself?"

"And my motive?" Callard asked, but he was rather pale. It looked as though Major Hardy had been right that Callard belonged to those criminals who never appreciate their danger, who rely for their safety on blindness in other people rather than on their own wits.

"Your sister comes into Mr. Armstrong's fortune by his will, made just after their marriage. You would have a very good chance, through her, of sharing in it."

Percy was really white now.

"You're getting up a case against me, faking it," he declared passionately.

"That kind of speech will hardly help you. I want facts, Mr. Callard."

Finally Callard agreed that he had taken the trees, knowing that his sister would see to it that there would be no prosecution. Lady Grail had suggested the taking as a joke—"on Major Hardy. She's wild that he no longer, cares for her, and, of course, she hates my sister," Callard said, as though that explained everything. He acknowledged that he might have intended, when he came back last night, to take the dwarf trees away, and dispose of them. But he maintained, with nothing of his usual languor, that he had left the wedding-chest empty, that the trees had been his only interest, that he was as horrified as any of the visitors when the dead body of his brother-in-law was found in the chest. As to any words of his to Lady Grail that had been over-heard earlier in the afternoon such as those that Pointer repeated, they had referred, of course, to showing the requisite amount of surprize when the chest would prove to be empty. Pointer gave him a very unpleasant quarter of an hour, but learned nothing more than he had known before. It was at the Yard, where he went next, that information directly bearing on the case was waiting for the chief inspector.

The man who had been sent to have a word with Mr. Larkin if possible, reported that that gentleman had closed his house yesterday evening. A telephone message had been received by milkman, baker, and newsagent, telling them to suspend all deliveries until Mr. Larkin let them know of his return from a hurried trip abroad for his health. Housekeeper and maids were put on board wages, however, which looked as though Mr. Larkin did not intend to stay away for very long. He was a widower, Pointer learned, and lived in a good deal of comfort. As Pointer had requested, all foreign police had been given his description and the same was true of the home counties as well.

Schofild at this point was shown in. He looked very pleased with himself. He gave a glance at the notes on Larkin, and then burst out:

"I've got hold of something really interesting, Pointer. Through Wilkins—"

The chief inspector was instantly attention. "Did he get anything out of young Wong?"

"Wong?" queried Mr. Schofild absent-mindedly. "Oh, yes, the handsome-young Chinese with the flute and the pet lark? No, he didn't have any success with him. Wilkins doesn't believe that he knows anything about yesterday afternoon, but there may be something else that Wong knows about." Schofild played the piano triumphantly on the table top. "For Wilkins has found out something that will interest you as much as it interested me. And Wong may know of it. It seems that some eight years ago young Lee married an English girl. She was a school teacher in a Limehouse board school. Old Lee really made the match. He was tremendously Anglophile at the time. The young woman—Alice Sydney was her name—ran away before a year was past. The man went by the name of Adams, but even those who called him that believed it wasn't his real name. No one knew what happened to the girl or the man. Young Lee got his divorce, and a year later married a Chinese girl, with whom he lives happily. They have four sons. That in itself would be enough to make any Chinese happy, I suppose.

"At the time the elder Lee took it tremendously to heart. It was his doing, that unfortunate marriage, you see, and for a long time he made no secret of his intention of having his revenge if it ever came his way. Now, the question is, has it come his way?" Schofild asked the question of himself, though he spoke it aloud.

"Has it come his way?" he repeated. "Was Adams—Armstrong? For Armstrong was working then on the widening of the London docks; was actually resident engineer on the construction. No one can say with certainty that he could not have put in some spare time playing around with Mrs. Lee. The only description Wilkins could get of Adams is vague. Unfortunately, the Chinese claim that they find it as hard to tell us apart as we do them, but still, it fits fairly, supposing him to have worn very heavy eyebrows and glasses. Wilkins is downstairs in my car, if you'd like to question him. He's got a few minutes to spare."

Wilkins was shown up through what seemed to him endless narrow corridors, past endless numbers of hurrying men in blue, and in plain clothes, and in uniform, coming and going, or typing, or working with heads bent over their desks, or sitting with headphones on and scribblung for dear life on papers spread out before them.

Pointer listened very closely to all that the missionary had to say. Then he sat a while thinking.

"What is your own opinion of the matter?" he asked finally.

"Mr. Lee is of the old school," the answer came almost regretfully; "best of friends and cruelest of enemies. Compound interest for kindness or for injury."

Wilkins would have hurried away, but Pointer wanted a word about young Wong. Here Mr. Wilkins believed that the chief inspector was off the trail. He finally thought that if Pointer were right in fancying that Wong knew more than his companion musicians, it could only be of this English marriage of Lee's. "Unless," mused Mr. Wilkins, "unless he has some reason to connect Adams with Armstrong... which I can't think could be the case. Wong only arrived in England a fortnight ago, and lodges with a Chinese family..."

"It's more likely to be something that connects the Lees with the murder," Schofild thought. He, too, was off for his own rooms, and now carried Mr. Wilkins away with him.

Pointer got out his car deep in thought.

Armstrong and Mrs. Lee? Was this why Farrant refused to return to Charles Street? Did he know that the murder was linked to an unpleasant scandal? He, more than any other, would have to talk to the widow, and try to explain things to her, and Hardy maintained that Farrant had been deeply attached to Armstrong. Pointer's thoughts returned to the dead man again. Yes, if he had been the lover of Alice Lee, the lover with whom she ran away, there might be something more than mere chance that the Lees were mixed up in this very puzzling crime. If! There was nothing whatever to bear out the idea—as yet. Or were the Lees connected with it, but acting under orders? Pointer could at any moment have got into touch with *The Winkle*, but if Rufus Armstrong stood for anything in this puzzle, he stood for too much to be frightened yet awhile.

"This must indeed be looked at the right way," Pointer murmured, with a pucker of his strongly-marked, short-haired brows—the brows of an observant man. "But I'm hanged if I know which way to look."

CHAPTER EIGHT

POINTER now mentally sorted out what so far was known from what was only believed concerning Armstrong's last day.

The facts were surprizingly few. Pointer was a quick and diligent worker, throwing himself with all his energies into a case, and, as a rule, getting some early result as his reward. But not here. No efforts of the police had traced Armstrong after he hurried out of his office for the second time yesterday morning. His hat, his gloves, the revolver that shot him, were still undiscovered, as much so as the motive for the murder—or the murderer.

And, more surprizing yet, nothing had been learned, in spite of every endeavor, of how Farrant had spent the hours until his dubious alibi began. Like Schofild, Pointer had expected that that young man must have known that his actions in the morning could be traced, but up till now he was safe.

That much for facts, now for inferences, or suppositions: If the chauffeur was right in his statement of the mileage shown on the speedometer when he brought it around yesterday morning, Armstrong had only used it to drive to his office, on to Herbert's office, back again to his own, and then to the lock-up. Certainly no long excursion had been made in it. It looked as though Armstrong had, after leaving it, at once met his death, since there was, all told, only one hour between eleven and twelve, the hour of the breakdown off Fleet Street. He had died apparently somewhere where his hat and gloves were not clearly in evidence, and where he had laid down his fountain pen. Now Armstrong was not at all the man to have gone to a doubtful haunt, not at all credulous... There was no house in which he was known to have any acquaintance that had not been examined by the police. All without result. It seemed impossible for his body to have been placed in the chest at any other time or place except at noon in the cul-de-sac, but everything connected with Armstrong just before and after his murder was still wrapped in unpierceable fog.

As to Mrs. Armstrong, Pointer did not think that she had utilized the moment when she had returned to the end room of the Chinese suite after the chest had been placed in position to open it. The reason for her faint when it was opened was, be thought, connected with something blacker, and more sinister. All else might be wrongly sucked into the vortex made by the crime, but that she, and the telephone message of the morning, were in the very heart of it, that it swirled around them, the chief inspector firmly believed.

Investigations had shown that Armstrong had suddenly altered all his plans for yesterday except the visit to Sir Ellis Herbert's office. The financial expert helping with Armstrong's affairs thought that that sudden alteration, one which Pointer linked with the telephone message, was connected with some secret reception of an all-important cable, a cable which had, so the expert thought, been taken from Armstrong's dead body, and to obtain which he had been killed.

Major Hardy said that the murder would either be connected with that cable or with the Lees. Farrant scoffed at both notions...

Then where had Armstrong gone after hurrying out of his office? What had Mr. Larkin said to him over the wire a few minutes before eight-thirty yesterday morning? Something that to Sir Ellis, at any rate, and—by his own instant flight, to Larkin himself—might have had some connection with his death, supposing it had been suicide. For Herbert had used the word murder when speaking of Armstrong's death in a tone that suggested a deliberate choice of that word. What had the stout little man who had been described to Pointer by Armstrong's office boy and others, what had he telephoned to the dead man? Pointer felt that this was a very integral part of the puzzle. He believed that it had influenced Armstrong's actions after its reception. That hunting up of the map, that mention of being out till late, had all taken place after it had reached him...

Mr. Armstrong's money matters were all in perfect order. Was there some charge of blackmail in disguise here? But Sir Ellis was no blackmailer, and Pointer did not suppose Mr. Larkin to be one either. The man had no need of that. He was earning a splendid salary. Another firm was going to take him on as soon as he should be back again, Pointer was told; a firm connected with Herbert, but not directly one of his. Sir Ellis evidently could not punish the blunder that had been made, but he would not forgive it either.

The position intrigued Pointer, who thought it over very carefully. Mr. Larkin stood for business. There was an important conference on. A question therefore to be laid before Armstrong? Or a paper to be signed? Was the idea to tell Armstrong something that would make him less single-minded, less alert than usual?

Pointer had got to this point of his meditations when word came to him over the telephone that a Mr. Larkin had been traced to Calais by the first night boat after Armstrong's death.

The chief inspector was just making up a package for Mr. Larkin when the information reached him. It made no difference to his little plan.

Half an hour later one of his men handed in a little package at the house in Willesden. "From Barbours, the jewelers of Regent Street," he said importantly, thrusting forward his book for the woman who opened Mr. Larkin's door to sign.

"He's not at home at the moment," she said, unwilling to take it.

"Left with us to have his initials put on a week ago. Wanted most particular. We were to hand it over to you all ready for posting, as it is, and you are to register it on to Mr. Larkin. Didn't he tell you himself?" The man looked as though Mr. Larkin must certainly have done so. The woman shook her head.

"Ah, well, the best of us forgets things," the young man said philosophically. "However, just you post it on to him—we've left the address blank, and it'll be all right." With that he made off. The woman stood a moment irresolute. A few minutes later, with her hat on, and the parcel in her hand, she hurried to the post office. So she had her master's address. Behind her came the chief inspector, a cane in his hand. A cane so awkwardly managed that, turning sharply to look into a shop window, it struck the box neatly from the woman's hand, flinging it some distance off. In one bound Pointer was on it, had picked it up, and was returning it to the very indignant woman with many apologies.

Mr. Larkin was at the Hotel Merveille, Vichy. Mr. Larkin would shortly get, or not, according to whether the postal authorities accepted the package, or insisted on a declaration with it—quite a nice cheap cigarette case with the card, "From a friend," enclosed.

Pointer decided that he must get to Vichy as soon as possible. A wireless message was sent to the French police. They replied that a question at the hotel in question showed that Mr. Larkin had stopped there only one night and then had been called to Paris, but he had left instructions that any letters should be kept for him, as he would return for his cure at the earliest possible moment. No, he had not kept his room on, but his luggage had been duly taken down and put into the Paris express the same day. Further questions brought further replies. Mr. Larkin had gone very early to the train. About an hour before it started. As the coach was made up in Vichy, his suitcase had been put into the compartment. No, no one had actually seen him in the train when it left the station. Yes, he was physically quite able to take the suitcase down and carry it about.

Now Pointer had found that Mr. Larkin really had been very strongly urged to undergo a treatment at Vichy or some similar spa by his Willesden doctor. The man needed it badly, in the medical man's opinion, very badly. Yet Vichy had been a blind, Pointer thought, for the French police had certainly not driven him away by inquiries.

Schofild, having heard nothing, returned as the chief inspector got out his Continental Bradshaw and saw that a train for Luxembourg passed through Vichy, and stopped there for five minutes just about a quarter of an hour after Mr. Larkin had reached the station en route for Paris.

No other train stopped during the hour that Mr. Larkin had so thoughtfully allowed himself.

Luxembourg! You couldn't summon a witness from Luxembourg... let alone have him arrested there... Luxembourg.

Pointer and Schofild, who had watched his moving finger down the time-table, looked at each other. Then Schofild had a chat over the telephone with the London office of the Belgian State Railways, with which Luxembourg is grouped. Mr. Schofild said that he was thinking of going to Luxembourg. Any spas in the little duchy? Most certainly. There was Mondorf for one. Mondorf had quite a large number of visitors. Its waters were very similar to those of Vichy.

A word to the Luxembourg police and Pointer learned that a Mr. Larkin was at the Hotel Splendide, had been there for some days, and was dutifully drinking the water.

"I'll take this on," Schofild volunteered; "just my sort of work—mental, not visible, clues." And he forthwith arranged for a seat in Imperial Airways machine that left for Brussels next morning.

At nine-thirty he was stepping into their car at the Haymarket offices, three-quarters more and he was at the Croydon airdrome, studying the weather map of

Europe with the anxious gaze of one who intends to fly across no matter what the prophecy.

The door closed at ten-thirty to the minute, and Schofild opened his window a thought more, arranged his luggage to his liking in the rack, ate a sandwich, and helped himself to some of the spearmint which the company thoughtfully provides as a solace for forbidden tobacco.

He felt the "car" running smoothly beneath him suddenly cease its vibrations, looking out he saw the ground slowly sinking. Schofild loved crossing in a plane. To watch the earth fall away until it showed a distant colored map was an ever new pleasure to him. That was Biggin Hill surely. He watched the altimeter until they were at a height of four thousand, when the climbing ceased. Far below was a tiny roll of cotton wool—it was the boat-train's smoke. He ticked off the familiar landmarks, then came the broad river of the Channel, another quarter of an hour, and Calais was left to the right and Lille took its place. Turnhout; Alost; Ghent. All gray blurs today with towers piercing the mist. Then, over the flat fields came the brown-gray smudge of spires and domes and roofs that meant Brussels. Five minutes at the Evère airdrome, a glance at the passport, another at his suitcase, and just three and a half hours after he left the Haymarket he was making for another plane that was waiting to take him on to Luxembourg. Thence a car drove him out to Mondorf.

He was told later that when a Belgian doctor recommends a cure at a native watering place to a lady, her husband gets in touch with him and implores him, as a man and a brother, to order Mondorf if it be in any way possible. There are no shops there, no theater, in fact, no anything except the water, a funny wooden shelter housing a reading room with a balcony around it, called the Casino, and some hotels. One of these looked so new, and so obviously the best, that Schofild was sure it was the Splendide. It was. He found the name that h. wanted in the visitors' book. Mr. Larkin was at the Casino, he was told.

Schofild was amused at the Mondorf idea of what that word meant. However, Mr. Larkin was not there, nor in what the guide book refers to as the "vast park"—a tract of wooded country with a few paths here and there in it. Schofild tried elsewhere. Finally he caught sight of a tea-room with an open-air loggia, and in the most comfortable chair was what, from the ground, looked like a big cigar and a Martini. Craning his neck, the private investigator saw a hand holding the Martini, and on that he mounted the steps. There sat the original of the descriptions with which he had been furnished, looking very sorry for himself.

Schofild came up from behind and tapped him smartly on the shoulder. The man jumped to his feet with a most betraying start.

"Wtat—*was*—*quoi*—" came in an indignant squawk from Mr. Larkin.

"I want a word with you, Mr. Larkin," Schofild said quietly, but with a coldly official eye. "I am acting for Mr. Armstrong's family in the inquiry into his death. I want to know from you yourself just what was the telephone message you sent him on the morning he died I suppose you know he has an automatic recorder fastened to all his telephones?"

But Mr. Larkin had not risen to his late position without keen wits. He had recovered himself now.

"Dear boy, you're being funny!" was his way of receiving the blow aimed at him. "Why not consult the damned thing then? There's no reason why my message to Armstrong should have brought you toddling all this way. I reminded him about the meeting with Sir Ellis, and made a mistake over the hour. Sir Ellis shifted me. That's all. And quite enough too. But no harm done—me or him. You must have wanted a change badly to come all this way on such an errand. Have a glass of something? There's nothing to do here but play tiddliwinks by yourself, or drink. My doctor sent me here, but it's not doing me any good." Mr. Larkin shook his head sadly. "Still, I must finish the cure."

"Long one?" Schofild asked.

"Depends." Mr. Larkin knocked off the ash from his excellent cigar, and rang for the waitress.

"On what?" Schofild asked.

"Symptoms that may develop," was the placid answer. "Sit down and have a cigar and a drink. I'm lonely. You're a godsend, Mr. Schofild, to see a fellow-countryman out here and get the latest news about Mr. Armstrong's murder"—he waved a plump hand towards some papers strewn around his feet—"old stuff."

"The police investigations are still going on," Schofild said, lighting up in his turn, "but even if I have come on a wild goose chase, you may be of help. You knew Mr. Armstrong, Mr. Larkin; what is your own idea about his death? You called it murder just now. Wasn't it more probably suicide?"

"Certainly not! Thuithide!" Mr. Larkin's contempt for the idea was so emphatic that he lisped.

"No, no, ath clear a cathe of murder ath one could wish to thee," he went on forcefully.

"Wish to see, Mr. Larkin?" Schofild seemed surprized at that way of putting it. Mr. Larkin's eyes looked angry.

"You know what I mean. It's murder all right. But as to who did it—well, who wanted to get him out of the way, eh? Some one who knew his little hours off, and where he was going, eh? Some one who knew them very well, from Mr. Armstrong himself, day by day, eh? Some one who knew about that wedding-chest coming along and knew that it would be a bit of a puzzle to find out about how, and when, and all that..."

Mr. Larkin fixed very enterprising eyes on the entrance to the park before them. He spoke with studied nonchalance, but he dropped no pearls before Schofild, though he invited him to dine with him at his—their—hotel. The private investigator promptly accepted. The dinner went a long way towards explaining one reason why the astute Larkin was willing to lie *perdu* here.

It was perfect in every detail. Mr. Schofild insisted on contributing a certain noble wine which—had Larkin known it—had been the subject of not a little talk with the wine waiter. Schofild had explained that it was a test of his friend's palate to see if he would detect the really noble vintage under its plebeian robe. Mr. Larkin, who had taken a glass perfunctorily, was delighted. The wine waiter promptly told him it was the very last bottle of that particular kind. It was strong wine, and Mr. Larkin had the bottle practically to himself, but he was as unsoundable after his last as his first glass. Schofild realized sadly that any further efforts would only run up expenses and lead to no result.   Mr. Larkin obliged with a song, and was apparently so willing to follow it up with a dance, that Sehofild bore him off to the bar below, out of which opened a ballroom. He continued to put away cocktails all evening with the same result, as far, as the investigation was concerned. Mr. Larkin got quite unsteady on his pins, he threw an arm around the other's neck and told him all about the girl he should have married, but he did not tell what it was that he had said to Armstrong, a message which, Pointer believed, had led directly or indirectly to his death.

Schofild had hardly started for Mondorf when there came a message on the telephone for Pointer, as the officer in charge of the inquiry into the death of Boyd Armstrong. It came from Rufus Armstrong, the dead man's cousin, and was not entirely unexpected. For Pointer had had one of his own men, sailing close by *The Winkle*, ask if some petrol could be spared him. Told to come on board, he had had a drink, and chatted a while of town news, ending up with the innocent inquiry, when he learned the name of the dispenser of petrol, "No relation of the Armstrong who's just been found murdered in a chest, I take it?" Begged to explain, he had given a brief summary of the accounts in the newspaper, adding that the inquest was to take place next day.

Rufus had looked, spoken, and acted throughout as an innocent man; but no criminal, unless the village idiot, acts suspiciously. And now from the station in town, to which he had hurried up, he was asking for the earliest possible appointment.

Pointer suggested Rufus Armstrong's house as the meeting place. He wanted to see servant as well as master. The former made a good impression as he opened the door. An elderly sailor man, if ever one was. Brown, alert, and useful in a tight place, was Pointer's summing up of him. No better man could a murderer choose than such a one, provided he were not to take part in any murder, but only to receive the police afterwards, and talk to them of his master. The chief inspector almost expected to hear him murmur, "Aye, aye, sir," when asked if Mr. Rufus Armstrong was at home.

Rufus Armstrong, who was standing with his back to the light when Pointer entered, was of quite another world. Tall, thin but wiry, he had a darkly handsome face. Below a good forehead looked a pair of brooding brown eyes; his nose was aquiline; his mouth discontented. The whole air of the man was one who had missed his path in life and knew it.

He met the chief inspector with the proper remarks of horror of the facts as related in the papers, regretted that he knew absolutely nothing that could assist the inquiry, and begged that the police would make any use of him they could.

First of all, Pointer asked him for his movements on the day of his cousin's death. Rufus mentioned that he had called at Charles Street to see a veryfline specimen of Chinese work—a wedding-chest which was to stand in a Chinese suite of rooms there, had learned that it was not expected to arrive until noon, and had left, after waiting in the library for half an hour in the hope of seeing Mrs. Armstrong, who had but just that minute left the house.

"Any special reason for wishing to see her just then?" Pointer asked.

"Oh, no," Rufus replied at once, "merely to hear what she thought of the chest—a very fine piece of work. Horrible"—he broke off to murmur—"horrible for it to be for ever connected with such a tragedy."

"Which of the servants let you out?" Pointer asked next.

"I walked out without troubling any one. There had been some sort of domestic upheaval —boiler, or pipe burst—I waited for a while, and then walked out without a word to any one." He sounded quite casual.

"Which room did you wait in, sir?"

Rufus looked surprized. "In the library. I expected to have Boyd walk in on me any moment."

"And what, exactly, is your connection with the Lees of Limehouse Street, Mr. Armstrong?" Pointer asked next. "You have invested money in the firm, we understand."

"Well—yes. I do not quite know how you learned that fact?"

By saying this he made it one instead of a mere guess on Pointer's part. As the other did not reply, he went on:

"Yes, I—eh—advanced them the money with which to start. I knew them as most respectable merchants, both of them. And knew that their own capital was either gone, or hopelessly tied up by the fall of silver. So, yes, I advanced them the capital with which to start. This is entirely confidential, and, personally, I think it should not have been brought forward at all." His dark, melancholy eyes looked down his thin drooping nose with the air of one surprized at an exhibition of bad manners.

"The only matters that will be brought forward by us are those connected with the murder of Mr. Armstrong," Pointer said politely, "but there is a great deal to be done in clearing up how people come to be connected with the case. These Lees, for example, you recommended them to Major Hardy, I think?"

"Yes." Something watchful came into the eyes fastened on his.

"And recommended the purchase of the chest in particular?"

The feet of Rufus Armstrong twitched into another position, with the effect of a start or jerk.

"I may have. It was the finest thing of its kind I have seen for a long time. But I fail to understand how this is connected with my cousin's death."

"The chest was where his body was found," Pointer said evenly. Rufus bit his lip. Bitter lips the man had, yet he had also a smile of great sweetness.

"Ghastly!" he murmured, "and that poor woman was there. Practically opened the chest herself and found him!"

"I wonder you could allow it to be sold to some one else," Pointer said now. "To a collector of Chinese things it must have meant quite a loss." He wanted to hear what the reply would be. It did not come at once.

"The chest was expensive. I happen to be unable to buy anything of the kind at the moment," came rather awkwardly from the man sitting opposite him, still with his back to the light.

Pointer asked a few more questions, chiefly about the Armstrongs, and rose to go. He glanced around him at the cases, still locked, as he did so. "I suppose I may not ask to see any of your collection, sir. I understand that it is most valuable?"

The dark face lighted. "I'll show it you with pleasure." And taking his keys out, Rufus Armstrong unlocked each case and expatiated on the contents. Now, quaintly enough, when Pointer was shown private collections, and that now and again happened in the course of some inquiry, he was always disappointed in them. For, being a man of the people, the only collections that he knew well were the finest in the world, those of our own great galleries and of the chief towns abroad. Compared with the exhibits to which he was accustomed, therefore, private owners, as a rule, had little to show worth a second glance. But he realized that that most fascinating branch of art in the world, Chinese art, was well represented here. Pointer worked faithfully through each case. There was nothing there that interested him, either personally or as the detective officer in charge of the inquiry into the murder of this man's cousin. Thanking his host, and mentioning the hour of the inquest, he walked away.

Something there was that stung Rufus Armstrong when that chest was mentioned... something also that vexed him when the question of his having advanced funds to the two Lees was referred to... This latter might be merely due to the fact that Rufus Armstrong did not care to have it known that he was financing the firm to which he so often recommended his friends. As he had openly shown his dislike of having his association with the Lees mentioned, it interested Pointer very little. Much less than the reaction that he showed when the wedding-chest was mentioned, for the latter, whatever it was, was suppressed.

And there was one other thing that was suppressed. Pointer thought that Rufus was in love with Mrs. Armstrong, and believed that he had successfully hidden that love when talking of her just now.

As for what Farrant felt about her, Pointer could not tell, except that in his case, too, it went deep, but with Farrant, Pointer would not have been surprized to learn that the hidden feeling was hate. As for Major Hardy, though he always referred to her with due words of compassion and friendliness, Pointer thought that if he felt anything about the woman one way or other, it was dislike.

The inquest came next, and was a purely formal affair, adjourned for a fortnight. Evidence of identification was given, but no reference to the breakdown of the van was made.

CHAPTER NINE

THE day Schofild was due back was June 4th—Derby Day, when new names can be made and old fortunes lost in less than three minutes on Epsom's famous mile-and-a-half course—the greatest test of a thoroughbred in the world.

Even to Pointer, as he waited beside his phone at the Yard, friends drifted in to murmur, "What do you think of Springy Ease? He gave Young Man seven pounds and finished four lengths in front of him?"

"A year ago he was running in selling plates," was Pointer's unkind remark.

"That's what I say," chimed in another voice, "he's about twenty-one pounds behind a good horse—"

Pointer threw out his hand in a warning gesture. In silence the men tiptoed out. The chief inspector had some message on the phone which he wanted to hear more than suggestions as to likely winners.

As Pointer had hoped, the vanmen had been found. He had counted on this, and their descriptions had been carefully circulated to the police on the course and to all bookmakers. Where else, he had asked himself, would men of their stamp go—Irish vanmen, with ample funds, when the greatest race of the year, for their kind, was close at hand?

At his request the two Lees had gone to Epsom as well, but their help had not been needed, except to confirm the identity of the three men.

All three of the vanmen had backed the winner heavily—for them—and arrived therefore at the Yard apparently in the mood of men from whom, whatever happens, that which they have cannot entirely be riven.

Two were just a thought the worse for drink, but the third was clear-headed enough, and when he was confronted with what was known, skillfully mingled with what was strongly suspected, Pointer got from him a detailed account of the chest's journey and of the arrangements for the breakdown.

Later, his mates, sobered by some skillful concoction of the doctor's, supplied missing links. All fitted in. But to a very extraordinary whole.

If what the men said was true, and Pointer, after very careful cross-questioning and many of his skillful verbal traps which again caught nothing, decided that it was true, then the body of Armstrong could not have been placed in the chest at the breakdown place. For Dummett, the man first questioned, maintained that he had slipped out from the publichouse, and, leaning against a lamp-post, had watched the taking out of the chest's contents from close beside the van. He it was who had helped Callard to lift the contents; done up in a white tablecloth, across, and stuff them into the hamper. Pointer asked to look at his hands. On the palm of one was a recently-healed cut. He had torn the skin on the wicker handle while doing it. Nothing, Dummett maintained—all three maintained—had been put in the chest in place of the lifted-out plants, let alone "a corp."

"Why, when the laundervan had driven off finally I looked inside the chest. It was as bare as your hand. Then my mates came on out, and they too had a look, then we locked it again, and sat in the van smoking and planning just what we'd do with the money. Lucky thing we backed Daddy Longlegs. There was half a word about putting it on Blue Ray, and then where would we have been?"

As for Mrs. Warnett, as he called her, his, or their, account tallied exactly with that given to Pointer, by Lady Grail. So did what Dummett had observed of Callard's movements fit into that young man's story. Nothing was new, except—and it was an absolute right-about-turn—the fact that no body had been put into the chest from the time it left the Lees place until it was delivered at Charles Street.

Pointer stood a while looking at his shoes after the men had left. They, had been warned to be silent until, or unless, they were called on to give evidence. The last thing that Pointer wanted just now was that that evidence should leak out, and dire threats as to fines of such magnitude that all their winnings would disappear, helped to make the three men assure him that not a word would they say on the subject.

Schofild arrived at this point, and, after a swift amplification of his own failure with Larkin, which he had already telephoned in brief, listened to what had just been learned. Its amazing import held him silent for a moment.

"So the hour of twelve is no longer of importance!" he said finally.

"As Farrant seems to have known all along," Pointer murmured.

"In my opinion," Schofild went on, "Armstrong was lured into that Chinese suite before the chest arrived, and tumbled into it when shot and that hasty return to his office..." For a second Schofild paused, head cocked on one side, bright eyes looking about him, like a bird intent on choosing the best available worm—"was very likely to secure something—paper, letter, cable—which was on him when he was shot, and which was why he was shot."

Meantime, Major Hardy had not gone to see the Derby either, and a telephone inquiry late in the afternoon by Miss Dickins found him in his flat off St. James's Street. She wanted very much indeed to have a word with him, she said. She was speaking from the Emerson Club. Hardy suggested calling for her at once in his car, and while they drove she could talk. May Dickins sounded very grateful as she accepted his offer. Lady Grail had taken her on since Mrs. Armstrong seemed to want to see no one connected with Charles Street these days, and had gone virtually into a retreat at a friend's house down in the country.

Hardy, as she stepped into his car, thought how pale Miss Dickins looked.

"I've just had a talk with Daisy Farrant." She spoke hurriedly, as though she were running. "She tells me that you and she—?" She stopped interrogatively.

He nodded with one of his swift smiles.

"Yes, she and I," he repeated. "Going to be married. Well?"

Now, in the beginning, when she first came to the Armstrongs, Miss Dickins had disliked Major Hardy, with one of those dislikes-at-first-sight that are as sharp as love, but sometimes as evanescent. But her feelings towards the explorer had changed. Little by little: she had grown to find his infrequent, rather teasing smile, attractive; the glance of those intent eyes of his, which at first she had thought so cruel, she now found merely full of character.

"Then if that's so, I want to talk to you," she said, with something almost desperate in her voice.

"Am I only being resorted to as Daisy's future husband?" he asked lightly.

"Yes" Her reply was blunt, but she looked as though she were suffering. "Oh, major," she burst out, "I must speak! I must consult you."

"About Farrant?"

She nodded.

"Does he know you're going to consult me?"

"He does not," she answered.

"Oh!" He stared hard at her. There was a little silence.

"If you're going to tell me anything, be sure and begin at the beginning," he said finally and not in the tone of a man very anxious to hear what was coming.

"You know I gave him a false alibi?" she whispered, leaning forward. "Oh, how I wish I hadn't agreed to back up what he said! But he told me he was in an awful hole.

You see, he and Mr. Armstrong—" She stopped, looking terrified.

"There's no use telling me half," he said.

"No. And as you're going to marry his sister—besides, you've stood up for him splendidly."

"Because I didn't want the murderer to escape while the police wasted time over him. Farrant had no hand in murdering Armstrong."

"At first I was certain of that, too. Of course! But— but"—she drew a quivering breath—"I can't stand the responsibility of keeping silence," she said finally. "You know—that telephone message that Mr. Armstrong got at breakfast had something to do with Willie. And I've felt —thought—somehow that message seemed to make such a tremendous impression, to be, so very important." She was getting bogged.

"How do you know that telephone message had anything to do with Farrant?" he asked in surprize. This was the first that he had heard of the idea.

"I was up early, putting some final touches to the lilies that were to go into the Chinese suite later on, and I took down a couple of vases for the writing-room. I heard the telephone bell ring as I was on the stairs that lead from the sewing-room past the library door into the street—you know I—I saw Mr. Armstrong go into the room, so I waited a moment where I was. I heard him take down the receiver and after a little while I heard him saying a word or two in a voice I never would have recognized as his. Never! It was so harsh and so— terrible. Then there came a pause, and finally he rapped out: 'Farrant? Indeed? You may be quite certain I'll look into the matter! That's quite enough, I think.' And the receiver was banged on again. Mr. Armstrong strode out of the room all in the same moment, it seemed to me. He didn't see me, he didn't look up, he just stood there clenching and unclenching his hands, and finally he struck one open palm with his balled fist—just like this!

The next moment he went on into the hall where I couldn't see him."

There was a short silence. Hardy had listened with what, in another man, would have been an open mouth. Finally he said, rather as though rousing himself from deep thought:

"You were going to tell me something about giving Farrant a false alibi?"

"Yes. We only met down on the links. Just before I got there. Close on four. He was quite unlike himself. All nervy and jumpy and silent. We just sat about and mooned. He said he felt ill, but wanted to rest in the fresh air. Then about half-past five he telephoned to a friend, a man who was at the reception, and when he heard what had happened—he had gone back by himself to telephone—he came out to me, and we walked off beside the seventh green, and there he told me that Mr. Armstrong had been found murdered, and that he himself was in as bad a hole as a man could be. That he had quarreled with him at the office and been dismissed about a cable which he hadn't shown Mr. Armstrong, and that every one would think he had a hand in the murder. I told him it was nonsense his thinking such a thing; every one knew that, quarrel or no quarrel, he was devoted to Mr. Armstrong. But he was fearfully stirred up, I don't mean outwardly, I mean inside, and he assured me that he hadn't a dog's chance as things were, unless I would back him up, and say that he had lunched with me at Harrod's, and that we had been together all the afternoon. Well, I—He quite swept me off my feet, and I agreed. But I thought it would only be for a day or two, until the truth should come out. It's horrible, major. I daren't say a word for fear something would slip out that would contradict something else I've said. I've blundered badly about what he had for lunch—or he blundered. And why—why won't he come here to the house?" she suddenly burst out. "I can't keep that question from haunting me. Night and day. Why? It—it looks—" She choked herself off, then rushed on, "He won't go anywhere. He'll hardly stir from his hotel. He just sits there in the lounge all day... brooding.

"I—I can't go to the police!" she breathed, "yet—I won't shield a murderer—I won't!"

"Farrant isn't a murderer," Hardy said with decision; "be quite sure on that point, Miss Dickins."

"Ah, but I'm not sure," she said, under her breath, "nor would you be when I tell you what I've just seen." She hesitated again, more to control herself than to get her thoughts together. They were together, though, in a seething ball.

"I went to see him this morning," she said finally, "went up to his rooms at the hotel. I felt I must have some franker explanation from him. We talked without any result, he only asked me to trust him, and—and— somehow I'm finding that very difficult, major. Then the telephone rang, and he jumped up to answer it. It was in the next room, his bedroom, and on the table lay a letter—open. He had thrust it half under another paper when I came in, and then I"—she bit her lip—"I walked over and looked at it," she said defiantly.

"Miss Dickins! Oh, I say!" murmured the major in a very shocked tone.

"When there's a question of wondering if some one you love is a murderer you don't care what you do!" she said fiercely, her nostrils quivering. "I knew that the paper was important. It was! It was from the offices of Sir Ellis Herbert, and—and—oh, there's no question but that Willie has been acting for them, getting information for them, keeping back a certain cable for them!"

Major Hardy whistled under his breath.

"What happened then?" he asked, as she said nothing. "I mean, did you say anything to Farrant about it?"

"I couldn't. But I left it lying out on the table, and I banged the door as I went," she said, with a sparkle in her eye. "And now, what to think, what to do, I cannot tell." She looked exhausted. "That's why I say it's beyond me—to feel sure of him, I mean."

"You don't think you misunderstood the letter you found?" he asked slowly.

"Oh, no!" Her reply was quite sure. "No one could. It was marked 'Personal and Confidential,' and it certainly was—"

"Then," he said, after a little pause, "I think I see an explanation. I believe Farrant is entangled in some very intricate piece of work on Armstrong's behalf."

"But that quarrel between Mr. Armstrong and him?" she asked breathlessly.

"I shouldn't be surprized," he said slowly—"this is strictly between ourselves, and Farrant, of course," he added with a smile—"if that quarrel were not all it seemed, Miss Dickins. I have an idea that Armstrong was laying a little trap—to catch some of the Herbert group. And using Farrant as a bait... If my guess is right, I've had it all along, then Farrant has nothing but his word to show for it that the kept-back cable you don't know about that? Well, it's too long to explain, but there was quite a scene at the office in front of one of Herbert's henchmen between Armstrong and Farrant, and, thinking it all over, I doubt that whole affair... It looks to me as though Armstrong was at one of his beloved little tests, and Farrant had entered into it with him."

"As he would!" she said, her eyes shining in relief.

He nodded. "Just so. But with nothing to show in writing. If so, Farrant has got himself into a dangerous position, no doubt. Far more so than we know, possibly. At least that's my idea, and if I'm right, he needs every helping hand he can grab. That's my idea, too. He can't, or won't, speak out, or else he thinks he won't be believed, and his very statements will seem like efforts to clear himself—I think the latter probably—and so he's lying low."

"But why won't he come to the house?"

"He knows that he will be in much more danger of being questioned here than where he is at a hotel—oh, he's right about that! I think that's what he wants. To be for the moment outside easy questioning. And he thinks another house is the only place for him until it's cleared up, and personally I agree with him."

"Oh, I hope you're right!" Her face had lightened and her eyes brightened. "And you may be."

"The best way is to ask him directly," he said. "Tell him frankly that you got the wind up and confided in me, once you knew that I was going to marry his sister, and tell him just what I've said. I think you'll find he doesn't deny it—and probably will confirm it."

"It seems to me the only straight thing to do," he added bluntly, as she looked very doubtful.

"But I can't tell him that I suspected him of murder," she said lamely, "nor did I suspect him. It never was as bad as that. I only—I only dreaded what might be the truth."

"I think you owe it to him," he repeated. "Besides, one word from him will help you more than any amount of talk from me. Otherwise, by this time tomorrow you'll begin to wonder if I was right after all. Whereas, if he tells you that I've guessed right or nearly right, you'll believe him."

"But I shall feel dreadful, letting him know that you believed in him more than I did!" she faltered.

"Simply because I know men better than you do," he said pleasantly.

"You think I ought to do it? It'll be fearfully painful."

"I do," he maintained stoutly. "I should expect Daisy to do it with me, in your place."

She said nothing for a moment, then she asked suddenly:

"What about the police? I thought they suspected him—and me—of being actually concerned in the murder—somehow. Can't you tell them your idea as to why he seems implicated?"

"It's no use telling ideas to the police," he said dryly. "As I see it, things are much too black against Farrant at the moment. You see, the police must go by evidence. Even the cleverest of them wouldn't dare act according to his belief in a person's guilt or innocence. They're not individuals at all, the police. They're the Law. Nor am I sure they do believe him innocent. Quite the other way. But as soon as they find something pointing to another person, as they surely will in time, then's the moment for Farrant himself to explain matters to them. At least that's how I see it. At present, neither he nor any one else would be believed."

'Have you any idea who did do it?" she asked, after thinking over what he had said and seeing its justice.

"Yes, but not for publication yet," he said to that, with a grim look about his mouth.

"I can't tell you what a load you've taken off my shoulders, or rather, my heart," she said gratefully. "I'm ever so much obliged to you. And I'll do what you say. Tell him everything—what I thought—and what you think—and—" She half faltered in the proposed task.

"There's nothing like frankness," he said again. "It may be hard on both at the moment, but it's the only thing that binds in the long run. Look here," he gave her one of his keen looks, "suppose I come along and we lay it before Farrant together?"

She accepted joyfully, but they found that Farrant was out. He had left no word at his hotel when he would be back. May Dickins decided to wait on the chance of his return, but after a quarter of an hour the major had to leave her. He had an engagement.

As May sat on, her spirits slowly fell. In spite of herself, what she remembered most clearly was not Hardy's hopeful words but Armstrong's voice as he replied to that early morning telephone on the day on which he was murdered, "Farrant? Indeed! You may be certain I'll look into the matter." Again she saw his face, and his gesture when he came out of the library and stood a moment, unobserved, as he thought.

Major Hardy's theory seemed somehow weaker, the longer she thought it over... Suddenly she heard Farrant's voice almost at her elbow.

Two people had come into the drawing-room, which had been empty but for herself. It was Farrant and his sister Daisy, a handsome, bold-eyed young woman dressed in the height of the moment's fashion. Just now her color was most unbecomingly real and not the shade that went best under coral rouge.

"Not another word!" she said under her breath, but in the tone of a woman almost beside herself with suppressed fury, and careless as to who hears her. "Not another word, nor another step with me either, Willie. I know now who shot Boyd Armstrong! Poor blind Bob, who trusted you so! Just as I believed in you—up to now." With a whirlwind action Daisy Farrant left the room. Farrant, imperturbable as ever, his light eyes staring straight ahead of him, followed after an interval. Neither of them had seen May Dickins in the big grandfather's chair. She sat on a moment. What had Daisy learned? Had she, too, seen some letter to Farrant? Well, May herself intended to write him one now—on the spot. She sat down at a little table, and after a minute of black immobility snatched up a pen and wrote swiftly and plainly. She told Farrant that she would keep her word, no matter what happened, that she had laid the whole matter before Major Hardy, who advised her to have a talk with Farrant, but that she felt too shaken in her conviction of his complete innocence in the matter to care to continue to count him any longer among her friends. She sealed it, and sent up word that she would like to speak to Mr. Farrant for a moment. He came down at once. She only handed him the letter—she dared not leave it for him—and without any but the barest of greetings for the sake of onlookers, left both him and the hotel.

It was just at that moment that Schofild was leaving Pointer's rooms at the Yard. But he was stopped by a constable entering, who brought in word that Major Hardy and Mr. Wilkins were there and would like to speak to the chief inspector.

Pointer had them shown in at once.

"Mr. Wilkins telephoned to me a few minutes ago, and what he had to say seemed to me so odd that I asked him to come at once and see you," Hardy began, before the door closed. He turned expectantly to the shabby, weary-looking man beside him.

"I would like to see the Chinese wedding-chest in which the body of Mr. Armstrong was found," Mr. Wilkins said. "For the first time today, I happened to see what purports to be a photograph of it in an old newspaper, and—well—I should like very much to see it."

Pointer was exceedingly interested. So was Schofild. Hardy evidently had had his surprize.

The chest was at the Yard standing in a bare room off Pointer's innermost room. They all four stood around it within the minute. Pointer could not imagine what was coming. Would it answer some of his own questions since his talk with the vanmen just now?

The little missionary only gave the chest one glance, then he turned.

"Yes, I'm right. This isn't a wedding-chest. It's a coffin. They've altered it in various slight ways: locks, hinges, and so on, but it's a Chinese coffin just the same."

"Are you sure of that, Sir?" Pointer asked, with but little question in his voice. Mr. Wilkins' whole manner said that he was sure of it, and also that he was not a man to speak certainly of what he did not know.

"They're often used as wedding-chests nowadays," the missionary went on, "but Mr. Lee must have known what it was he was selling you."

"A coffin!" muttered the major, looking long at the present which he had sent in to the dead man's wife.

"Just so," Schofild nodded meaningly. "Young Lee's wife goes off with an Englishman, and the elder Lee sells this coffin to be given to a man who is found lying murdered in it when it is opened; who may, for all we know, be the very man who ran off with his daughter-in-law. In my opinion there's more than a possibility of a connection here."

"Any objection to my taxing him with it?" Major Hardy asked. "I'd like to hear what he has to say. And then I want to go on and hear what Rufus Armstrong has to say!"

"Would any ordinary collector of Chinese things know it for what it is?" Pointer asked. At the question, Major Hardy turned and gave him one meaning look.

"If he knew anything at all of China itself, he must have known what this was," Wilkins said. "Of course, if he's never been to the country itself—"

"Both Rufus Armstrong and the two Lees knew what it was, all right," Hardy said fiercely. "As for me, I never pretended to know anything beyond the usual Chinese things, and—the Armstrongs were in the same position."

Pointer had no objection to Lee being questioned on a point of which he must have full knowledge. It rather explained to him why the two Chinese had not been over pleased to see Mr. Wilkins... they might well have thought that he would at once learn from the talk what the real article was that had been sent as a chest.

But did it mean more than that? And why had Rufus Armstrong let the deception pass? If indeed he had not instigated it! He finally asked the major to leave the matter of the wedding-chest being really a coffin in his, and Schofild's hands. The major gave way with a tightening of his lips.

"My little chat can come afterwards just as well as before," he said significantly, and left them.

Schofild, turning and re-turning the pieces of the puzzle in his mind, and rejecting each incomplete picture, also hurried away. He wanted to question the vanmen for himself.

Before going to the Lees, Pointer asked Mr. Wilkins to drive with him to the house in Charles Street, and there run a very careful—and experienced—eye over the double doors leading into the suite.

"I want to make quite sure there is no secret panel, or anything of that kind," Pointer spoke quietly enough as he drove off with the missionary beside him, but he felt almost desperate. Mr. Wilkins' interest in the chest had not advanced matters.

Outside the great doors on the first-floor landing Mr. Wilkins peered intently at them.

Gong doors, he called them, referring to the noise they made when opening or shutting, and after that he settled down to a steady inspection. The result was an assurance from him that they were what they seemed— temple doors of solid unity.

The same inspection was made at the little side doors. Here again Mr. Wilkins could find no sign of cut or division, or possibility of entrance. And this time, with many thanks, he was allowed to go.

Pointer telephoned to Rufus Armstrong. He was away at the races. He left a message that he would be obliged if he would ring him—the chief inspector—up as soon as he returned, as the latter had something to say which would, he felt sure, interest Mr. Rufus Armstrong greatly.

CHAPTER TEN

WHEN Mr. Wilkins left him, Pointer stood for a moment with head bent, hands in pockets, eyes on his shoes, as, deep in thought, he paced the length of the Chinese suite back and forth.

He had tested and re-tested, and just now tested again, the possibility of a silent, unnoticed entry into these rooms, and, as always, had been told that such a thing was impossible. He had had an architect, one whose specialty was hidden passages, go over the house and corroborate his own belief that there was no possibility of an entrance into these three rooms by way of papered wall, or wooden floor, or dragon plastered ceiling. Yet if an entry, unnoticed, were possible—as he thought the case over in its present form, with the breakdown of the van carrying the chest standing for nothing in the circle of the crime, instead of being, as hitherto considered, its hub—he saw a straight theory of the murder which explained all the known facts. Yes, he said to himself, eliminate the idea that Armstrong's body had been in the chest when it arrived at Charles Street, and the whole case becomes logical—according to this theory—*provided* an entry had been possible. He put it on one side and tried for other theories of what had happened, and tried in vain. Many theories would fit many points, but he found only one that would fit all. Yet for it to be right in this case meant that there must be some way into that suite, which seemed so well guarded. Bar that apparent impossibility, his theory explained everything so simply. Supposing he were to test it, would he find other material objections beside the doors that no one could open or shut without every one in the house knowing of the fact?

Armstrong was said to have been fond of testing theories, with Pointer, too, it was liking as well as the necessity of his calling that made him prove his ideas up to the hilt.

He decided that he would see where each step of his theory would lead him, and whether it must be abandoned—even before he got as far as the impenetrable suite. His theory rested on the belief that Armstrong had been murdered in the house itself. Well, yes, even apart from his theory, it was hardy possible for a dead body to have been carried into the house from outside in broad daylight except in that chest. Pointer's men had already made most searching inquiries about all hampers and big bundles received at the house. Yes, he told himself, he might safely assume that the murder had taken place in Armstrong's home.

His theory suggested the library... According to it, Armstrong must have reentered his house unnoticed, using the side door, from which a passage passed the library door leading to the narrow stairs which joined the main stairs at the first landing just outside the little sewing-room. A heavy gold damask curtain across part of the landing hid stairs and sewing-room from the view of the rest of the house. Yes, granted that Armstrong had returned to his house from his office, the library would be the natural choice, and since his return had not been noticed by the passing servants, then his library was the one room one would expect him to have entered —where one would expect the crime to have taken place.

Quite apart from the chief inspector's idea of the march of events, Armstrong's bedroom was next to his wife's, and Mrs. Armstrong's maid had been in and out of the latter preparing and altering the frock that Mrs. Armstrong wore at the reception.

It was almost out of the question that Armstrong could have been shot and his body carried down the corridor with the maid passing every minute or sewing with the door of the room open, as she said that she had kept it. But though to carry a dead body up the stairs from the library would take physical strength, it passed no other doors on the way. Granted that the sewing-room, off the Chinese suite, had been as deserted as it undoubtedly was until four o'clock on the day of the murder, then the body could have been carried up into it with the minimum of danger. Yes, Pointer felt that he could pass the theory of library as the place where Armstrong had been shot. Shot in the library, then carried upstairs in what?

Pointer eyed his shoe tips very closely indeed. No bloodstains anywhere in the house... Supposing, as his theory did, that nothing had been brought into the house in which to carry up the body, what could have been used? It would have to be something which would not be missed if taken away. Yet the library, though well furnished, had no spare draperies. Then it was still in the house, for the man who wrapped up the body, lest bloodstains should betray its passage, would not have roamed the house to hunt for something suitable. Whatever was used must have been already in the library or in the writing-room opening out of it, and would, in all likelihood, be still in it. One of the Yard's plain clothes men was still on duty, and nothing of the size that Pointer had in mind had left since the chief inspector had arrived, for his theory did not connect the Chinese musicians with the murder, and they alone had passed out unnoticed. If you wrap a dead man up to carry him, you need a good deal of spare length to sling over your shoulder, and a good deal of spare width in which to roll him... and the material must be stout...

The eye of Pointer's roaming mind settled instantly on the crimson hanging curtains each side of the big library windows, curtains of patterned wine and rust color. Stiff damask... admirable for the purpose. They hung, he remembered, in close folds against the walls banded back with strips of their own material, and since the day of the murder had not been drawn, as the lowered blinds were ample shield from observation for any one going in there at night, and, barring the police, no one had entered the room since the tragedy, except in daylight.

If his theory were right, there would, there must be, bloodstains on one of those curtains, rather high up...

Anywhere else in the room? It was possible that the top sheet of the blotting pad had been taken away because of blood spatters on it. But not necessarily so. His theory pointed to another reason for its removal as still more probable.

He left the Chinese suite, clanged the door shut behind him, locked it with the sound of exploding rockets, and went down into the library. He was just about to turn the key on himself there when Schofild was shown in.

"I've seen the vanmen. Like you, I'm satisfied they're telling the truth, and nothing but it, and the whole of it, as far as they know it. Well" —Schofild flung himself into a chair that creaked wildly—"I shall soon begin to see into this case. Don't think too hard of me, chief inspector, if I don't clear it all up immediately when I do. I must have certainty first. And who knows, you yourself may meantime get a line on the criminal, too."

"No knowing," Pointer said cheerfully, as he locked the door and went into the farthest of the three rooms, returning with some library steps that he placed near the window. After one glance up inside the helmet, he chose a curtain that had one ring not properly hooked in place, undid the band, mounted the steps, and proceeded to take the curtain down.

"Helping with the spring cleaning?" Schoffici asked, puzzled.

"Yes, in a way I suppose I am," and Pointer let the heavy mass slide to the floor, then, springing down, he straightened it out on the parquet.

Schofild, with an exclamation, was beside him, feeling the material inch by inch, just as he was feeling it. Almost simultaneously they touched something stiffer than the rest of the red and rust-colored material. Fairly near the top, just where Pointer had expected it to be, was a large-ish patch of about a foot in circumference. A curious feeling came over Pointer as his fingers rested on it. It would be analyzed, of course, but he knew the touch of dried blood.

The private investigator murmured something under his breath. It sounded like "But this is impossible! Impossible!"

He got up, and together with Pointer they walked the room inch by inch. Schofild noticed afresh how the flooring creaked under their steps. Any one moving in here could easily have been heard in the hall outside. There were no bloodstains on the boards, but when Pointer turned over the third of the three, rugs, they found on the back of it several places varying in size from a half-crown to a dinner plate, where the color showed up under Pointer's electric torch as slightly different from the rest. The chief inspector chalked each place so found.

"Good God!" Schofild knelt staring at the rug, "Armstrong was shot here in this room! That's what those marks mean, Pointer. And bloodstains on the blotter, too, probably. Yes, Armstrong was, in my opinion, sitting in that chair there by his desk when he was shot, or perhaps he was standing by his writing-table. In either case he had his pen in his hand... I think it fell to the floor, and rolled out of sight until the murderer put the room to rights. Congratulations."

He jumped up. "There's nothing like quick eyes for detail to help to conclusions. I told you that, together, we should solve the mystery! If so, Major Hardy must be in it, too." Schofild went on very gravely, with genuine regret, "I don't see how else... in fact it can't be done otherwise. That Chinese suite can't be entered except by the main doors that make such a racket, and which are in full sight... the chest must have been brought in here for a moment... Armstrong was already dead, lying wrapped in that curtain, probably under the Empire couch over there... I'm sorry about the major... though, as I told you, I learned that there was some gossip about him and Mrs.

Armstrong last winter in Biskra. Armstrong wasn't there.
It has died out lately. You agree with me, I suppose?" His
tone was equivalent to certainty.

. "I don't think it's possible for Armstrong's body to
have been put into that chest before it was placed in the
suite," was all Pointer would say, "there were too many
eyes on it."

"I should like to think so," Schofild spoke almost
wistfully, "but what's impossible is impossible. There's no
way into the suite, remember, except by what I might call
the public way. No, the major is in it. Pity!"

They looked over the second-room, the writing-room,
and found nothing whatever to detain them in it.

"Better look in the third room, if only for form's sake,"
Schofild said, a little grudgingly.

He disliked searches, and the first room was all that
mattered in this case, he thought.

As for Pointer, whether he found any marks to
support it or not, his theory pre-supposed that a man had
hidden in the farthest of the three rooms on the day that
Boyd Armstrong was murdered.

Together they now entered the musty, dusty little
den. The one door leading into it from the writing-room
was in the middle. All the walls were lined to the ceiling
with double book cases, that slid to and fro at a touch on
narrow, three-foot-long rails let into the floor, so as to
permit of the books in the back shelves of the cases, and
on the wall shelves proper, being reached.

Each case in turn was now pulled out, examined front
and back, the shelves behind it examined, and then the
case slid back and the next one taken. They had begun at
the left of the central door. Only when they were nearly
round again did they have their reward. But like many
things that come late, it was worth waiting for. On sliding
out the case nearest but one to the door, both men
stopped for a second. Behind it, the wall shelves had been
removed for some distance, the books tumbled into a pile
under the window belonged here, they saw. The shelves

that had been taken out had been forced on top of other shelves above and below. This made a niche where a man, or woman, could have sat in comfort.

Pointer stooped instantly, and nodded on rising. "Bootblacking on the lowest books."

"From the heels of whoever made this hiding-place and sat here—look at this!" Schofild had now slid forward the very last bookcase, and was pointing to what it had concealed—an unsmoked cigar lying on the edge of a shelf where it would have been handy for a man sitting in the little niche. Pointer picked it up gingerly with his flippers. By the mark it left in the dust around it when lifted, it had not lain here long. Say three days, Pointer thought. Evidently whoever had to attend to this end room scamped his or her work and did not pull the sliding cases out daily, or even weekly. The niche, on the other hand, was quite clean.

They both studied the cigar closely. It had a curious, sickly, sweetish smell.

"Opium in it," both murmured.

"The proof!" Schofild chortled under his breath. "At least, I think it will turn out to be that. It looks as though the man who sat here —I can't name him yet, Pointer, not for a while longer, had thought of a smoke, expecting a long wait apparently, but had suddenly remembered that the smell might betray him. He took out the cigar and laid it down after remembering where he was. You see, this is where I come in, in reconstructing the crime from the clues we find together. 'Cigar'—I'll call him that for the present—'Cigar' wanted to hear something— wanted that intensely. He doesn't merely try to hide," Schofild continued; "he wants to hear what is going on... I confess I don't know what—nor why."

Pointer's theory covered this too. But he said nothing.

"Will you talk in the adjoining room as though to some one else, and I will see how much I can hear?"

The chief inspector, shutting the door between them, talked conversationally to himself, now high, now very low. Schofild, with his ear against the wall, was able to repeat even the softest spoken word, and his hearing was not as keen as Pointer's.

They went back to the library proper.

"I wonder why there is no clock on the mantel," Pointer said suddenly. "Yet there's an empty place as though one had stood between those two bronzes."

"Perhaps Armstrong disliked the sound of ticking," Schofild suggested without much interest.

"It's quite possible. He has no clock in his room at his office. And there, too, there's a space that seems made for it over the fireplace. There's a bronze clock here in this cupboard," Pointer took it out, a charming piece of French work, "but it's not going. There are a few fingerprints on it. The latest look to me like those of Armstrong himself."

"There you are!" Schofild had turned away. "I'll just put it back, all the same, and have a word with the butler."

"Why? Routine?"

"No, curiosity," was the reply, and the chief inspector pressed the button.

When the butler answered it, he was alone in the house except for a couple of under servants. Pointer asked him where the library clock was. The man seemed surprized. He turned towards the mantel and stopped in perplexity. His eyes roamed the room.

"It was in its usual place on the mantel the day that Mr. Armstrong—died. I laid lunch in here, because of the other rooms being more or less in confusion—yes, lunch was in here, and I remember the clock striking one o'clock. I went by my watch. But I remember hearing it strike the hour. I can't think what's happened to it, I'm not used to the things in the establishment yet," he went on apologetically. The staff had been in Lord Nunhead's service. "I can't be sure what kind of a clock it was, but I think it was bronze." Suddenly he pounced on something in a cupboard that Pointer negligently opened. "This is it, sir! Been put in here, I see. This dreadful affair has upset the household. I shall be thankful when the place is closed." He set the clock on the mantel and pulled out his own gold watch.

"It's stopped. Funny! It's an eight-day clock, and I wind them every Saturday morning. And it is wound." He tested the winder, and shook the clock.

"You're sure it was going at noon on Saturday?" Schofild asked with no real interest.

The butler repeated, again, that he had heard it striking just before he served the luncheon.

"Ah, well," Pointer said, as though it were of no importance, as indeed it was in Schofild's eyes, "a man is coming from the Yard later on who understands all about clocks. I'll get him to have a look at it."

The butler set it in its place and closed the door after him. Pointer looked the clock over carefully. He put his gloves on to do so. There were many fingerprints on it, as he had just said to Schofild, the latest looked to him like one of Armstrong himself. He next opened the back. In the main-spring a sliver of paper had been inserted. Removing that, he found that the clock went perfectly. Some one had wanted to stop it. The some one— Armstrong—presumably, who had placed it in a cupboard. He was puzzled... This tiny item was outside his theory. Or was it tiny?

"Going to be sent off somewhere, evidently to the clockmakers." Schofild rose. "Well, I must hurry away. I'm going all out on that cigar trail. In my opinion it'll lead us home." He paused at the door. "I feel I ought to give you a leg up in return for that curtain you happened on. To the men who are already in the crime circle, we must add the man who sat listening in that furthermost room, and who intended to smoke that cigar. Remember he must have known the house, known all about the bookcases sliding forward, and known that he could hear what went on in the center room. And here ends my lecture." Schofild gave a little laugh as the telephone bell rang.

It was from Rufus Armstrong. He could see the chief inspector at once, either at his house or at the Yard. Pointer chose the former as being more convenient. He asked if Mr. Schofild might come too.

"You do want to see Mr. Rufus Armstrong, don't you?" he inquired suavely, as he hung up, on hearing that Mr. Schofild was welcome to accompany the detective officer.

Schofild eyed him.

"I'm not so sure about you, Pointer," he muttered. "You seem to have a knack of guessing things."

Pointer only hurried out to his car.

They found Rufus polishing some jade with his hand, rubbing the smooth patina to a still silkier sheen.

"It just this," Pointer said, after, the briefest of greetings all around, "we are told that the wedding-chest in which Mr. Armstrong was found is in reality a Chinese coffin."

He purposely made his sentence as short as possible so as to give the other no time to arrange his reply. Yet Rufus Armstrong took time —plenty of it.

"It is both," he said at length. "Nowadays in China the wedding-chest is often the coffin too. I recommended this particular one, of which you are speaking, to Major Hardy, simply because I thought it the most beautiful piece of work I had seen in years. It was to stand at the head of the Chinese suite, and whether called coffin, or wedding-chest, would be a superb sight, seen from the big double doors."

He spoke quite easily, and went on stroking his jade circlet.

"Will it be one of the four articles you are to select from Mr. Armstrong's objects of art?" Pointer asked in the same tone.

Rufus Armstrong's dark eyes rested on him thoughtfully. "Yes," he said finally, and offered his guests their choice of cigars and cigarettes.

Schofild, who smoked the former, bent over the boxes with interest.

"Nothing Chinese," he asked, "nothing with just a whiff of poppy to sweeten the nicotine?"

"You'll have to go to Callard for that sort of thing." Rufus spoke almost contemptuously. "He's trying to introduce that sort of a cigar very discreetly. I confess I find them pretty deadly."

Schofild seemed able to console himself with one of the brands in front of him, and for a few minutes the talk was general and vague about Armstrong's last days and general character. Rufus spoke of his cousin with decent though tempered affection. Of Mrs. Armstrong he spoke not at all, unless directly, questioned. When they rose, Pointer turned to his host.

"We want to ask the Lees some questions about that coffin—chest. Will you be kind enough to come, too, and check his answers?"

"Quite unnecessary!" Rufus said promptly. "You'll find him absolutely reliable."

But Pointer was insistent on having him come too. Pointer did not want Rufus Armstrong telephoning to the Lees before he could get there.

Finally Rufus yielded, though he professed to be in a great hurry. Arrived at Limehouse, they found the father in.

Mr. Lee bowed profoundly. He realized, he said, of course, that coffins did not head the list of presents to valued friends in this country as they did in his own, and that Mr. Rufus Armstrong, when he referred to it as a wedding-chest, had not seen it clearly in full daylight, and that therefore he, Lee, should have—

Rufus Armstrong cut him short.

"I take all responsibility for the sale of it as a wedding-chest. I knew that what my cousin's wife wanted was a beautiful place in which to store her Chinese embroideries and shawls, and beautiful the coffin was, and is. A noble piece of work. Personally, if I had my way, my cousin should be buried in it."

"I feel sure that he would realize much pleasure," murmured Mr. Lee sincerely.

Armstrong hurried off. Schofild and Pointer seemed to have time to spare. Mr. Lee brought out his cigars and cigarettes and offered refreshments as before, yellow wine from Shoa-hsing served in warmed, dainty handleless cups, and wine that looked like water, but which was supposed locally to make a tortoise frisky. Both were declined.

Schofild looked over the cigars and recited his little, piece about poppy-sweetened nicotine.

"I had a box of those," Mr. Lee murmured in what looked like hospitable regret, "but Mr. Rufus Armstrong bought them. These, however, poor though they are, are supposed to be bearable smokes."

Schofild took one and was enthusiastic; then he left them. He had scribbled the words, "Going on to Callard" on his cuff, and, as he stretched out his arm for a cigar, the words had come into Pointer's view.

The chief inspector sat on after the other had gone. He had not taken either cigar or cigarette. He could not be quite sure what the interview would bring to light.

"Mr. Lee, will you forgive me touching on a very delicate family matter?"

Mr. Lee's eyes seemed to withdraw themselves like the head of a tortoise into his shell.

"Any interest shown will be considered a compliment," he said imperturbably.

"It's about young Mr. Lee, and"—Pointer hesitated, but he went on—"and his first marriage."

"Yes?" came calmly, "yes, Mr. Chief Inspector?"

"The name of the man who ran away with her was Adams, was it not?"

Mr. Lee nodded, his eyes were on the other's face.

"Could you describe him to me?"

Still the old eyes looked steadily at him.

"It would be a most inauspicious day if you bring news of him—or her," he said finally. "This morning my fifth grandchild was born to me. It would be a most unfortunate day on which to hear news of old family misfortune."

"I only want a description of his looks," Pointer repeated. The eyes dwelt on him, then the thin lids fell.

"I think I see where the light of wisdom is falling," murmured Mr. Lee. "Permit my saying it is not falling on right spot. You think there was connection between my family and the man who was found dead in chest we sold Major Hardy? Mr. High Police Officer, this must be looked at the right way. There was no connection. The man who, for a time, ruined my family's happiness, was short, thin, and had hair the color of unclean copper. For a time there was hatred of him and of her in this family. But that was because the matter was not looked at in the right way. Now we are wiser. Now we know that great happiness can wipe out old disgrace. This man Adams did my son great service. My son is a happy man, a father of four beautiful boys and one beautiful girl child. I am a happy grandfather."

Pointer listened intently. Unless Mr. Lee was a really remarkable actor he was speaking out of a very full heart. As a rule the chief inspector kept his beliefs and his conduct as strictly apart as any weak-kneed believer who sings hymns on Sunday and picks pockets on Monday, but he had come to a pass in this case where he must break through somehow to the light.

"You know Chinese teaching of man?" Mr. Lee went on, as though half to himself, "the animal world on one side of us, the celestial world on the other, and man the link between the two, capable of living in either, as he chooses, but intended to serve as union of both? This family's old feeling about my son's first marriage belonged to animal kingdom, but now opinion and feeling belongs to Higher Kingdom." He smiled with what looked like real benignity.

Pointer rose. He determined to venture his last cast.

"Then will you come with me and have a look at the house where that chest was delivered, Mr. Armstrong's house? I want you to see if you can suggest any possible way that the body could have gone into the rooms except through the main doors. It must have been done. But— this is in strictest confidence, Mr. Lee—I still cannot see how it could have been done."

"Impossible that my little eye should see what your enormous orb does not," murmured Mr. Lee, but he got up with alacrity.

"The doors are Chinese, Mr. Lee. Each man to his own country. I still have an idea, for instance, that the chief flute player of that orchestra, Mr. Wong was his name, saw something that I missed, and still miss, and that every one of us Europeans who have examined the doors have missed. Perhaps you can help me to find out what it was."

"The eyes of age see inward, not outward," Mr. Lee murmured deprecatingly, but he followed Pointer very quickly to the car. In the house he stood before the great doors with a deep breath of pleasure.

"From my land, as you say. Not a copy." He touched the wood with a gentle old finger. "A beautiful land that I shall never see again. But my coffin will take my body back so that my dust will be its dust." He smiled as though at a delightful prospect. Pointer explained the noise that the door and the key made. He demonstrated his words. Mr. Lee nodded. "That is generally the case," he murmured, "much noise so that all may know when one enters by these doors of ceremony."

"There's no way known to you of getting in without that sound?" Mr. Lee shook his head.

"It is intentional. Part of the way the hinges are cut," he told him.

"Now in here," Pointer led him into the farthest of the three rooms, the one where the coffin had stood, and pointed to the wall, "here is another smaller pair of doors. As far as I can find out, there is no way of opening them or getting in through them. They are locked and we know of no key in existence. Besides, to all appearances, the lock has had no key inserted in it for years, let alone turned in its wards."

Mr. Lee examined the doors, tapped them carefully, and shook his head. "Little eye sees nothing," he murmured regretfully.

"Then will you look at them from the other side?" Pointer asked. He led Mr. Lee into the sewing-room. The room where Mr. Wong had been.

Mr. Lee bent close to the doors, he had put on his second pair of glasses. He now added a third.

Suddenly he turned, taking off two pairs. "This lock does not open with a key. Keyhole only made for look. Real way to open is secret. This is rare court puzzle-lock."

He explained to Pointer that though this particular kind was unusual, such locks were not uncommon in China. No keys were ever made to fit them. To open them, you had to press some part or parts of the elaborate decoration in regular sequence, generally three times running. The sequence would be given to the purchaser of the lock in the first place and by him handed down to some member of his family.

Pointer asked him if he were certain that this was such a lock. Mr. Lee explained that, as a rule, the thickness of the lock, the distance the keyhole from the side of the door, and the elaborate high relief of the ornamentation on the sides and top of the lock all told an experienced eye—such as his own—what kind of a lock he had before him, but in this case he only could have recognized from especial knowledge. "Mr. Wong brought a family chest away from China with him, from his father's palace, that has a similar lock. Much smaller, of course, but made on the same plan. It was a gift from an Emperor to his grandfather. It has a prayer in Chinese engraved around it as part of the puzzle. This lock made by same man, I think."

"Do you think you could open it for me?" Pointer asked. Mr. Lee said he could not. "Could Mr. Wong?"

Mr. Lee had been about to suggest him. "He is a great mathematician, but he now earns his living as puzzle-maker. He makes very good puzzles. He could find out this secret if any man can."

"Certainly it needs to be looked at the right way," Pointer murmured, abandoning any further effort on his part to solve the mechanism.

Mr. Lee chuckled, and hurried off in a taxi, promising to bring Mr. Wong back as soon as possible.

He was as good as his word. They arrived before Pointer had dared hope to see them.

Mr. Lee had a word or two with him in the musical Mandarin tongue. Wong looked at the door and gave a sudden shrill laugh.

"You have found out the truth," he said to Pointer, and Lee translated. "We say truth is drawn to a true man." Then he bent over the lock...

"Honorable work. Highly honorable work. Honor to me even to try to find out such well-devised secret. Hopeless without my family knowledge of similar piece."

Pointer asked Mr. Lee how long Wong thought it would take him. Mr. Wong in answer, pulled some tables out of the pocket of his bright blue suit. Counted the bosses of the lock, the scales of the dragon, the petals of the flowers, did some calculations on an abacus which Mr. Lee had in his pocket, and then said:

"If lucky, it might be done in two hours. If unlucky, it might take me two days" And with that he set to work, touching here and touching there, pressing this and trying to move that, and each time referring to his tables of calculation and his abacus that clicked like western knitting needles. Mr. Lee seated beside him inked in notes as the younger man worked. He had colored chalks with which Wong marked strange dots and stars here and there on the ornaments of the lock as he fingered it.

CHAPTER ELEVEN

THERE is a curious law in crime detection. A sort of doubled rule of "unto him that hath," and "from him that hath not"... Once let a step forward be taken with great difficulty, and let there be no longer acute need of help, and along comes assistance in plenty. A herbalist, as he called himself, a street seller of groundsel for canaries and lavender in its season, had been off in the country. No reader of newspapers, the man had only just been told of the murder of Mr. Armstrong by a maid opposite, to whom he sold a weekly bunch of green stuff for her bird. She showed him the picture of the murdered man, the house, and the inmates. He promptly made his way to the nearest police station.

His story was that on the day in question he had been in the street on which the side door opened, and had seen a man walk very quickly down the street and hurry through the door in question, letting himself in with a key which he took from his waistcoat pocket. The hawker said that there had been an effect of careful avoidance of noise both about the way, the door was opened and the way it was shut. He positively identified Farrant as this man. He was quite certain of him, and supplied details of his dress which had not been furnished to the press in order to check up any statements. Pointer had a long talk with the man. It was just a little before two that he had brought the servant in question her bird food, and it was while he was ringing the area bell for her that he had seen Farrant.

A few test questions as to men passed on the way into Pointer's room, showed that Anderson had the keen eyes and faculty of remembering what they have seen, which generally accompanies good wits and a lack of reading matter. The world about him had to be Anderson's library and daily paper. It supplied him with serials and short stories in plenty. Schofild, too, put him through his paces, but nothing could shake the hawker. He had noticed correctly, even the color of Farrant's hat and of his gloves.

"Which makes me wonder afresh where Armstrong's are," Schofild said, as the man had been thanked, rewarded, and dismissed. "As for Farrant, well, we now know what we suspected all along that he had a very good reason for his alibi only starting with the afternoon hours." Schofild thought the case over in silence for a few minutes, then he said, "About that cigar we found. I came round to tell you that Callard bought a consignment of them from another firm of Eastern importers—not the Lees—after trying one at Rufus Armstrong's. The consignment isn't paid for yet."

"You do surprise me!" came from Pointer.

Schofild laughed. "He's selling them on commission. They're not really doped, barely a hint of opium. And apparently Callard started business by giving some away to all his friends—I mean acquaintances, he hasn't any friends—for them to sample. For which reason, the finding of that cigar proves nothing really, except that it was some one possibly who knew Callard... In my opinion, as I say, it may very likely have been Callard himself, in which case he was not the murderer, Pointer, but heard or saw the murder done, and is keeping his news to himself for purposes of blackmailing Farrant. That eavesdropper's niche looks very like Percy to me."

Pointer took down his receiver as the bell rang. He hung it up swiftly and fairly leaped from his seat.

"Wong has opened the door!" he said, as he, too, performed the same act, but with considerably less time and trouble. Down the stairs the two bounded like boys, to fling themselves into Pointer's car and whiz off. But the door between the sewing-room and the Chinese suite was not standing open when the two men let themselves into the little side room and locked its door behind them.

Wong and old Mr. Lee were sitting talking; the lacquer double doors looked as usual, barring tiny dots of color on the decorated lock.

Both Chinese bowed. "He waited for you," Lee explained, waving a fan towards Wong and again bowing, but this time much lower and in the direction of his compatriot.

Wong took a step forward, his back to the others. His rather, good-looking young face was tense but beaming. His eyes seemed like glittering jet as he ran his yellow fingers in a certain succession over rosettes, petals, and dragon scales. Without a sound, much less without a click, the door stood open. Mr. Wong waved his hands towards the opening. Old Mr. Lee now produced his diagrams and tables and explained the sequences marked in colored chalks. It was a great moment. Pointer shook hands with Wong, and thanked him warmly. He asked him to let him know his charge for the help that he had given. Mr. Lee smiled and translated a sudden gush of words from Wong.

"He says," the older man murmured, "not to speak of money. This was done with pleasure because Mr. Rufus Armstrong asked us to help you in any way. Mr. Rufus Armstrong"—he hesitated, and then went on hurriedly and running his words together as though afraid that Wong might understand them if spoken clearly —"he helps Chinese. He helped me and my son start. He helps refugees such as honorable son of noble house standing beside me. That was why we wanted his cousin to have the chest. To keep it safe."

"To keep it for Mr. Rufus Armstrong?" Pointer nodded casually.

Lee bobbed his head. "He would not let me take it out of shop. But by selling to his relation, he could arrange in time to buy it from them if they not pleased. That why, whether wedding-chest or coffin seemed of not much importance in my foolish mind. But my tongue is talking too much."

In spite of all Pointer's pressing, Mr. Wong refused to take a penny for his work, and he and Mr. Lee left the house together, smiling long smiles of content that made their dark eyes mere slits in their pale faces.

Behind them the two investigators solemnly shook hands.

"What luck!" Schofild said fervently. "What amazing luck! But I suggest the writing-room for a talk. That squeaky floor of the library gives excellent warning of any one coming near the door. Now, let me see," Schollld said, as they made, their way there. "I'd like to tabulate for you the facts that we now know. This is how we stand. Armstrong was murdered in the library. Farrant was in the house at an hour that would admit of his having done it. Armstrong's corpse was carried upstairs in the curtain you came on, and laid in the chest after the men had placed the latter in position and left. Whoever put the body in knew the secret of the lock. Now, who would know that? Nunhead for one."

"It seems that Lord Nunhead had practically completed the arrangements for the sale of the house before his death," Pointer said. "Lady Nunhead has written to me to say that the papers connected with the purchase of the Chinese fitments and objects were handed to Mr. Armstrong personally by her late husband."

"Ah!" Schofild came out of his theory for a second. "Then Farrant, as Armstrong's trusty aid, could have seen the papers giving the written directions of how to open the smaller doors. But there's another man who also came to Charles Street the day of the murder—and may, or may not, have left before it. He was a great friend of Nunhead's... helped him fit out that Chinese suite... it's much more than a guess that he knew..."

"Mr. Rufus Armstrong told us both that he knew of no way into the suite except the obvious one;" Pointer agreed.

"What people say interests me very little, Pointer, in comparison to what they think. But there's one more item you ought to know. Little Billy—Nunhead's only son— used to be a pal of Callard's. Billy and he started some speed-boat racing venture somewhere or other, and lost their respective pennies over it."

"Lord Nunhead's son is dead, I understand?" Pointer asked.

"Yes. Went to Southern Rhodesia and had to race a lion back to camp one night. Poor Billy lost." This was Schofild's short way of relating a really nasty tragedy. "So then," he went on, "it's quite likely that Callard, too, knew of the lock. And he would know that the chest was empty. Whereas we have no reason to think that Farrant knew of this latter point. Hardy may have known of the empty chest, for he had the opportunity, I still think, to look inside it when it arrived, but I don't think he could have known about the lock. And I'm glad to say that I think his air of being simply appalled at the tragedy was not acting. How long do you imagine it would take to work that combination and get the door open?"

"Mr. Lee has written down here 'Three minutes if well known'."

There came the sound of a ring at the door.

"Look here," Pointer said quickly, "that's probably Farrant. I phoned him to come on here as soon as I heard the doors were opened. Will you take him on and keep him here talking over the ease for half an hour after I leave? I shall slip out soon after he gets in. Probably while he's inspecting the opened door upstairs."

Schofild asked no questions; he merely nodded. "Even if he knows all about it, he'll have to pretend to be dumbfounded," he added under his breath.

A moment later and loud squeaks on the floor of the library heralded a servant. It was Farrant whom he announced. Farrant certainly acted to the life the man amazed beyond words when Pointer and Schofild told him of the latest development. They took him up to the sewing-room, and there Pointer showed him the way the lock worked. They even worked at it together, Farrant apparently incredulous of the existence of such a mechanism. Then Pointer slipped away, and Schofild discussed with the former private secretary the new avenues opened up by this discovery. They talked them over in the morning-room, for Farrant had turned away from the library, to which Schofild would have led the way, with a slight but quite definite air of preferring another place for a conversation.

A servant came in with something glittering on a salver. "We found these lying in the hall, sir. I don't know if they belong to either of you gentlemen or to Mr. Pointer?"

Farrant snatched up the bunch of keys with a pounce.

"Mine! I can't imagine   " His hand flew to his pocket in swift dismay. "Why, the chain's been cut!" He stared white-faced at Schofild.

"You said something about having come by tube," Schofild murmured, "those crowds in the lifts are the haunts of pickpockets. Did you lose anything? Or was it just an attempt that didn't come off?"

Farrant ran a most perfunctory pair of hands through his pockets. "No, nothing is taken. But I can't think when these tumbled out—"

"I heard something drop just now, when we crossed the hall, but I thought it something below stairs," Schofild lied chattily, and began again on his ideas as to what the opened doors into the suite might mean.

He had barely re-started when Pointer came in again, this time with Major Hardy. Once more the lock was shown off, this time to a man who made no attempt to show amazement, but who only nodded with a dark and set face.

"So Armstrong wasn't murdered out of doors—nor on the way, but here—in this house!"

It was at Farrant that he stared with those penetrating eyes of his. But Farrant, looking oddly shaken, did not meet his glance.

"By the way," Pointer threw in now, "I want you both to come into the library for a moment." The three followed him into it.

"It's about that clock on the mantel," Pointer said. "The butler tells me that it was in its present condition when he laid lunch in here on the day Mr. Armstrong died. Do you remember seeing it, major?"

Hardy gave it a look, but his mind was too full of what he had just heard to make it easy for him to consider clocks.

"Yes," he said vaguely, "I went by it when worrying Lee about those plants and the chest. Why?"

Pointer explained where it had been found, and about the piece of paper inserted to stop it temporarily.

Hardy barely listened. Farrant seemed to pay close attention. "I understand that Mr. Rufus Armstrong is taking it," Hardy said, almost impatiently. "Perhaps Armstrong had intended giving it to him as a present. He may have admired it in his hearing. Armstrong was a very generous chap as we all know,"

"How do you mean 'taking it'?" Schofild asked the major.

"He's sent in the names of the four things he wants from the house. Most moderately chosen they are, too. None of them works of art, barring that accursed chest. That heads the list—of course he wants to have it destroyed. Second came this clock as a souvenir of Armstrong. The other two are portraits of no value except to a Border Armstrong."

"I suppose it really is just a clock," Schofild said, examining it while thinking of other things of Farrant chiefly and of Rufus Armstrong's list.

"It's going, isn't it?" Hardy asked, as though tired of clock talk. "It was on Saturday, for I heard it strike the half-hour, when I left the table and telephoned again about that chest."

"Yet it isn't striking it now," Pointer said quietly.

Schofild started. "My jove!" he eyed the clock carefully. "The striker, too, been deadened?" he asked. Pointer shook his head.

"It's not a striking clock. I had our Yard expert give it a look. Not that I expected that result. I merely wanted to know everything about it that I could. At first, when only the butler told me it had struck, I paid little attention to the statement, because I think him a thoroughly unreliable witness, not intentionally, but due to the fact of being a slovenly observer. Major Hardy, however, is another affair altogether. And he says he heard it strike on the day that Armstrong was murdered. Which apparently means that there was another clock in the room that day."

"Farrant, you must know," Hardy said impatiently. "What about it?"

All present glanced at Farrant. He did not see them. With distended eyes he stood rigid, staring at the mantleshelf, and at the clock on it. His face was quite white. Schofild could see a blue vein beating hard near his eyebrow. Then he seemed to recollect himself with a jerk.

"It's the clock all right," he said now, "It must have got into the cupboard by mistake... some one must have cleared away things..." He was talking rapidly, like a man trying to cover up a slip.

Hardy looked at him intently under his pent lids. And then Farrant took a very abrupt leave. Hardy followed after him, with a lifted eyebrow in Schofild and Pointer's direction, as though asking what they made of things.

"Though he is engaged to Farrant's sister, for the first time Hardy is beginning to doubt," Schofild said promptly.

"Yes, for the first time Hardy is wondering whether he hasn't been too certain of Farrant's innocence," he went on. "If he knew about his return at two on the day of the murder, I think he might feel no doubts whatever. But now what about those keys, Pointer? I hope you won't have me up for defamation of character if I connect you with that cut chain? If so, it's lucky you joined Scotland Yard. What did you do with the keys?"

"Used them," came the happy reply. "One of them, as you saw, was the key to a safe. I have had to do some stiff negotiating before the safe authorities would even listen to me. But I finally got their promise that if I presented myself with the right key I might be allowed to look into Farrant's safe. I wasn't to be alone with it for a moment," Pointer added, with rather a glum twist to his mouth, "but I was to be permitted to look into it surrounded by officials. Nor was I to use my knowledge publicly. But in spite of all these efforts, mine eyes have this last half-hour been permitted to rest for a moment upon what I am certain is Armstrong's felt hat, his gloves and something wrapped in a handkerchief which I feel sure is the .38 automatic that killed him, and a sheet of blotting paper which I am also certain came from that blotting pad there. From the hour, it would appear that Farrant drove to his safe and deposited those relics on his way to tell you about Armstrong's desire to see you beside the chest. The commissionaire says he was only a second in the little cubicle put at his disposal. And he noticed, too, how ill he looked as he came in. Ill and shaken, he thought."

"Just as he looked a moment ago," Schofild muttered. "Are you going to arrest him first and then have him open the safe before you? Or trick him into trying to shift those damning relics, and then arrest him? In my opinion the latter is the better move. More dramatic, too, and the public loves drama."

"It would make quite a nice headline, wouldn't it?" Pointer agreed, "but first I want to know about that clock."

"I don't understand about it at all," Schofild said handsomely. "Where are you off to?" he asked.

"Armstrong's office. I fancy Farrant was making for it. He's being followed, of course, and by others than Major Hardy."

Schofild seated himself beside Pointer in his car. He could not understand this fuss about the clock, but it had certainly moved Farrant in a most amazing way.

"You think the two clocks, office and study, may have been changed? Ah, that parcel of family papers that was heaped on the mantel and sent off by Farrant—you think the clock that was actually on the mantel the day of the murder may have got swept into the packing-case with them by mistake? That's quite possible. And a bullet may have hit the one in the house? Ah, yes! That might account for that feeling of tension that I had in the library just now. If so, in my opinion—"

He stopped and bent forward. Both Pointer and he were looking at Farrant, who was walking swiftly along the pavement. They were close to Queen Victoria Street. Evidently the jam, in which Pointers car was also stuck, had been too much for Farrant's impatience. But Pointer's eyes went behind Farrant to one of his men who was trailing the private secretary.

"Shall we get down and walk too?" he asked.

"The head clerk has had a telephone message—when I went off with the keys—to detain in talk any one from our little circle who might want to go into Mr. Armstrong's private room, and to keep any visitors under observation. One of my men is working at the office as a 'volunteer' these days."

Pointer turned into a side street just before the office building. His sleuth, a plainly-dressed, commercial-looking person, followed.

"Well?" Pointer asked.

"Nothing to report, sir, except that another man is following him. Chink, I fancied, by the glimpse I caught of his face. There he is!" He indicated a slim figure that passed the opening of the street, walking swiftly. The day was raw, and the muffler and felt hat left little of the face to be seen, especially as it was partially turned away, but there was a suggestion of a slanted eye setting, of an Orientally high cheek bone. "He got into a taxi, and kept now level with mine, now in front. He was following Mr. Farrant without a doubt."

"Call up Burton and have him follow the man. You stick to Farrant. He's not to be left for a moment. Call on Grimsby and Carlton if necessary."

"The Chinese element once more intruding," Schofild murmured, as they stepped out into the main street again. The Chinese, if it had been one, was nowhere to be seen.

Pointer stopped. "I wonder if you'd go back to Charles Street, in case Farrant only pops in here for a moment, and then dashes back there? If he doesn't find that clock here he'll certainly have a look there."

Schofild lifted his stick to a taxi by way of answer, and with a nod was off.

Yes, the head clerk told Pointer that Mr. Farrant had just arrived, and was very much put out at not being allowed access to Mr. Armstrong's private room. "I told him it was kept locked nowadays, and that you had the key." The man handed over this latter as he spoke.

"Thank you, Mr. Castle. I'll join him in a moment. But first, who unpacked the parcel that came from Charles Street the day after Mr. Armstrong's death? The parcel containing business papers and so on?"

Mr. Farrant had. He had handed over to the head clerk the papers bearing on present matters, and put the others in a cupboard after docketing them. They could all be seen. Had all been seen many times. Pointer now passed on into the passage and Mr. Armstrong's private room.

"Isn't the clock back yet?" he asked as he looked inside. As he had told Farrant, he had not seen one when he had been in the room before.

The clerk shook his head. "Not yet. Probably away being overhauled—oiled, regulated, and so on."

"It was a striking clock, wasn't it?"

"Yes. Very clear and most unusually sweet note."

"Hours?" Pointer seemed very interested, in clocks, Castle thought.

"And half-hours."

"When did you see it last?"

The clerk could not say. Either just before, or on the day of Armstrong's murder, he thought. "Who, took it to the clock-maker's?"

"Mr. Farrant or Mr. Armstrong must have." The head clerk spoke carelessly.

"Can I have the address of the repairers?"

Not from the head clerk at any rate. That good man had no idea where the clock was. He had been too busy with more important matters to find out.

They stepped on into the room where Farrant stood, twisting nervous fingers together by a window. He whirled round on his heels at their entrance.

"That talk of clocks at Charles Street reminded me— I'm not sure where an office clock of Mr. Armstrong's has got to that he valued very much. I haven't seen it for days. I suppose you'll think it cheek of me, chief inspector, but unless it turns up I wish you would have your men keep an eye out for it," he said genially.

Pointer looked great surprise.

"Has it been stolen?"

"Stolen or missing," Farrant said shaking his head as though uncertain which.

Pointer asked some more questions of Farrant, of Castle, of the office staff generally. .

No one could say when they had last seen the clock.

"Yes," Farrant repeated earnestly, "Mr. Armstrong valued that clock immensely for sentimental reasons, and so, for his sake, I do too. I'd gladly offer a reward of a hundred pounds for it, if you'll let its description be circulated among the police."

Pointer said he would have to think that over and consult his superiors at the Yard.

"But you might give me the description in case they permit the reward," he said.

Farrant handed him a sheet of paper on which he had been writing. Pointer glanced it over.

"The clock is the duplicate of the one in the library in Charles Street then? Except that it is a striking clock?"

Farrant nodded. "They are a pair. Armstrong had the office one copied from the other which he used to have at one time here in his room. But he preferred a striking clock for business."

"My idea is that Mr. Armstrong may have taken it home with him," Pointer suggested. "It strikes the hours and half-hours, so it seems as though he may have wanted to be very sure not to miss some set moment... If stolen, I shouldn't be surprized if it had been stolen from Charles Sheet."

Farrant looked extremely, sceptical. Quite carefully so.

"But it's not in Charles Street," he objected, "the house has been very carefully looked over since Armstrong's murder. Nor was it ever there. I'm certain it was lost or taken away from here."

"Could it have slipped in among those papers you sent from the houses" Pointer asked Farrant again said that such a thing was impossible. No, the clock had never been at the house. He could not understand why the chief inspector fancied that it had ever been there. And he fastened his light eyes on the officer as he spoke. Very keen indeed his eyes could be at times, Pointer saw.

Farrant, as he spoke, was searching the room again. Pointer, giving no reason for his idea about the clock having wandered off to Charles Street, helped him search it and the remainder of the two floors of offices. It was not found.

Farrant was rushing off when Pointer stopped him.

"Before you go, just make me up a bundle of newspaper which would roughly be the size and could contain the clock you want us to find for you."

Farrant hastily bundled something together and held it out, then he was off. Pointer tied the papers neatly in another and carrying it carefully under his arm left the building, after a word to the office boy. He had not gone a yard when a man walked level with him as though passing him, seemed to slip. His hand, a claw-like hand, very small and yellow, came down hard on the paper parcel.

"Sorry!" a voice breathed. Pointer covered the hand instantly with his own. He looked into a semi-Chinese face.

"Sorry!" the man breathed again in perfect English, "I slipped. Sorry."

Pointer let him go, and walked on. The Chinese now knew that there was no clock in the paper parcel, and Pointer, for his part, knew now that the Chinese wanted to be sure of that. Had the clock been found at the office what would have happened? In case it had turned up there, and because he thought that danger would surround its finding, Pointer had asked Schofild to return to Charles Street and wait for Farrant there. He himself now got into his car and drove to the house, where he found Schofild helping Farrant search the library rooms. Fortunately a clock, even a small one, has many places where it cannot be hid, but Farrant hunted with desperate eagerness in unlikely, as well as likely places. Remarkably so, for a man who had professed such scorn of the notion that the clock had ever, been at the house.

Finally he left—left in a way that suggested a continuance of the hunt in some fresh spot that had just occurred to him.

Pointer was glad that his sleuth would have ample help. Farrant needed watching, very close watching—and would get it.

CHAPTER TWELVE

MRS. ARMSTRONG was a charming, pitiful vision in black and silver. But the woman herself looked ghastly under her paint. Her cheeks were as hollow as her eyes. Though she wore no mourning, yet in deference to the recent tragic loss of her husband there were no guests stopping with Sir Ellis Herbert and his sister except herself. Miriam Herbert, a clever, easy-going woman of around forty, was sitting drinking her after-dinner coffee and eyeing Mrs. Armstrong with the sort of look that a large dog gives a lap-dog, as though wondering for what purpose it had been created, and why it is considered a dog at all.

Mr. Farrant was announced. It was just half an hour after he had finally left Charles Street.

Miss Herbert removed herself.

"It's about that box of letters sent down to you from Charles Street," Farrant spoke hastily. "I think some articles were put in by mistake that we rather need. Armstrong's office clock, for instance. Can I take it back with me?"

"The box hasn't been touched." She spoke with the look of one to whom the mere thought of it was horrible. "If any clock is there, it must stay there until—well, until I feel like facing them. Just at present, I want to forget. I must, the doctor says, or go dotty. Sir Ellis has been no end kind. I'm going with him and his sister on his yacht for a bit, as soon as the weather gets a bit steadier. I'd go to Cannes, only people are still so narrow-minded."

"Is there any truth in the rumor that you and Rufus Armstrong are going to be married?" Farrant asked almost fiercely.

Something like absolute fear showed in her eyes "No, how absurd! Certainly not!"

"The company states that there is no truth in the rumor," Farrant said bitingly under his breath He was about to say something aloud when Major Hardy was announced.

He looked at Farrant speculatively as he shook hands with Mrs. Armstrong. "Who's the Chinese-looking individual by the front gates, a retainer of yours?" he asked the other. "I think I've seen his face before, recently too..."

"So have I. Quite recently," Farrant said dryly. "He's my shadow. My follower."

"Good Gad, d'you mean it really?" Hardy asked, with a look of interest. "Now I come to think of it, it was while at the Lees that I saw him. Do you really mean he's following you?"

"I do. Quite really."

"Then my advice would be not to keep to the highways and avoid the byways," Hardy said promptly. "The middle of the street, and the broadest of the streets at that! But am I interrupting you and Mrs. Armstrong?"

"Not at all," Mrs. Armstrong said tonelessly. "Mr. Farrant has merely come down to look at a box of letters from Charles Street. He thinks an office clock has got among them. If it has, who cares?"

There was a look on Farrant's face as of one who cared very much indeed, who would give a very great deal to stop the speaker, but who knows that the attempt would be useless.

"Yes, we all think that clock ought to be back in Armstrong's office," Major Hardy said. "So let's have a look at it, do you mind?"

"Of course I mind. The box is full of my old letters to Boyd."

"It's only the clock that's wanted." Hardy seemed unimpressed by her dismay. "Just tell us where the box

is; we'll make no further trouble." Something rather
sardonic gleamed in his vivid eyes.

"I'll ring," she said indifferently. "Meade may know
about it." There followed a colloquy between herself and
her maid.

"The box is up in town," she announced as the result.
"It was sent to Percy to take care of. I overlooked it when
leaving. You'll need a note from me." She spoke in the odd
tremor which she seemed to be in throughout the
interview.

"With Percy?" Hardy gave a short laugh. "Nothing
needed with Percy but firmness, Phyllis, and both
Farrant and I have plenty of that quality."

"Are you both going for the clock?" She looked
bewildered, and also vaguely alarmed. "Apparently."

"But what interests, you about Boyd's office clock?"
They did not reply. Indeed each hardly troubled to say
good by to her before he hurried from the room.

When they had gone, Phyllis Armstrong rang for her
maid again. "Meade, get Mr. Callard at once on the
phone."

This proved to be impossible. "No, I can't wait. Try for
Mr. Rufus Armstrong." The maid was successful this
time.

"Rufus"—Mrs. Armstrong still had a tremor in her
voice—"will you do me a great service? Very great? Oh, I
do know it, Rufus. I *do* count on you always. I want you to
go to Percy's rooms at once and take away a box"—she
described it—it had her name on it—"and is full of old
letters. They know you there, and will let you have it. At
any rate, get hold of it at once, or if you can't do that,
then stand by it and see that no one touches it until Percy
comes in. He'll give it you, of course. It sounds silly, but
it's really very, very vital to me that no one should touch
it. Oh, thank you, kindest of faithful friends!"

She turned away with something trickling down her
cheek. But after ten restless, uneasy minutes she rang
once more for her maid.

"I'm going up to town," she said to her. "No, I shan't want you. And there's nothing to pack. I want a thick driving coat and a hat."

A moment later she had a word with her host. She wanted to get to town to see her brother at once. It was most urgent. Would Sir Ellis spare her a swift car and a chauffeur?

In the end she dashed off in Sir Ellis's new Bentley with Herbert himself at the wheel, delighted to show what it really could do on occasions. For in his opinion, a Bentley was wasted under eighty miles an hour. People who wanted to crawl along at anything less than that, should buy some other make. But his was not the only car racing on the roads to town that evening.

Farrant and Major Hardy were each out to get to Knightsbridge first.

Herbert won the race, as Herbert generally did. Mrs. Armstrong rushed up the steps of the little house where Percy Callard had his bachelor service flat and rang the bell feverishly, while Herbert said that he preferred to wait for her in the car.

"Is Mr. Callard in? I must see him at once. I'm his sister, Mrs. Armstrong," she said to the very respectable-looking man who opened the door.

"Mr. Callard is out, madam. Would you care to wait for him? There are a couple of gentlemen—"

"Yes, yes!" She spoke hurriedly. "Mr. Rufus Armstrong has just been here, hasn't he?"

"No, madam. Not today. Not yet." He let her into her brother's rooms. The man felt very sorry for her. Every one knew what a devoted couple she and her murdered husband had been.

She refused to be shown into the sitting-room, and made for the bedroom. She whipped through the door with a speed that looked like sheer terror, he thought. Nerves, he told himself later, as he went down to his own rooms again. But his former word was the true one. Mrs. Armstrong was in deadly fear. Moved by fear, summoned by fear. The box in question was in the bathroom. As she slipped into it she heard the sound of a key being fitted into the front-door lock. It was Percy himself. He caught sight of her through the open door.

"Phyllis! What on earth—?"

She did not answer. Hurriedly opening the box before her with the key tied to it, she thrust her hands down in it and lifted out the contents helter skelter. There was no clock in the box. Again the front door bell rang.

"Don't let any one in!" Mrs. Armstrong almost shrieked. "Don't let either of them in!"

She rushed past Percy into the narrow passage, but he had already opened the door. Farrant stood before them. She faced him with panic on her face.

"What do you mean by coming here?" she choked. Even she felt that the words were meaningless. She had herself told this man and Major Hardy where the box was. But that was before she had had a sudden awful thought as to what the clock might stand for...

"No use, Mrs. Armstrong, there's something in that box that belongs to me—or at least, I intend to have it."

"I won't give it you!" she said in a shrill, twisted voice as distorted as her face. "I won't! Do your worst. I won't!"

"My worst?" There was a nasty edge to his tone. Putting his hand in his pocket he drew, out a flat thermos flask which had been bulging his coat since he entered. With one twist he unscrewed the top. "Now then, Mrs. Armstrong, take me to that box or have this vitriol in your face. I'm an absolutely desperate man." He certainly looked it. "Let me have that box and nothing will happen to you. Stop me, and you'll be sorry." He was standing with his hand on her arm in a grasp of steel.

"Dear me," drawled Percy, "I've evidently forgotten to remove my *tarnkappe* this evening. Allow me to make myself visible, Farrant, and recall to you that this is my flat."

"Be quiet, you fool!" Farrant's usually level tones came like the hiss of compressed steam. "There's enough in this bottle for either or both of you. One step nearer me, and she gets half it!"

At that instant there came another, furious ring at the bell, and a knock like a combined postman and policeman. As Farrant drew Mrs. Armstrong farther into the passage, Callard stretched out a hand and pulled back the door. Major Hardy stepped in.

"Cocktails going?" he asked lightly, his eye on the flask. Phyllis Armstrong shrank back as far as Farrant's clutch on her would let her.

"I'm like a prisoner between the two of you! A creature on the rack," she half sobbed.

"Well, Phyllis, I too want that box, and as I don't approve of the purpose for which Farrant wants it, I think, under the circumstances, you'll hand it over to me. Stand back, there!" Something gleamed in his hand. Percy Callard languidly, stepped in front of his sister, but the revolver was pointed at Farrant, not at her.

"There's vitriol in this. You may kill me, but I'll blind you." The two men were shed of all conventions. They were both primitive savages.

"Can I be of any use?" asked a pleasant voice. It was the voice of Chief Inspector Pointer; behind him stood Schofild. They had been in the sitting-room.

"You can!" Hardy said instantly. "Arrest that man there for the murder of Armstrong. He's fooled me just a thought too long. In that case is a clock. In the clock is a microphone which, in my belief, will give him away completely. That's why he wants it."

"What are your reasons for such an absolute change of opinion?"

"You mean, rather, what were my reasons for being so blind?" Major Hardy said bitterly "I was ass enough to think he was carrying out some orders of Armstrong's, and only pretending to be acting against him. But I know the truth now. He was—is—Ellis Herbert's creature, bought by him, acting for him—"

And on that came yet another ring at the bell. This time it was Herbert himself.

"Ready, Mrs. Armstrong?" He stared at the group in the little passage.

"Please come on in, Sir Ellis," Pointer said, closing the door behind him, "I very much want a word with you."

Sir Ellis frowned.

"I've no time to waste, chief inspector," he began, in a tone that said he had no liking for his company.

Pointer only led the way into the bedroom.

"What I want from you," he said at once, "is some idea of what your head clerk telephoned without your sanction to Mrs. Armstrong. It was something about his wife. The point is—whose was the other name?"

Sir Ellis looked at him. Pointer looked back coldly.

"The case is very near its end," the chief inspector went on. "In a very short time I expect to be I able to prove who murdered Mr. Armstrong, and we want, as far as possible, to set aside those who, though apparently implicated, had no real share in his murder—or, say, no intentional share. Such as you," Pointer finished, as the other said nothing. Sir Ellis started.

"Naturally, as head of a rival financial group, there would very likely be a good deal of talk," the chief inspector seemed to be murmuring to himself.

"All the fault of that damned idiot Larkin! I'll tell you the truth, chief inspector, and trust to your good sense to keep me—us—out of anything disagreeable. We had a conference coming off with Mr. Armstrong at eleven. Mind you, he and I got on capitally together. Our rivalry was purely a business one. Personally, we liked each other. Well, this conference—Larkin had the idea that if he could rattle Armstrong we might get him to sign an agreement we had drawn up which none of us thought him likely to pass otherwise. It seemed a possibility, so we left it to him. Larkin has pulled off some clever things before now, but this time he went too far. At first it seemed all right. Armstrong came in at eleven and

rushed things through as quickly as possible, but he
refused to sign at all. Said he must leave that till the next
day. Stuck to that, and rushed away. Next thing we heard
was that he was found dead. And some people—lots of
people at first—said it was suicide. Nice position for us,
wasn't it! We liked Armstrong, I tell you. Until it was
clearly established that it was murder, I don't think any
of us slept a good night's sleep. That damned Larkin had
been too clever, we all thought. But as it was murder—"

"What, exactly, did he telephone? I quite understand
that you had nothing to do with devising the message,"
Pointer insisted.

"That Armstrong had better watch his wife and
Farrant, and he quoted some stuff from a letter which her
maid had quoted to him. Mind you, I knew nothing of this
at the time. I only got it out of Larkin after the murder. It
was an absolutely baseless calumny... that poor little
woman... there's absolutely nothing in it. Just like Larkin
to try it on, though." Sir Ellis dilated at length, or was
prepared to dilate at length, on Larkin's black mind and
Mrs. Armstrong's white reputation, when Pointer asked
another question.

"Now about Farrant, I understand that he is working
for you? Oh, this is no betrayal of confidence. We have a
letter found in his flat that showed as much. I understand
he really is one of your men?"

Ellis Herbert nodded. "One has to use all sorts of
tools," he said apologetically. "He offered himself to us—
at a price—well, he'll get his price and be damned as far
as we are concerned. If we hadn't taken advantage of his
offer the next man would have."

A few more questions were asked, and then Sir Ellis,
duly thanked, made his way at once to Mrs. Armstrong.

"Let me take you away," he begged under his breath.
"This is no place for a woman just now—let alone for you.
Come."

Somewhere, in the house above them, a clock struck the half-hour, two notes, sweet and clear and unusually musical.

Percy Callard's eyes blinked more like a cat's than ever. With a gasp, all but Sir Ellis turned and looked wildly around the room. Pointer was the first out of the door, and calling to the steward.

"Mr. Callard lent a friend, who has rooms upstairs, a small bronze striking clock, didn't he?"

"Say nothing, Tarrant!" called Callard, "it's none of their damned business."

"Look here," Pointer said quietly, showing his card, "I am investigating—"

"Lor' bless you, sir, I know your face from the papers—"

"I believe that clock that struck just now may be Mr. Armstrong's office clock. If so, I want it immediately."

The man felt in his pocket.

"Well, sir, Mr. West's away, and left his key with Mr. Callard, who's his great friend, and, of course, I can't say what he's put there and what he hasn't. Mr. West's own man sees to his rooms. He's away, too, at the moment."

Pointer put a whistle to his teeth and blew it softly. Instantly the bell of the street door rang. The steward opened it. Two tall men entered and looked silently at the chief inspector. He made them a sign to come with him, and the three ran with the steward up to the floor above, where he unlocked a door.

At the same moment that Pointer and Schofild, followed by the two newcomers, hurried in, there came a crack from some room inside, and, through a burst door that had originally been a servants' stairway, for this house was old and had been turned into service flats with the minimum of expense, tumbled Callard, Major Hardy, and Farrant.

Unfortunately, they were nearer the door of the room from which had come the sound of the striking clock than were the police force. In a second they were in the room.

Pointer jumped. One of the men went down. Even as he did so he fired, and all but hit the clock. He kept his finger on the trigger, which sent a stream of bullets up into the ceiling as Pointer twisted the hand up and away. First from the clock, then from himself, and finally from the man's own head. Fighting and firing until the little magazine was exhausted, the handcuffs were clicked on Major Hardy's wrists. Then Pointer rose and picked up the revolver. Farrant had snatched the clock from the mantel and crawled with it under a couch. It was a beautiful small French bronze, an exact copy, as far as looks went, of the one in Charles Street. Both showed a merman seated on a big shell leaning his ear against a boulder in which the dial was embedded.

A plain clothes man tapped at the door.

"What about the lady, sir? She's going in for hysterics," he asked prosaically, "and the gent with her doesn't seem to know what to do beyond fanning her."

Motioning to his two men to keep firm hold of the prisoner, Pointer stepped into the hall and asked the gaping steward if he hadn't a wife, or if there wasn't some woman on the premises who could help Mrs. Armstrong. His wife, it appeared, was only too willing to be in the picture, and Pointer dismissed Mrs. Armstrong from his mind for the moment. Her turn would come later.

Major Hardy, raging like a tiger, and as silent, was next sent off in a car between two very vigilant men. A third hurried away with the precious clock clasped in his arms like a baby.

Pointer waited behind to clear matters up with Farrant.

As the three of them, Farrant, Schofild, and he, stood around a table in the absent West's sitting-room, the chief inspector knew that he must pry open any doors himself.

"Mr. Farrant, I think the explanation of your conduct throughout is that you had given a promise to Mr. Armstrong not to betray Major Hardy," he began therefore, "which means that you found Mr. Armstrong alive when you slipped into Charles Street close on two o'clock on the day he was murdered. I am certain that it was you who laid him in the chest."

Farrant stood silent. But when he lifted his light eyes they shone with an exultant glare.

"If you gave some such promise," Pointer went on urgently, "I think you'll be carrying out Mr. Armstrong's real wishes best by now telling all you know. If you do so, we, on our part, will do everything we can to keep Mrs. Armstrong's name out of the case."

"You can't break your word, because it would make things easier for the wretched woman who was the cause of it all," Farrant said fiercely.

"But you may have to clear yourself from the suspicion of being in with the murderer," Pointer said dryly.

"In my opinion, that's by no means an unlikely suspicion," Schofild added weightily.

Farrant looked longingly at the two men. It was easy to see that he wanted to yield.

"A very clear and detailed statement now might save you from a shadow that would darken all the rest of your life," Pointer spoke persuasively. "As far as possible, anything you tell us will be considered confidential but I think the arrest of Major Hardy absolves you from your promise."

"I oughtn't to've given it," Farrant said slowly, "but he was dying—and when he asked me the second time to say nothing—" He broke off, and then went on in a vehement rush: "I swore to myself that I'd keep silence as long as possible. Until you'd arrested some innocent person—I thought it would be me. Well, as it happens, it's the right man—".

"As it happens—!" Schofild looked indignant and hurt.

Farrant did not hear him.

"Suppose you begin at the beginning?" Pointer suggested. "I think it probable that all this apparent betrayal, this going over to the enemy's camp, Sir Ellis's camp, was part of a plan arranged with, or rather by, Mr. Armstrong himself?" In fact, Pointer thought just what Major Hardy had told Miss Dickins to quiet her fears.

Farrant nodded.

"Yes. But it was Hardy whom Armstrong was after," he said triumphantly, "Hardy whom he suspected of having gone back on him and of having secretly joined Herbert's camp. To prove it, he devised this plan of getting information to him through Herbert. Information which I was to sell. It was of a kind to have finished Hardy financially—had Armstrong lived—in, say, another two weeks' time. If he was honestly in with Armstrong, as he claimed, it would do no damage. However, that's not the point. As you know so much about things, I think it will be better to tell you everything about that last day.

"In accordance with the plan I had left Armstrong's office and house the afternoon before. I was not to go near him until I had a telephone message from him which would mean something quite different from what it seemed to. I had some work to do for him till around one, and passing near Charles Street, I saw him on the opposite pavement. He didn't see me. His face looked terrible. Altered from anything that I had ever seen. I knew something very bad must have happened. I had to go on and finish my commission, but that face stuck in my memory. I had a feeling that something was all wrong, that I must see him at once. Finally, I gave way to it and let myself into the house. It was ten minutes to two exactly. I went in by the side door and slipped into the library and found him sitting at his desk, shot in the head from behind, with a revolver lying on the floor, as though it had dropped from his hand; a piece of paper was in front of him and his, fountain pen was stuck in its holder. The paper, in what looked just like his writing, ran:

"*Darling Phyllis,—My head is going. I must take this way out. Forgive.*"

"That was all. He himself was still breathing. I lifted him up in my arms, and to my surprize he recognized me. 'Hardy and Phyllis,' he just breathed. Then, when I thought they were his very last words, came 'Promise—promise—you'll say nothing.' I didn't promise. I was trying to lift him to the Chesterfield and get to the bell, but he held me. 'Promise—promise,' he kept murmuring, his eyes fixed on mine. "I—I"—Farrant's voice broke for a second; his own light eyes looked more than ever like those of a wolf dog—"I had to promise, though I hated to. And on that he died. Then I looked about me. I saw that that devil Hardy, after shooting him and while he was still alive, though helpless, had arranged everything to look like suicide. That note purporting to be in Armstrong's writing had been blotted on the new top sheet of the blotter... I had given my word to say nothing, but I hadn't promised to let it seem that he had killed himself. Armstrong was no coward! I remembered the *tomasha* for the afternoon, the big chest Hardy was sending the Armstrongs, and I decided that the man he had murdered should accompany his gift. I knew of how the Chinese lock worked. Armstrong had been shown it by Nunhead, and I knew where he kept the directions locked in his desk. I took the paper out, slipped up into the sewing-room, opened the door, saw the chest—I knew nothing about any plants inside, but I unlocked it, found it as I expected—empty, ran downstairs again, took down one of the curtains, wrapped Armstrong's body in it, and got him into the sewing-room and ultimately into the chest. Closed the door. Slipped downstairs again, put everything right in the study—the curtain in its place, changed the rugs, took the top sheet off the blotter, and carried it and the note away with me. The revolver I wrapped in my handkerchief and took that off too. Mopped up the rug with my own handkerchief and put all these things together into a package. You see, I didn't dare come forward at once, because of the position I was in myself. I had nothing to show that Armstrong was behind me in the so-called revelations that I was making Herbert. Though I had a fancy, at the last, that Hardy was too sharp to be taken in by them... that he suspected a snare was being set for himself... Anyway, to the world it would look as though I had betrayed Armstrong, for Hardy would scarcely speak up for me, even if he did suspect the truth! I knew that I was playing with my life. But anything, barring my own arrest for it, was worth Armstrong's murder not being taken for suicide. Then I went to you, Schofild, and arranged for you to be present at the opening of the chest, because I hoped you might get at once on Hardy's trail. I would have given you a hint afterwards but for your being in with the police, and I was terrified of a mistake. I don't mind ordinary danger, but to be hung—and for murdering Armstrong! No, I couldn't risk that. That's why I roped Miss Dickins in. She, too, began to waver after a while. But she didn't let me down. I had no right to put her in such a position, but I was desperate. As to the presence of a microphone in the room, I never thought of it until the talk came up about a different clock having been in the library that day. And then I recollected, in a sort of flash, how I had more than once suspected that Armstrong had one hidden in that clock. I didn't know for certain, but I suspected. I thought it might have been sent to Mrs. Armstrong among her papers and letters... so I tried to get it by force. You see, once I had it, I expected to have proof. And then I could afford to drop you hints that would lead you home. I don't know what it will tell, but it can't be anything to incriminate me, and trust Armstrong to see that it would catch Hardy!"

"And the vitriol you threatened to throw over Mrs. Armstrong?" Pointer asked severely, but there was a twinkle in his dark gray eyes which he only let his shoes see. He had been quite sure of the harmless contents of the thermos, both from the way in which Farrant had unscrewed the top, and from the fact that there was a cork in it.

"Water." Farrant looked extremely foolish. "I was desperate. I—well, any means, I thought, were allowable to get hold of that clock before Hardy could destroy any record there might be in it."

"How do you think he knew there was a microphone inside it? Supposing of course that there is one. We are all supposing that," Schofild asked.

"In the old days he had probably heard something from Armstrong that made him—like me —think that occasionally Armstrong used one to record important conversations with slippery customers. Just as Mrs. Armstrong evidently had a vague recollection of something of the sort. Armstrong rightly banked on no one noticing the difference in the clocks on the mantel, but once Hardy had a suspicion of such a thing having been in the room, obviously he must get hold of it."

He looked done, and they let him go, after one more word. He had tried to tell his sister of his certainty of Hardy's guilt when she had announced her engagement to the explorer, but she had chosen to adopt the attitude that he was trying to throw suspicion on an innocent man, and had appeared to see in it only a proof of his own guilt and treachery.

She had not wanted to believe what he told her. The chance of marrying Major Hardy had seemed to her so wonderful. Far above anything that she had hoped to secure. Daisy Farrant would have overlooked any crime if, by being blind, she could have made a really good marriage. If it came to selecting which—brother or fiancé—she would choose to believe guilty, there would not have been long any difficulty in her mind.

Callard was the next man questioned. He urbanely mentioned that, liking the clock, which he had always admired, he had taken it back with him on the day after Armstrong's murder. He had simply sent down word that Mrs. Armstrong wanted it to set her watch by, and, on being handed it by the constable on duty in the house, had kept it. As at that time the murder of Armstrong was considered to be an outside affair, there had been no orders given that nothing was to be removed. But in his rooms he disliked a striking clock, he found, and, on his friend West much admiring it, had promptly presented it to him.

"Just as well you knew that the box with Mrs. Armstrong's letters had been sent by her to her brother's flat," Schofild said, when Percy had finished his nonchalant account and left them, or we might have missed the boat." Pointer had known that it had been sent, but it was only just now that the box of letters had any interest to him. That there was no clock in it, he was fairly certain, but since it seemed to be the center of interest at the moment, Pointer, had at once made for Callard's flat, where it was housed, on Farrant's leaving Charles Street to rush down to Mrs. Armstrong in person and try to carry off the prize.

The telephone rang. Pointer, listening took down in shorthand just what it was that had been reeled off the microphone which the Yard had found cunningly hidden inside the shell on which the merman sat.

"What does it tell?" Schofield asked tensely, when the chief inspector finally hung up.

"Everything we need to know. Almost nothing of the talk between Mrs. Armstrong and Major Hardy."

"She's lucky," Schofild said darkly. "But, of course, Armstrong overheard their conversation himself from his niche in the end room. Which, in my opinion, was why the, microphone clock was put in the one room where he couldn't overhear the talk. Well?"

"The microphone records the laying of the table," Pointer read from his notes, and lunch proceeding, with nothing of interest until Mrs. Armstrong says 'You're very odd today, Bob. Why weren't you in this morning, as I expected?'

"'I knew I was coming on here about this chest,' is the reply. Then she says in a voice that suggests great indignation kept in bounds with some difficulty, 'Let's have our coffee in the writing-room. I much prefer it to this gloomy Abbot's Chamber.' You hear her and his steps going across the squeaking floor to the second room, where they would expect to be absolutely safe from eavesdroppers. Next comes an interval when the table is being cleared and taken away, and you only now and then catch the murmur of talk from the other room. Then comes the sound of the door between opening, a woman's steps crossing the library floor again—Mrs. Armstrong—for she evidently turned just before opening the door leading out of the library into the hall and said:

"'So you've thrown me over! It's a lucky thing for you that Boyd has no suspicion. He'd find it very easy to get his divorce if he read those letters I have locked away, and knew where to find that maid I paid off in Lucerne.'

"'Lucky for yourself, too, Phyllis.' Hardy's voice had an edge to it. 'You've no settlements, remember. You're entirely dependent on him.'

"She bursts out with a sort of sob. 'I hope to God never to see you again!' and his reply in a very mocking voice, 'That might be too sudden a change. For both our sakes, I shall do nothing so foolish. Nor will you!' And there's a very grim tone to the last three words. They're a command. Then the door into the hall closes. Next comes a period when a match is struck, evidently, Hardy lit a cigarette and then you hear a surprize 'Hello, who's in there? What, you, Armstrong? Didn't know you were here.' 'No, I know you didn't,' and very deadly a voice replies. 'I know you didn't. But you will know it from now on—you unutterable cad. You'll never get that post you're so keen on. Oh, not only about my—her—but about Herbert too. I'll hound you out of every club in town. I'll close every door to you—every door that you care about. I'll—' The voice is the voice of a maddened man.

Apparently Hardy was at the writing-table; there's a sound of a drawer opening with amazing speed, and, to the natural ear, amazing soundlessness. Next comes the report of a small automatic which would have been almost unheard to any one in the house as a heavy car was passing at the moment. While at the same time Hardy says, in a low and steady voice, 'I think not, Armstrong.' Next you hear him shifting his place. I take it he was writing those few words to be found, apparently in Armstrong's writing. There's nothing easier, as we both know, than to imitate the writing of some one who will be supposed to have been laboring under great excitement at the moment. You can hear the pen moving over the paper, and you can hear a very low groan from Armstrong, or more accurately described, a sort of sigh, and, Schofild, the pen of the murderer doesn't even pause!" There was a quite unprofessional note of horror in Pointer's voice.

Both men looked at each other. "No," Pointer repeated, "doesn't even pause, though Armstrong had been his best friend!"

Schofild made a grimace. "So it really was a murder from fear," he said slowly. "Major Hardy, who's supposed not to know the meaning of the word! Those letters must have been pretty bad ones... that maid's testimony a bit worse than usual. And then the Herbert transactions... And yet Armstrong didn't want Farrant to give Hardy up to justice! He must have loved his wife!"

Pointer said nothing. He thought that Armstrong was one of those men whose pride would be lacerated if it were known that they had been successfully hoodwinked by another. He would, so Pointer imagined, much prefer to have his death be considered an act by his own hand even than let it be known that Hardy had duped him, and that his own wife had tricked him.

"Then you hear the door close, and at long intervals a low moan from the dying man," he went on. "Then, within ten minutes from the time the shot was fired, just before the clock chimes two, the door opens, and the rest is exactly as Farrant has told us, or very nearly so. There are some words of his, very, moving last ones, to Armstrong which he didn't mention. And now, I must see

Mrs. Armstrong—I take it she's on the rack not knowing how much was recorded in that microphone and how much not."

"I'm sorry for her," Schofild said impetuously. "In my opinion, she's had an awful punishment. Light she is, but not, I think, a criminal. And Hardy evidently sprang the fact that he had shot her husband on her and told her she'd be implicated unless she upheld the fiction of suicide. I can see why she fainted when she saw enough of her husband's body in the chest to guess that he lay there, instead of the plants she expected to see—but her manner to her guests?"

"I think Hardy gave her some mixture of heroin that he takes himself at times," Pointer said thoughtfully. "I fancy she may have taken it when she stayed alone a moment in the Chinese suite. Like you, I think she's had a terrible punishment."

Again the telephone rang. "Yes?" Pointer asked into it. "Mr. Rufus Armstrong speaking? Yes, this is Mr. Callard's flat. Hold the line a moment, please."

Percy was summoned. His words were a casual, "Your taxi had an accident in crossing the street? Not a bad one, I hope? Oh, don't trouble about the box. Phyllis is here. Yes, been here some time, and likely to stay for quite a while. Coming on here? Oh, certainly. Going to take her back to a quiet place for supper? Splendid idea. Don't apologize. I'm due elsewhere. Phyllis will be delighted. Or if she isn't she can tell you so herself." And Callard, with the air of a man whose home ties are pressing a little too closely on him, wandered again to the door. Pointer asked for explanations.

"Mrs. Armstrong asked Rufus, too, to come and fetch that clock. Pity he couldn't get here in time. He's missed quite a show." And this time Percy succeeded in getting gracefully out of the room. But he threw over his shoulder, "It may all be part of a bright idea, but otherwise Mrs. Armstrong is just a bit on tenterhooks until she sees you, chief inspector, and knows just what that box recorded. Pity Armstrong never used it to catch the echo of some of my opinions of himself. It might have done him good."

Pointer was only a moment or two alone with Mrs. Armstrong. When he returned to Schofild, he looked as though a very painful part of his duty were over.

"She says, and I think its the truth," he reported, "that just before leaving the house Hardy told her that Armstrong had overheard their talk together, and had shot himself. But that he had written a message saying his brain was going, so that no one need ever know the real reason for the deed. That he was in the study, that she was, on no account, to go near the room, but let some one else discover Armstrong's body and meanwhile carry on just as always, and to help her he gave her a pellet. The rest is as we thought. Since then she has suffered agonies of remorse, she says."

"Agonies of apprehension, more likely," Schofild said bruskly. He was always afraid of becoming sentimental.

Pointer agreed. "Even the best of us," he added, "can't always separate those two, and I'm afraid Mrs. Armstrong doesn't come under that heading.'

"Is she going to marry Rufus?" Schofild asked with frank curiosity. "She says, and at any rate at the moment thinks, that the only man she really loved was her husband. As far as we are concerned, she may not be drawn into the case at all. The prosecution may quite easily say that the quarrel between Armstrong and Hardy was caused by the latter obtaining and using against Armstrong the information which he got as Armstrong's friend."

"Let alone what he learned through Mrs. Armstrong," Schofild agreed. "So the chest was a parting present to her, as she began to guess on the day of its arrival. Well, that's over! In my opinion, Hardy forced Mrs. Armstrong to agree to a future engagement with Rufus Armstrong lest their own old relations be suspected. Just as he hastened to get engaged himself to that little huntress,

Daisy Farrant. He chose her, of course, so as to still further close Farrant's mouth."

Something in Schofild's tone suggested that his thoughts were not on what he was saying. What was occupying them was apparent after a second's silence, when he broke out with, "Look here, Pointer, when did you first suspect the truth of the Farrant mix-up, and when did you guess that Armstrong was, himself 'Cigar,' the man who sat listening in that end room niche? You must have felt very sure of your grounds, or you would never have ventured to arrest Major Hardy as you did—"

"It would have been a case of no Major Hardy if I had let him out of my sight, I thought," Pointer said. "He knew that the game was up once we had that microphone which was why he called on me to arrest Farrant, so as to get just a few minutes' start, probably to tear up some incriminating papers we shall find among his things, and then shoot himself, or take a prepared pellet...

"As to how I came to suspect him—well, he seemed to fit the facts best of all the men in the case," Pointer said evasively. But Schofild would not let him off.

"I really would like to know what clue put you on the right track, with so many side tracks?"

"Well" Pointer tried to make the beginning clear, "the van breakdown held us up for some time, of course. It suggested so many possibilities that had to be allowed for—murder outside the house, a way of disposing of the body so that it might be difficult to prove the place of the crime, and identity of the murderer; Armstrong's own statements about being away till late in the evening, his great financial interests all supported it. The Chinese end of the string seemed to get a bit knotty too"

"Altogether it was quite a compact chain of apparently vital links," Schofild summed up "Well?"

"As soon as we learned that the chest had arrived at the house with no body in it, all these links, as you call them, were swept away, and one thought as in the beginning, that whereas Armstrong's death would have lent itself to a staged suicide effect, the opposite was so clearly being aimed at. By putting that body in that chest which was opened in public, it was practically posted to us at Scotland Yard"

"I fancied at first that might have been spite," mused Schofild

"That was always possible," Pointer thought, "but by the time we knew that the body had not been put into the chest on the way to the house, we also knew that no efforts to stage clues had been made so that it looked to me as though whoever had put the body into that chest knew it was murder and had found the body in circumstances that made him sure either that an attempt would be made to dispose of it so that it would never be found, or under circumstances that suggested that suicide was being staged. We had found no traces of the first possibility, which would have been very difficult, whereas the nature of the wound made it look as though the murderer had had the second idea in his mind. The missing hat and gloves suggested that whoever put the body in, wanted the crime to be thought an indoor one. We found it to have been so. This confirmed the notion that nothing was being done to mislead us by the man who laid the body in the chest. That pen in the drawer... that changed top sheet of the blotter... even the missing weapon all suggested swift attempts to alter a suicide setting. Whoever put the body into the chest didn't come forward, and had given no alarm when he found Armstrong, which showed pretty clearly that he was in such a position that he would himself have been suspected of the murder. Though he kept the letter supposed to have been written by Armstrong and the blotting paper. There are Armstrong's fingerprints on the revolver, by the way. Another ghastly bit of Hardy's thoroughness. They, too, were made by him while Armstrong was still alive. But to go back, we find a man who has given an alibi that fits the time when the hawker saw Mr. Farrant come back into the house. A man who speaks of a telephone call so as to give us the idea that Armstrong was alive at that hour. The man in question can let himself in and out unnoticed, and knows the house and may know the secret opening into that suite. Also, he fetched you to be present when the chest was opened. But he had carefully refused to incriminate any one except—possibly—by his choice of the chest. It seemed difficult, however, to believe that out of the small number of people who could have murdered Armstrong in his library, Farrant should have no suspicions of the criminal. If so, what hindered him from sending us anonymous letters? Or placing clues? Altogether, if Farrant was the man who put the body in the chest, a promise of silence made by him to the murdered man was suggested.

"That shot was not immediately fatal, the doctor said. Farrant could therefore have had a word with him..."

"Yes, yes," Schofild agreed, "Farrant may have been indicated as the man who put the body in the chest, but how did you come to suspect Hardy?"

Pointer thought this very obvious.

"That telephoned message which made Armstrong alter all his plans and which Sir Ellis Herbert feared might have made him commit suicide, suggested some tale-bearing about Mrs. Armstrong. If so, that suggested the possibility instantly of Armstrong having given out that he would be away all day and yet having returned secretly to some place where he could watch his wife."

"That niche! Evidently Armstrong was told some detail by Larkin which he knew applied to Hardy—not to Farrant! And the cigar must have been one given him by Callard to try. I take it he only sat there playing with it to help get rid of some of his emotion." Schofild was deeply stirred.

"Just so. Well, the only person who lunched with Mrs. Armstrong that day was Major Hardy... and his efforts to keep suspicion from falling on Farrant fitted the idea of his guilt. You see, Hardy knew that only Farrant could have put the man he had shot, and left for dead in the library, into that chest in the Chinese suite. Though he must, and was, immensely puzzled as to how he got him into it. But he made no mistake as to why his chest was chosen! He was certain that Farrant knew the truth. I think he guessed that the latter—when he did not speak —might have given Armstrong just some such promise as he did, once Hardy knew that Armstrong could have recovered consciousness after he left him in the library"

"Yes, that necessity to shoot him so as to have it be thought a suicide rather put him off his aim. But I confess I wonder at Armstrong's magnanimity!"

"It may have been that. And it may have been an intense dislike to have it known that Hardy had apparently won the rubber, and that his wife had been deceiving him so successfully. I think Farrant rather believes it to be due to this latter reason, or I doubt if he would have spoken at all."

"I wonder how much Callard suspected of all this," Schofild said after some moments.

"Something very near the truth, I think. But he probably thought that Hardy would marry his sister. He would look on the respective engagement as what they were, mere figments. I think Hardy would have been quite willing for suspicion to fall on Percy, but he dared do nothing openly to bring this about, as he knew the sister wouldn't stand for that! So he finally chose the Chinese as the safest suspects."

"Who was that Chinaman who followed Farrant?" Schofild asked.

"A detective employed by Hardy. I think he was trying very hard to find out any shady stories about the Lees. The very fact that the man has been traced to the Lees' place in Limehouse makes me very sure that he did not come from there."

"I wonder Hardy didn't kill Farrant. Too risky, perhaps?"

"Farrant didn't give him much chance," Pointer said, with a little laugh. "He wouldn't stay in the house. Nor leave his hotel easily. My man agrees that he seemed to enjoy being followed by him. I think Hardy thought that Farrant—my belief is that before he was shot Armstrong let him know that he had some piece of evidence against him. Armstrong would mean the microphone. But Hardy could not be sure that Farrant had not got hold of it—whatever it was."

"In my opinion," Schofild said slowly, "Hardy possibly attributed Farrant's silence to an old attachment to Mrs. Armstrong."

"Either way," Pointer thought, "he was very careful that no strain should be placed on whatever it was. Let the private secretary be accused of murder, Hardy reasoned, I think, and he would speak. Yes, I shall always remember this case as the only one I have ever had where the murderer nobly refused to let suspicion fall on an innocent man."

"It did indeed require to be looked at in the right way, though," Schofild said appreciatively, as the two left the room.

THE END

Other Resurrected Press Books in *The Chief Inspector Pointer Mystery* Series

MYSTERIES BY ANNE AUSTIN

Murder at Bridge

When an afternoon bridge party attended by some of Hamilton's leading citizens ends with the hostess being murdered in her boudoir, Special Investigator Dundee of the District Attorney's office is called in. But one of the attendees is guilty? There are plenty of suspects: the victim's former lover, her current suitor, the retired judge who is being blackmailed, the victim's maid who had been horribly disfigured accidentally by the murdered woman, or any of the women who's husbands had flirted with the victim. Or was she murdered by an outsider whose motive had nothing to do with the town of Hamilton. Find the answer in... **Murder at Bridge**

One Drop of Blood

When Dr. Koenig, head of Mayfield Sanitarium is murdered, the District Attorney's Special Investigator, "Bonnie" Dundee must go undercover to find the killer. Were any of the inmates of the asylum insane enough to have committed the crime? Or, was it one of the staff, motivated by jealousy? And what was is the secret in the murdered man's past. Find the answer in... **One Drop of Blood**

AVAILABLE FROM RESURRECTED PRESS!

THE EDWARDIAN DETECTIVES
LITERARY SLEUTHS OF THE EDWARDIAN ERA

The exploits of the great Victorian Detectives, Poe's C. Auguste Dupin, Gaboriau's Lecoq, and most famously, Arthur Conan Doyle's Sherlock Holmes, are well known. But what of those fictional detectives that came after, those of the Edwardian Age? The period between the death of Queen Victoria and the First World War had been called the Golden Age of the detective short story, but how familiar is the modern reader with the sleuths of this era? And such an extraordinary group they were, including in their numbers an unassuming English priest, a blind man, a master of disguises, a lecturer in medical jurisprudence, a noble woman working for Scotland Yard, and a savant so brilliant he was known as "The Thinking Machine."

To introduce readers to these detectives, Resurrected Press has assembled a collection of stories featuring these and other remarkable sleuths in The Edwardian Detectives.

- The Case of Laker, Absconded by Arthur Morrison
- The Fenchurch Street Mystery by Baroness Orczy
- The Crime of the French Café by Nick Carter
- The Man with Nailed Shoes by R Austin Freeman
- The Blue Cross by G. K. Chesterton
- The Case of the Pocket Diary Found in the Snow by Augusta Groner
- The Ninescore Mystery by Baroness Orczy
- The Riddle of the Ninth Finger by Thomas W. Hanshew
- The Knight's Cross Signal Problem by Ernest Bramah

- The Problem of Cell 13 by Jacques Futrelle
- The Conundrum of the Golf Links by Percy James Brebner
- The Silkworms of Florence by Clifford Ashdown
- The Gateway of the Monster by William Hope Hodgson
- The Affair at the Semiramis Hotel by A. E. W. Mason
- The Affair of the Avalanche Bicycle & Tyre Co., LTD by Arthur Morrison

RESURRECTED PRESS CLASSIC MYSTERY CATALOGUE

Journeys into Mystery
Travel and Mystery in a More Elegant Time

The Edwardian Detectives
Literary Sleuths of the Edwardian Era

Gems of Mystery
Lost Jewels from a More Elegant Age

E. C. Bentley
Trent's Last Case: The Woman in Black

Ernest Bramah
Max Carrados Resurrected:
The Detective Stories of Max Carrados

Agatha Christie
The Secret Adversary
The Mysterious Affair at Styles

Octavus Roy Cohen
Midnight

Freeman Wills Croft
The Ponson Case
The Pit Prop Syndicate

J. S. Fletcher
The Herapath Property
The Rayner-Slade Amalgamation
The Chestermarke Instinct
The Paradise Mystery
Dead Men's Money

The Middle of Things
Ravensdene Court
Scarhaven Keep
The Orange-Yellow Diamond
The Middle Temple Murder
The Tallyrand Maxim
The Borough Treasurer
In the Mayor's Parlour
The Saftey Pin

R. Austin Freeman
The Mystery of 31 New Inn from the Dr. Thorndyke Series
John Thorndyke's Cases from the Dr. Thorndyke Series
The Red Thumb Mark from The Dr. Thorndyke Series
The Eye of Osiris from The Dr. Thorndyke Series
A Silent Witness from the Dr. John Thorndyke Series
The Cat's Eye from the Dr. John Thorndyke Series
Helen Vardon's Confession: A Dr. John Thorndyke Story
As a Thief in the Night: A Dr. John Thorndyke Story
Mr. Pottermack's Oversight: A Dr. John Thorndyke Story
Dr. Thorndyke Intervenes: A Dr. John Thorndyke Story
The Singing Bone: The Adventures of Dr. Thorndyke
The Stoneware Monkey: A Dr. John Thorndyke Story
The Great Portrait Mystery, and Other Stories: A Collection of Dr. John Thorndyke and Other Stories
The Penrose Mystery: A Dr. John Thorndyke Story
The Uttermost Farthing: A Savant's Vendetta

Arthur Griffiths
The Passenger From Calais
The Rome Express

Fergus Hume
The Mystery of a Hansom Cab
The Green Mummy
The Silent House
The Secret Passage

Edgar Jepson
The Loudwater Mystery

A. E. W. Mason
At the Villa Rose

A. A. Milne
The Red House Mystery
Baroness Emma Orczy
The Old Man in the Corner

Edgar Allan Poe
The Detective Stories of Edgar Allan Poe

Arthur J. Rees
The Hampstead Mystery
The Shrieking Pit
The Hand In The Dark
The Moon Rock
The Mystery of the Downs

Mary Roberts Rinehart
Sight Unseen and The Confession

Dorothy L. Sayers
Whose Body?

Sir William Magnay
The Hunt Ball Mystery

Mabel and Paul Thorne
The Sheridan Road Mystery

Louis Tracy
The Strange Case of Mortimer Fenley
The Albert Gate Mystery
The Bartlett Mystery
The Postmaster's Daughter
The House of Peril
The Sandling Case: What Would You Have Done?
Charles Edmonds Walk
The Paternoster Ruby

John R. Watson
The Mystery of the Downs
The Hampstead Mystery

Edgar Wallace
The Daffodil Mystery
The Crimson Circle

Carolyn Wells
Vicky Van
The Man Who Fell Through the Earth
In the Onyx Lobby
Raspberry Jam
The Clue
The Room with the Tassels
The Vanishing of Betty Varian
The Mystery Girl
The White Alley
The Curved Blades
Anybody but Anne
The Bride of a Moment
Faulkner's Folly
The Diamond Pin
The Gold Bag
The Mystery of the Sycamore
The Come Backy

Raoul Whitfield
Death in a Bowl

And much more!
Visit ResurrectedPress.com
for our complete catalogue

About Resurrected Press

A division of Intrepid Ink, LLC, Resurrected Press is dedicated to bringing high quality, vintage books back into publication. See our entire catalogue and find out more at www.ResurrectedPress.com.

About Intrepid Ink, LLC

Intrepid Ink, LLC provides full publishing services to authors of fiction and non-fiction books, eBooks and websites. From editing to formatting, from publishing to marketing, Intrepid Ink gets your creative works into the hands of the people who want to read them. Find out more at www.IntrepidInk.com.